OLEG SA...

AN IDEAL WORLD
FOR A
SOCIOPATH

Enjoy the adventure!

BOOK ONE

MAGIC DOME BOOKS

An Ideal World For a Sociopath
Book #1
Copyright © Oleg Sapphire 2023
Cover Art © Alexander Rudenko 2023
Cover Design: Vladimir Manyukhin
English translation copyright © Colin Parker 2023
Published by Magic Dome Books, 2023
ISBN: 978-80-7693-230-2

ALL SERIES
BY OLEG SAPPHIRE:

The Hunter's Code
A Portal Progression Fantasy series
by Oleg Sapphire and Yuri Vinokuroff

An Ideal World for a Sociopath
a LitRPG series by Oleg Sapphire

The Healer's Way
A LitRPG series by Oleg Sapphire & Alexey
Kovtunov

TABLE OF CONTENTS:

CHAPTER 1

PROLOGUE

I AWOKE WITH A GRINDING PAIN in the back of my head. *Damn, how much did I drink yesterday and why do I feel so bad?*

My head was filled with a wild stubborn knocking sound which would not let up and was trying its best to either finish me off or drive me insane.

With difficulty, I reached for a bottle of warm water and, ignoring the unpleasant taste, chugged the remaining half liter in one gulp.

"Now that is one freaking hangover," poor little old me groaned as I stared into space and attempted to shake off the brain fart.

I hadn't had a hangover like that in a long time, and it was particularly strange because I hadn't had anything to drink yesterday.

The lousiest thing was that the delirium was

1

not about to let me be. Incomprehensible symbols and figures swam before my eyes.

"Hallucinations be gone, I did not summon you," I said, trying to laugh it off. What if I really had guessed the code word and they'd left me in peace and moved on to my neighbor, who had long since tamed these wondrous creations after seeing them every other day?

Shoot, the horrible knocking sound in my head was still there. Or, hang on, maybe it wasn't in my head? Struggling, I turned it in the direction of the corridor.

Definitely. Someone was knocking on the door, and with their feet by the sounds of things, such was the racket they were making.

That was all clear then. One of my neighbors had drunk themselves into a state and was trying to break into my den. *Give it your best shot. I fitted an armored door last year to keep out woodpeckers like you.*

Heaving myself to my feet, I staggered over to the long-suffering door. Such behavior was nothing new in these parts and my door had seen more than one attempt to break it down. One time, a drunken neighbor broke his axe against it and threatened to sue me, first for destruction of his property, then for smacking him around the head and catching his neck lightly on the follow-through.

Not good. In my current condition I was more likely to get hurt myself than be able to pacify a disorderly drunk.

"Get lost, you freaking glitches! What's going on with me? Am I being drawn into the matrix? Where did all these bizarre digits come from?"

After I'd said this, the figures began to disappear, but just as I was delighting in my normality and not having to call for the white coats, they reappeared, bringing their girlfriends along with them this time.

Welcome to the system. Your world will no longer be the same. Evolve or die! All the system's functions are henceforth unblocked.

I saw this and then I heard it, enunciated by a lifeless robotized voice.

That's it, this is the end. I've gone freaking mad, I thought to myself.

I felt even more nauseous now, despite the lettering disappearing. Perhaps I still had a chance?

"Pack it in with the fucking knocking!" I shouted, grimacing with pain. "Otherwise I'm gonna give you a knock on the head, you fucker."

I made skittishly for the door and yanked it open.

"Aaaaargh." It was the end for uncle Grisha, who also seemed to be suffering from barrel fever, if his appearance was anything to go by.

The thing that had sometime been a human was now nothing short of a walking corpse, its eyes bloody and its forehead smashed up after its encounter with my door. The body staggered towards me.

"Piss off," I said, and, without understanding

what I was doing, slammed the thirty-kilogram door shut as hard as I could, giving my ex-neighbor a lesson in flying backwards in the process.

That's made me giddy, was my first thought. *Although actually, I reckon it's made him giddier.*

Congratulations on First Kill. You are the first survivor in your world to kill an infected since the commencement of action was announced.

You have earned a reward: A unique-quality trinket casket.

A light popping sound came from beneath my feet, and I lowered my head to see a trinket casket with faint golden sparkles running along it.

It dawned on me that this was impossible.

"Status," I muttered to myself, unconvinced any words would come out. "Jeez, it came out."

New text appeared before my eyes:

Name: Igor Vargov

Level: 1

Skills: none

Inventory: 2kg (capacity)

What to make of all this, huh? Had I been thrown into a game or something? Or perhaps a game into me?

Wait. I've got it. Television.

I grabbed the trinket casket — how could I not? After all, it was probably loot — and ran towards the old television set, which ought to show me what was going on around here.

I reckoned if no one knew what was going on in the world, the television would explain the situation.

No signal on channel 1, channel 2 likewise, same with channel 3, and so on up to 9. Only channel 10 had a signal. But what a signal it was!

Clamor, shouts, and the chomping sounds of flesh being guzzled. The camera lay on its side, focused on a female reporter being devoured by her cameraman.

"Fun nonetheless." I switched off the television and fell deep into thought.

What do I do now? Yearning and melancholy overcame me. I had practically no food left, and no money to spend on it. Although thinking about it, money was no longer relevant, and a smile crept onto my face. It would seem poverty was no longer a primary concern.

So, I would have to work it out as I went along. And first up was the matter of the trinket casket. I inspected it thoroughly, turning it over in my hands.

A regular trinket casket, expensive looking and made of an unknown material.

I played practically no games, but I did read books, and I understood roughly what to do.

But no, I did not understand.

The trinket casket did not want to open. *Maybe I should hit you with a hammer? No? Fine, stay intact then. I haven't got a hammer anyway. Pity, it would come in handy for the zombie apocalypse. Actually, a light machine gun would be handier. Although you'd need a portable munitions factory to go with it.*

"Open," I said, no nonsense, looking at the box and wondering where I could get an angle grinder from.

Hmm, it worked! There it was, the great power of thought. Thought about an angle grinder, something I had never before held in my hands.

You have received: skill — Invisibility, level 10.

The trinket casket opened and I looked inside. I saw a card, seemingly a regular playing card, only it wasn't plastic, although truth be told, I couldn't tell what it was made of.

Is this definitely a book? Okay, let's have a look. I extended my hands towards the card and removed it from the box, when suddenly with a dull "pop", it transformed into a book.

Hmm. I scratched my head. No doubt I needed to flick through it in order to gain the skill. *Yes, definitely, that must be it. But I'm not actually going to have to study it, am I? Or am I?*

Silence in response. Very interesting. Who was I expecting an answer from?

I turned the book over in my hands, as I'd done with the trinket casket, and saw nothing new. Then I tried to open it, and suddenly saw a new message before my eyes.

Do you want to study a skill: Invisibility? Yes/no.

"Well yes, how could I not?" I didn't understand such a silly question. How could you refuse invisibility?

You have studied a skill: Invisibility, level 10.

Cool. I was delighted as I thought what to do next.

I called up my status, and there in the *Skills* column it said impressively: Invisibility. *Excellent. So how do I find information about it?*

Well yes, how do I do that? I asked myself, smiling dryly.

I concentrated my gaze on the word "skill" and barked:

"Information!"

Information is inaccessible at your current level. You can read information with the help of the skill: **Evaluation**.

Cool. I laughed and reminded the system ironically that I had no such skill.

I spent the next hour trying to get to grips with all this nonsense. Although I must say it was actually quite lighthearted nonsense. Outside the window, an alarm wailed and there were fewer and fewer people. But the most impressive sound was the visceral snarlings. I lived on the third floor and was not overly concerned that a beastie might climb in through my window.

Using trial and error, I discovered that at this point I could call up two windows: Status and Inventory. I had no life or mana bar. Or other similar game baloney.

My inventory was interesting yet strange. I could put a two-meter picture in it, but not a twelve-kilogram kettlebell. Evidently my limit was two kilograms, as mentioned by the system, but the size of the object was unimportant.

"Uh-oh, old ma Zina's in trouble," I said, hearing the screams cease in the apartment above.

It was nothing less than she deserved. She was an old witch who loved to make life difficult for everyone. Countless were the times she had dropped the dime on her neighbors for ridiculous reasons, such as they'd stolen ten thousand from her, or flooded her out.

The first few times, the gallant police had answered her calls, but then they'd stopped bothering with the old cow, and now she'd probably been finished off by zombies. Or maybe not zombies but her neighbor Nikolai, whose car she'd scratched out of spite.

I also understood how the skill of invisibility worked. You just had to give a mental order to activate it, and it was ready. I could see myself clearly, but the mirror could not see me anymore. I experimented with the skill and bumped into the doorjamb. My invisibility hadn't deserted me, continuing to shelter me. I even pricked my finger with a needle, thinking the wound might open invisibility, but that work seamlessly too.

Since that was the case, then excellent, I could go on a recce mission without fearing for myself.

I selected the longest knife in the kitchen and headed out into the hallway and straight for the front door.

Just in case, I first put my ear to the door and listened. There was some noise, but it was distant. After opening the door cautiously, I saw nothing but a zombie.

"Wow, what's this?" My face burst out in a radiant smile.

Beside the corpse lay a gray box, about twenty centimeters long and twenty wide.

This was my loot, which I had earned fair and square but forgotten to collect.

I looked around once more before calmly approaching the box. It would be stupid to open it on the landing, so I went back into the apartment.

Back home, I decided to conduct another experiment. With my status set to *Invisible*, I held the box up to the mirror. It was also invisible. Interesting.

I placed the box on the floor and gave it a mental command to open.

Hmm, no cards this time. Instead, the box contained a packet of buckwheat, a can of olives, and half a pack of cigarettes.

Apparently the system understood I was not exactly weighed down with food, and had decided to bung me a bonus.

Although why only half a pack of cigarettes? Was the system tightening the belt?

I went through to the kitchen to boil up the buckwheat.

It just so happened that, since I'd polished off the remains of the edible supplies a few days ago, the only food left in the house was a couple of bags of pasta which even a Chinese person would have turned their nose up at. I had no money. I had no job either.

In the last six months I'd lost everything, including the desire to live. First I'd been set up in the competitions, then banned from the sports association, and then I was out on my ear. Then I was kicked out of my job for some trumped-up reason. I guessed my trainer, the one who had set me up, decided to play a dirty trick on me, so acrimoniously had we parted company. Old bastard.

Turned out the apocalypse wasn't so bad after all. At least it would inject a bit of zing into my boring life.

I did understand, however, that it wasn't all quite so simple. If the zombies were now spending days hammering on my door, then sooner or later they would break through.

And apart from the zombies, there were creatures even worse. Humans. I had received an interesting skill from the system, and in return it had received a + to karma from me. However, other people would also receive its gifts and then start laying down their own law.

The thing was that I lived in a human anthill. Thirty stories high, five below ground level, and all this stretched for two kilometers in length.

I suspected all kinds of motherfuckers were already ganging together and discussing how to screw over everyone else.

Which meant I had to become strong enough to overcome them.

Since loot dropped from zombies, that meant I had to kill them, and in large numbers, in order to get food and, possibly, weapons and skills.

I was distracted from these thoughts by a gut-wrenching scream from below the window.

I looked out to see what was happening, and winced. The beasties were tearing some poor thing to pieces against the wall under the window. The victim had gone quiet, doubtless dead, and the beasties were howling blue murder, which made others come running.

"What are you shouting about? Shut the fuck up!" I yelled at them. My head hurt as it was, without all this hullabaloo.

In response to my request, one of them began bawling all the louder, which made me really mad.

"Right, you're fucking dead," I said, totally losing it and diving into the cupboard. "Going to carry on screaming, are you, you asswipe?"

I stuck my head back out of the window and aimed my bow at the bawler. The beastie showed no sign of stopping, and I was liking it less and less. There were at least a hundred zombies crowding beneath my window. Children, old men, girls. Anyone you could think of.

My arrow landed bang on target, directly between the zombie's eyes, killing it stone dead.

The zombie fell silent and crashed down on its back, but its place was immediately taken by another, albeit not a screamer. Perhaps this one would be smarter.

As the zombie collapsed, alongside it appeared a box, which I was not destined to take.

"Now that's annoying. One arrow down and I

miss out on the loot."

I had just deliberately killed a human-turned-monster, my hand had not shaken, and I had experienced no qualms nor pangs of conscience. Maybe because I did not especially like people. Or maybe because I'd been an archer for the past fifteen years, since the age of ten.

It was no boast to admit I was the best archer around and rarely missed. Were it not for my poverty, I might even be able to think about a trip to the Olympics, despite not having been given the opportunity to win at the state championships. Victor Pavlovich, that asshole, my trainer. He sold himself out, the louse, planting a bag of performance-enhancing drugs on me. He went to the judges himself and wrote an official complaint about me.

I'd never even seen performance-enhancing drugs, if only because I could never have afforded them. But I was disqualified from the final, and all the medal places were given to their guys, who afterwards looked down on me sneeringly. I'll remember those looks until the day I die. One of them looked me right in the eye and said, "Know your place, worm!"

You sold out, Victor Pavlovich, and you sold out your student, together with his bright future. I hope you've already been devoured. Otherwise I shall find you, and then nothing will stop me from restoring justice. I'll shoot you with my bow, and how very symbolic that will be.

It was probably then that my love of people

finally died. I could forgive much, even the time my grandmother was tricked into exchanging a decent apartment in the city center for this pile of shit. I couldn't care less about not knowing my parents, who, according to grandma, had taken me to her as a two-year-old and announced they had neither the desire nor the time to raise a child. They added that if she didn't need me either, she should give me up to an orphanage and be done with it.

My parents didn't even have the grace to give me their surname. Grandma registered me under the surname of her husband, my grandfather, Ivan Vargov.

These thoughts and recollections made me want to go kill a couple of zombies. But first there was buckwheat.

The buckwheat was tasteless without butter, but it was all there was, and I was grateful to the system that had provided me food. I finished all the olives as well. After lunch, I stepped out onto the balcony for a smoke, to the accompaniment of the zombies' screechings.

Done smoking, I flicked the butt right onto the top of a zombie woman's head, and went to get ready.

In all the zombie movies, people don motorcycle safety gear, arm themselves with baseball bats, and go in search of rotting skulls to crack. My situation was different. I had no protection, what with having no motorbike, nor even a bicycle, and I'd broken my baseball bat over the head of some lowlife three months back. Plus, these zombies' skulls looked in no way rotting or infirm.

It took me ten minutes to come to a decision and devise a plan.

I put my bow out in the corridor and lay two dozen arrows in a row for ease of access.

Running up and down between the floors of the building and shooting zombies was dangerous, at the very least because they might pen me in from both sides.

I opened my door and looked out. Nobody. I stepped out onto the landing, breathed in two big lungfuls of air, and gave a loud whistle, announcing my whereabouts to the walking dead.

Judging by the loud stamping that came from both downstairs and up, my had plan worked.

The main thing was that there shouldn't too many of them, for my supply of arrows was not endless, and they broke quickly when they pierced anything other than polystyrene.

I went back into the apartment and put the door on the chain, leaving a gap of no more than ten centimeters.

The zombies came and came, giving no thought to stopping. They fell, rose, and surged on, trampling the heads of their own kind underfoot, seeing no obstacle in them.

Then the first of them guessed where the aroma of tasty human was emanating from and tried to grab me with its crooked arm, shoving it through the gap and scraping some nasty-looking skin from its hand as it did so.

I now had a closer view of them. I wasn't worried about the chain holding out. It was thick, like a padlock shackle, and I'd bought it last year, after my rampaging neighbors had ripped out its feeble predecessor and knocked my door down.

The lower floors were occupied by paupers and boozers. Anyone who had money would find themselves a place on the higher floors.

The zombies were completely different to those I'd seen in the movies. They were not listless with empty eyes. They knew precisely what they wanted, and judging by their bloody foaming spittle, they wanted me.

The first onlooker, clearly taking me for a tasty morsel and trying to seize me, received an arrow to one of its eyes. The second got the same treatment, as did the third, the fourth, and the fifth. I missed the sixth zombie and the arrow got stuck in the wall. Shooting a moving target was harder than shooting a static one, and its zombie comrades gave it a shove, making it fall face first into the gap, where it got stuck, and the arrow had shot past over his head.

Not good. I had competition arrows, which broke on impact with walls. If I'd had sharpened hunting arrows, things would have been very different.

A small box appeared right by the door. Excellent, it would just squeeze through the gap.

Quick as a flash, I went to get a mop handle to pull the box into the apartment.

It was quite small, red and shaped just like

the gray one. After a brief moment's thought, I opened it and was disappointed.

Bullets. Bullets for an archer. An *archer*.

It did not take a genius to understand what I'd been given: twelve 5.56 mm rounds and fifteen 9 mm rounds. Was I supposed to pelt them at the zombies or something?

"Fine, who cares?" I brushed off fate's little joke (or the system's?) and continued to shoot beasties.

Not wanting to waste arrows, I took careful aim and shot accurately. The only bad thing was that I couldn't see how many zombies were left. I'd been thinking the flow would stop somewhere on the first floor, but a vague feeling now took me that some idiot had forgotten to close the main door downstairs, or given the code to the zombies. There were too many of them and the flow kept on flowing.

After my twentieth arrow, I began to see the futility of my endeavors, and after downing twenty-five beasties, I became concerned for my arrows, of which I had another twenty-five before I was clean out.

However, something interesting happened.

You have gained level 2. Your body has become stronger.

Hmm, that is interesting. Very interesting in fact. Although I didn't have time to test out my strength yet.

So, I get not only trinket caskets and other boxes, but also abilities which should make me

16

superhuman.

Encouraged by the news, I continued to shoot the zombies coming at me.

It did actually occur to me that pulling back the bowstring had become easier, although in truth I'd never particularly had problems with it anyway.

After sticking yet another zombie in the eye, I leaned wearily against a chest of drawers in the hallway and accidentally knocked over a vase. It fell to the floor and smashed into tiny shards, renewing the zombies' vigor in their attempts to squeeze through the narrow gap, clattering on the door with redoubled force.

Sound. They were very attracted to sound. As it transpired, gunfire was not so effective around here, probably even dangerous. Each shot attracted newer and newer enemies and gave everyone in the vicinity to understand your location.

Screw gunfire! I needed to find more arrows. The smolderings of hope arose that the drawers might contain arrows from the system, which would mean I had to kill as many zombies as possible.

But it soon became impossible to shoot more zombies, as a whole mountain of them now lay by the door, completely blocking my view.

For some reason, I had thought I'd be able to shoot them all and collect my trophies.

Disconsolate and weary with the day, I closed my apartment door and went to the kitchen, where

I sat down at the table and reflected on how to stay alive.

I spent all evening preparing for the next day, inspecting whatever might come in handy. Why did I need this collection of music discs and children's clothes that lay for some incomprehensible reason in the wardrobe?

Everything I had no need for I simply chucked out of the window without fanfare. In my hour of need, I did not want find myself looking hastily for something I needed, to find only a pile of useless trash.

CHAPTER 2

I WAS AWOKEN SEVERAL TIMES during the night by the sound of distant gunshot. Each time, I got up and went to check the apartment door just in case. You never know.

The zombies had ceased their drumming on the door in the evening. If that were to continue, I was done for. Or rather it was my door that was done for, followed by me.

In the morning I sat drinking tea in the kitchen. The last freaking bag. The other morning news was the electricity outage. That was it, people were toast, too long had they played the potentates of life. It was a good thing I had a regular kettle and an old gas stove. Although if this kept up, the gas would disappear too, and I would defenestrate the stove and possibly fell a couple of deadmen.

The only joy left was the water in the pipes and the working sanitation. If one thing was worth hanging on to, it was being able to relieve oneself in comfort.

After lunching on the remains of the buckwheat and using up the last teabag, I went to get ready.

Opening the door on the chain again, I had a good look around. Before this, I had spotted just two zombies through the spyhole.

Using the mop handle I began dismantling the corpse mountain, and managed to regain three arrows. No sooner had the pile of corpses shrunk slightly, than three monsters came at me and reached out their hands to grab at my body. In the old-fashioned way, or rather, as I had done yesterday, I dispatched them to kingdom come, or wherever they would end up. Valhalla perhaps.

I took the risk of activating my invisibility and opening the door, the long knife clutched in my hand.

No more moving zombies were within eyeshot, but I could distinctly hear them on other floors.

Trying not to make a sound, I stepped out onto the landing and had a good look up and down it. A number of zombies had been eaten by their fellows after I'd killed them. I hoped gorging on their brothers would not make them stronger.

Then I got busy with the most important task, the gathering of trophies to top up my battle reserves. Of the nearly thirty arrows I'd spent, I was able to retrieve just fifteen, the rest being damaged beyond repair. I realized how uneconomically I had fought yesterday. On the other hand, how could I have fought better in a situation like that?

I had no desire whatsoever to engage in hand-to-hand combat with them.

A silly smile emerged on my face, and I wanted to laugh as I recollected how the other children had always teased me. Why do you want to do archery? You're better off signing up for boxing or karate. What are you going to do if you have to face off with a boxer? Boxing is strength and power. Hahaha!

I would love to see what those boxers were capable of now. Breaking zombies' jaws and knocking them out?

Kicking one of the zombie corpses, I noticed a Zippo lighter fall out of its pocket. It went straight into my inventory.

After the arrows, it was time for trophies from the system, which was clearly not feeling generous today.

There were approximately thirty zombies, but only ten boxes, trinket or otherwise.

Gathering these goodies, I darted back into the apartment and, by force of habit, slammed the door. The slam echoed up and down the stairwell. Fuck.

Never mind, screw it. There was loot to check out.

Five gray boxes had dropped, which pleased me immensely.

As I opened them, my head buzzed with the hope of finding food. I would not last long without it. If only I didn't live in such a densely populated area, I might be able to venture out to the store, but that was not an option here: too many zombies.

I opened the boxes and smiled. My catch consisted of: one salami stick, two packets of buckwheat, four cans of fish, two bags of potato chips, three kilograms of potatoes, two bags of pasta, five bottles of drinking water, and one packet of black tea. Mmmmm.

I'd completely forgotten about water. Since there were zombies everywhere now, the water in the pipes might with time become infected. If a couple of deadmen fell into the water at the purification station, it was the end for all of us, you wouldn't even be able to brush your teeth.

One more problem to add to the list: conserve water as much as possible.

Then came the turn off the two red boxes. More bullets, three 5.56 mm and four 9 mm. Garbage, if I was honest, although I could keep them for the purpose of exchange. *Yeah right, and then get shot with them?*

There was another trinket casket, blue this time. As I'd guessed, the trinket caskets were system objects, while the others were terrestrial.

The blue trinket casket was flatter than the others.

Opening it, I found another card. The prospect of another book stirred my spirits, but it was not to be.

You have received a card: Fact-Clue.

Fact №1: Infecteds can sense humans at a distance, and walls are no obstacle to them. They will take great pains in their attempts to get at the living.

Half a minute later, the message disappeared, as did the card from my hands. *That won't help me get the whole collection,* I thought with a heavy sigh.

On the one hand this was a bummer, but on the other hand it was useful information. It seemed I could learn more about the system by killing zombies. Bad luck for the deadfolk. Now I had a greater incentive to kill them by the boatload. All I needed was more arrows.

I had two trinket caskets left, one red, the second brown.

I opened the brown one first.

You have received: a tent.

For fuck's sake.

Do I have to go and live in the woods so I don't lose my goodies?

Still, at least it had remained in the card instead of pitching itself. I threw the card into my inventory. It was better off there for the time being.

Then came the turn of the red trinket casket, which I had high hopes for.

Red. It would be a weapon, if I understood correctly, and potentially that meant arrows.

I opened it, and saw a new notification.

You have received: a short iron-bamboo spear, level 1.

Freaking terrific. A spear for an archer. Fuck.

My first thought was to bury the spear card deep in my inventory and forget about it. Then I thought for a moment, decided against that, and opened it.

The card turned into an interesting spear.

Less than a meter long, perhaps seventy centimeters, and cast entirely from iron. The shaft was fashioned to look like a bamboo cane, and the twenty centimeters of spearhead were leaf-shaped.

An elven spear, if ever I'd seen one. Taking it in my hands and waving it about, I was surprised how light it was. I figured it must have been hollow inside. Or maybe I really had grown stronger.

With this in mind, I approached my kettlebell and lifted it to test my strength. It seemed lighter. But then again, maybe not. Then I did some push-ups. A hundred. Excellent. I used to push fifty or seventy, depending on my mood.

I was stronger, and that was pleasing.

It was time to check out my idea.

I went out into the hallway and squinted through the peephole. All clear. I took a comfortable grip on the spear and began pounding the blunt end of the shaft into my neighbor's metal door. The visceral snarlings began immediately and were followed by footfall. It sounded as though there were zombies behind three of the neighboring doors. Bad news for my neighbor. I'd never met him, as he'd only moved in a week ago and he hadn't managed to track me down yet.

Then I darted back into my apartment and closed the door on the chain once more.

For the next hour, I was to the zombies as Van Helsing was to vampires. They approached, and I pierced their heads with my spear. It was quite sharp and penetrated eyes and throats smoothly. One time I missed and caught a cheek instead, and the zombie merely twitched and caught the spear between its teeth, nearly robbing me of it. After that I took aim more carefully, not wanting to lose such a convenient weapon.

How many I killed in that hour I do not know, I wasn't counting. But I was exhausted. The spear was caked in blood, which was also running down my arms. In fact there was blood everywhere, even a small puddle out on the landing.

And as ill luck would have it, my mop handle was broken.

The mountain of deadmen outside my door was no joke, so I had to figure out where to get rid of the corpses. Shoot, why can't they just disappear by themselves? That would be cool. Maybe I could throw them in my inventory and then out of the window? I wouldn't have lasted long at that rate. I was fearful for the door, even though it was standing firm against attack so far. I now understood it had probably been the best 53,999 rubles I'd ever spent. If my juicehead neighbor had been able to knock down my old door, it would have been a cinch for the zombies.

I could not now collect any loot, and I was unlikely even to be able to open the door because of the zombies barricading it with their bodies.

Having worked up a hunger, I went to the

kitchen to fix myself some food. Fried potatoes.

Sitting at the table, I shoveled them into my mouth, and chased them with more potato, in the form of chips. Chemicals, which I had to spare, and which had no particular value anyway.

As I made tea, I pondered my next move.

I had to think of a way to collect the loot from out in the corridor. The only way I could think of was to climb from my balcony to the neighbors' and approach the landing via the neighbor's apartment. The question was, who or what might be waiting for me in the neighbor's apartment?

I stepped out onto the balcony and took a look around. The distance between the balconies was negligible. The problem was the windows of my neighbor's glazed balcony.

"Hey, neighbors, anyone alive in there?" I asked, knocking on the window with the remains of the mop handle.

Silence.

Not for long, however, for it was broken by the ruckus of the balcony door being smashed. It was old and had a large pane of glass in the center. My zombie neighbor came to investigate the noise and got stuck against the door. However, eyes on the prize, as they say. He slammed his whole body against the window, and then hung there on the frame, skewered on the remaining glass shards.

I thought he would die there and then, but t'was not to be. Zombies were resilient, but they could be killed by damaging the head.

I quickly smashed some more of the glass and

sank a bullet — meaning an arrow, but bullet sounds cooler — into the wriggling zombie.

My neighbor went limp hanging on the frame, and half the battle was won. I cleared the window frame of the remaining shards and threw an old blanket over the frame, just in case I'd missed a chunk of glass sticking out. The chances of being able to call an ambulance were extremely thin.

Although, zombie medics? That would be really something.

Joking aside, I had to clamber onto my neighbor's balcony.

No hassle. Then I entered his apartment, but not before throwing the stinker down onto the street. He flew like a butterfly, and then went "kersplat."

My neighbor's apartment was no different to mine. I gave it the once over just in case and found no guests. He'd lived alone.

Then I remembered the first rule of the apocalypse: if the world is fucked, then bring on the pillaging. And nothing here was of any use to a deadman.

Another interesting question: what were the chances of me becoming a zombie like everyone else? Everything about the apartment pointed to my neighbor having become a zombie in his sleep. Which meant he hadn't been bitten, and the bite-chain theory didn't cut it here. The water perhaps? Also ruled out; I'd cleaned my teeth and drunk tea that day.

I quickly scoured my neighbor's rooms, of

which there were two, and found practically nothing of interest.

I took his stock of matches and all his kitchen knives, although frankly I don't know why, but what the hell. While I was rummaging along his shelves, I heard a noise from beneath the window. The sounds of smashing glass had attracted the attention of the local zombies.

I had a gift for just such an occasion. Wheezing, I picked up the large television, hauled it out onto the balcony, and rested it on the window frame, before tipping it over the edge. Crash. Kersplat. I peeked out to see what I'd done. Three down. Not bad. I wondered if I should perhaps follow it up with the fridge. But then who would be able to treat my slipped disc? Not an option.

I went back inside to continue my plundering, but found nothing more of interest. He had no food to speak of, just a lone pan of soup going bad in the fridge, so I quickly closed it.

I did not have to search for the keys to the apartment, for strange though it may seem, they were in the front-door lock.

Now came the sketchiest part of my plan. Using my indivisibility, I had to open the front door carefully and attack the zombies. The problem was that I still didn't know whether they would sense me by sound or by smell. That said, I had noticed I could barely hear my own footfall when I was invisible.

Cautiously and very slowly, as though my life

depended on it, which it did, I opened the door. The piercing squeak penetrated the entire stairwell. The zombies were knocked sideways. I was knocked sideways. The zombies, spraying spittle, ran at me.

I had no idea I could run so fast. I ran back to the balcony, leaped like a cat back over to mine, grabbed my spear, and was ready to face the beasties again.

"Shit," came my commentary on the situation. There was no zombie-free space on my neighbor's balcony.

At once, three of them tried to climb over to me. They didn't make it, resulting in three downward kersplats.

Throwing economy to the wind, I grabbed my bow and began shooting as I'd never shot before. I cared not about arrows, spears, or loot. The main thing here was to survive.

I straightaway rejected the spear as my weapon of choice. There was such a crowd of zombies that I simply didn't have the experience to take them all down. With my bow, on the other hand, I felt absolutely at home. In the past I'd been victorious in many a speed shooting competition.

Five down, ten down, twelve, fourteen, eighteen. *How many of you are there?* My supply of arrows dried up. There hadn't been all that many on the balcony.

I'd left some in the corridor, but there was no time to dash and get them now. I grabbed the spear and began to stab, chop, slice. And sweat.

"AGRKH," said a zombie almost right into my face, after running nimbly over its fallen brothers and jumping over to my balcony. In my surprise, I walloped it with the spear, and it flew down and landed badly.

The battle had been epic, testament to which was the system's new notification.

You have gained level 3. Your body has become stronger.

My body was strong enough for another half hour, after which I was exhausted. One of the vampires very nearly got its teeth into me, and I was lucky to fend it off with the spear. My arms felt like cotton wool, my eyes were awash with sweat, and the zombies kept on coming and coming, although the flow had eased somewhat.

I understood I had to retreat, but where to? My balcony door was also a regular Soviet one, whose glass would be smashed with ease to allow unhindered access to me.

The only thing that came to mind just then was my skill. While the zombies were still no less than three or four steps from the edge of my balcony, I mentally activated my invisibility. It worked. Hurrah. The zombies came to an abrupt halt and began looking around, growling menacingly as they did so.

I stood there for at least five minutes until I was sure they couldn't see me. All I had to do was make the slightest move and they would hear me. Or maybe they wouldn't, but it wasn't worth the risk.

Stand perfectly still it is then, I decided, shrugging my shoulders. It was still better than fending them off. An hour later, the zombie population of my neighbor's balcony had thinned. When the last one had vacated it, I figured I could leave my own balcony at last. Sidling, I jumped back into my apartment. I did not close the door, so as not to make excessive noise.

What a dolt! I would now have to fight my way through them to close the door to my neighbor's apartment, otherwise I wouldn't get a peaceful night's sleep. They would come and chow down on me.

And how much loot would there be?

I had a raging thirst for either tea or vodka, perhaps even tea with vodka, but I couldn't afford to make any noise. I still had to close the freaking door somehow.

I sat quietly down in my armchair for a rest. A few hours later it was time.

I took the remainder of my arrows from the hallway and went out onto the balcony. All clear. Not good. It would have been better to shoot them all in one place.

Once again I climbed over to my neighbor's balcony and, trying to maintain balance, stepped over the corpses there. The journey was complicated by the shards of glass and wood shavings from the smashed-up windows, and I came dangerously close to stepping on one. It was a good thing I was checking carefully beneath my feet, for I might easily have trodden on a ten-centimeter shard. It was interesting to note that as I stepped over the bodies, I felt nothing, no emotions. It was of absolutely no concern to me that these bodies had once been people.

I entered my neighbor's apartment noiselessly and in the first room immediately came across four zombies. Standing immobile, heads tilted backwards, they were gazing at the ceiling and growling softly. *What are they looking out for?* I wondered.

I looked up as well. What were they looking at? There was nothing there, they were having me on.

What, are they battery powered? I quipped to myself. *Maybe they've broken down?*

I did want to keep living, however, and preferably not get eaten alive.

Spear in hand, I got to within striking distance and plunged it into the skull of the nearest enemy. Wasting no time, I pulled it sharply back out before the body fell to the floor, and struck again, felling another.

Two collapsing bodies did not go unnoticed, and the other two zombies turned in my direction and adopted poses of readiness, growling louder and louder.

It struck me, however, that they could not see me, and so, stealthily and cautiously I tiptoed closer and jabbed the leaf into the eye of a bald zombie. After that it was plain sailing, only one left. It died in the same manner.

The other room was empty, but in the hallway

there were two more, soon dispatched.

Then, lightning fast and no longer concerned with stealth, I ran to the front door and slammed it thunderously shut.

"Mission accomplished," I said quietly to myself, before leaning against the wall and slipping down it in my exhaustion.

CHAPTER 3

AFTER YESTERDAY'S SHENANIGANS, I stumbled back to my apartment, fell onto my bed without undressing, and was out like a light. I slept right through till morning, and was awoken by the sun's rays and birdsong, against a background of car alarm, gunfire, and human screams.

Genially, I asked the system, "Please don't give those jerkoffs any more bullets. They disturb people trying to sleep."

The system appeared to have heard me.

"Aaaaaaaa." From somewhere up above, someone flew down.

Now then.

I was wide awake in an instant and running for the window. I made it just in time for the second failed pilot. Then there was a third... all the way up to six.

Hmm, they didn't jump by themselves, did

they? They were buck naked, so I doubted this was a means of escape from zombies.

Obviously, power was already changing hands.

I wasn't overcurious about watching spread-eagle bodies being surrounded fast on all sides by zombies. As I've already mentioned, I do not hold humans in especially high regard. They've never done anything good for me, but bad stuff: more than my fair share.

Then again, I was human myself, and therefore nothing human was alien to me. I noticed one person still twitching. He'd probably broken his spine and was as good as dead, even if I tried to save him. But the crowd of zombies running towards him would only prolong his suffering.

Picking up the bow I'd left on the balcony yesterday, I fitted an arrow to it, took aim, and shot the guy, putting him out of his misery. The gift of a quick death, not to be eaten alive by monsters.

Mind you, I don't feel bad about this either, and I've just killed a human, I thought to myself.

"Whatever." I shrugged my shoulders and went to get some food.

You have killed a survivor.

The capacity of your inventory is increased by 3.5 kg.

So that's what you're fucking doing to me, is it, system? You do understand I've got to kill them now? Or not? I thought. Never mind. I'll just grab a bite to eat. What a lovely day.

I'd decided today to chuff some pasta with a couple of cans of fish, and while I was cooking them up, I gave some thought to my situation.

If your inventory was enlarged for killing people, then things looked bleak. We would soon annihilate each other, without any need of zombies.

Secondly, the zombies were looking worse than yesterday, which meant they were rotting and decomposing all the while, which in turn meant disease and other crap. On top of which, the stink of them was something else.

The main news was that my bow weighed 4 kg, while my inventory would hold 5.5, which was simply terrific, because there was no room for the spear. But never mind, it was nothing vital just yet. After my big feed, I could prepare myself for some dirty work. The cannonade on the upper floors had not died down; the party was in full swing.

I found an old sheet in the cupboard, tore a strip off it and wound it around my face, covering my nose and mouth. Then I went out onto the balcony.

The smell of the dead zombies on the balcony was not fragrant, to put it mildly. To put it not so mildly, the stench was eye-watering. I dashed back into the room, rummaged through the wardrobe, and changed into some old clothes which it would be no shame to discard later.

Climbing over my balcony, I surveyed the scene. All quiet. So I got busy heaving corpses over the edge.

The first twenty bodies, which I had killed with the spear, plummeted down. Then came the zombies with broken-off arrowheads stuck in them. Bastards. Those were my arrows.

After fussing about for a good half hour, I'd managed to rescue just seven arrows. Seriously not good. I had a total of fifteen now. An urgent plan required hatching.

I'd killed around fifty zombies, but convinced myself it had been a whole hundred. Plus, there were the corpses on the landing to drag in and launch from the balcony as well. It was heavy work, and a fair pile was already building up down on the street. I hoped the stink would not reach my windows, for I had little desire to be inhaling those deathly vapors.

The next step was to clear the landing. To my deep surprise, there were no walking dead out there. Plenty of dead ones, mind, looking pretty dreadful with their bodies all gnawed. First I had to drag them into my neighbor's apartment, and then, after closing the door, drag them out to the balcony. A fair mound had piled up.

The work soon began to tire, and I was dying for a shower.

The rewards, however, only delighted. A whole pile of various boxes, including trinket caskets, now lay on the table in the living room.

I was not up for dealing with them just yet, however. I took a shower, giving myself a good scrub with a loofah and trying not to miss a single centimeter of my body.

As I was washing, I made a mental note to myself that corpses needed throwing down onto the street straightaway and not leaving until later. Clean and happy, I settled myself comfortably in the living room, and busied myself with what had recently become my favorite hobby: sorting loot.

Today was a turning into a veritable holiday, as I found myself looking at boxes in colors new to me.

I opened the new ones first. Two pink trinket caskets.

You have received trading coins: 2 pcs.

You have received an inventory-expanding scroll: 1 pc.

The scroll brought a contented smile to my face. It was not in a card but simply lay in the trinket casket. I picked it up, turned it over in my hands, as was my habit, and immediately wanted to use it.

Your inventory is increased by 2.5 kg. Its capacity is now 8 kg.

Also not bad. I would have to kill a couple of zombies and then my spear would fit in the inventory.

There were twenty-five gray boxes.

I opened just five, figuring any food in them wouldn't spoil. The boxes weighed just 200 grams apiece, while the food would weigh several kilograms, so I put the remaining twenty boxes in my inventory, intending to open them as and when necessary.

You have received: 4 cans of stewed meat, 3 cans of beans, 2 packs of cigarettes, 6 kilograms of potatoes, 5 liters of bottled sparkling water.

Not bad at all. I also noticed the system's messages sometimes differed from one another, as though it was trying to adjust itself to people individually but wasn't quite there yet. I did not want to think about the nature of the system.

I didn't even know if I would see tomorrow, what there would be to eat, nor even where I could get more arrows, so why would I want to think about the system if I could change nothing in my life?

Next came the red boxes. Which contained something of interest.

You have received: M16 rifle, 1 pc.

You have received: 5.56 mm bullets, 22 pcs; 5.45 mm bullets, 12 pcs; 9 mm bullets, 17 pcs.

What the hell did I want with all this? An automatic rifle which I couldn't shoot, and not exactly a generous amount of ammunition.

A weapon like that was only good for killing other people. Which meant I would have to close the curtains just in case. How could I now not think there was some idiot with a sniper rifle in the apartment block opposite, leveling up his inventory?

It was a shame to risk it for the sake of a bunch of useless garbage. And if I started firing a machine gun, every zombie in the anthill would come running to smash down my door.

Okay, it was time to calm down. I knew what would lift my mood, and that was facts, definitely useful. So, I picked up the two blue boxes.

You receive fact № 22: there are skills that consume mana, and there are skills that do not consume mana.

"Thank you, system, for that very detailed fact. You really didn't waste any letters there," I said, complaining to myself again about the system.

At least I now knew that mana existed, and that my skill did not eat it away.

I opened the next trinket casket.

You receive fact № 32: a bite or scratch left on your body by an infected will produce a low-level infection and turn you into an infected.

"Oh, that's news to me," I chuckled. I'd seen that in a thousand films, it was nothing new. Even without that fact, there was no way I would go anywhere near their teeth or claws.

Speaking of zombies' claws, they really did seem to have become slightly longer.

Just five red trinket caskets remained, and I figured they would be the most interesting.

Without giving it too much thought, I mentally commanded them all to open.

You receive a card: guardian's shield.

You receive a card: hired gun's crossbow.

You receive: bone arrows, 57 pcs.

You receive: short dagger.

"Arrows!" I jumped for joy and proclaimed that joy to the whole apartment.

This was it. This was what I needed.

And I didn't care that they had bone arrowheads. They could have been stone for all I cared, I would have been delighted anyway.

"Thank you, system," I said from the bottom of my heart.

On that note, I grabbed the arrows and ran out onto the balcony. It was interesting that the system did whatever it wanted, writing differently about loot each time, and indeed issuing loot as it wanted. I also had questions concerning demand, but it was clear enough anyway that no one would give me anything for nothing. It was no doubt some holy random at the helm.

"Hey, dipshits! Form an orderly queue," I shouted from the window, despite this being absolutely unnecessary, what with the crowd of onlookers standing around anyway.

I felt an arrow to check the shaft was true and in good condition and the fletching well made. Only the arrowhead was made of bone, but I didn't see it as a disadvantage. The bone tip was hard and sharp.

I considered I had gotten lucky. Yet it was still worth testing the water.

The first arrow hit a zombie's eye, rather than the nose I was aiming for. Dammit, bone was light, I would have to aim above the target. My second shot hit the spot.

Turned out it was great, shooting zombies

from the balcony like that. All I needed was a few thousand arrows and I'd be happy.

I spent five hours on adjustment of fire, but I still had fifty-two left. Excellent.

Bam, Bam.

Gunshots nearby, perhaps the seventh or eighth floor of my block. What a cretin. Did he not understand all he was doing was attracting attention to himself? *Take a knife and stab them. Or better even yourself.*

The arrow experiment successfully over, it was now time to have a look at the coins.

Sitting comfortably on the sofa, I turned a coin over in my hands. It was obvious what to do with it. There was, of course, the option of giving it to a peddler or throwing it into the heavenly piggy bank. But how little information there was about the system and its items, and it was in no hurry to share its secrets.

I hoped the system behaved the same way with everybody, not just with me. It would be very upsetting otherwise.

I sat there in contemplation for approximately two hours, I reckoned. My phone went dead and I had no other clocks. I managed to work up a hunger in that time, and I saw no reason to deny myself the little things.

I stuffed myself. Hell, did I stuff myself. Then I stretched out contentedly on the sofa, reflecting on the fact that my storeroom, by which I mean my inventory, contained twenty boxes of food.

I could afford to sit on my ass for ten days and

do nothing but stuff myself and chill. Although if I did, the probability of my being killed would rise dramatically. Each box or casket increased my strength and provided me new information about the system. Without them I was a goner. And that was to say nothing of levels. I really had become stronger, and I was only at level 3, so what would I be like at level 20? I hoped my skin would be bulletproof, because now it was too scary to go out for a walk, what with the system giving rewards for killing survivors.

Anyway, that's enough rumination. Let's finish this tea and go kill some zombies. I really hope I get lucky again and don't get eaten.

This time I fell back on the old door-chain-spear routine.

Once again I summoned the zombies by hammering on the neighbor's door. Silence. How disappointing. Here I was, all ready to flee, and they didn't even show up.

Did that mean the zombies were ignoring me now? *What, am I not tasty enough for you? Hey, come back, all is forgiven!*

So what do I do? As it is, reconnaissance is dangerous.

The whole problem was that I lived in a damn anthill. Every floor in the building had no fewer than three stairwells, with four elevators each, and on every fifth floor there was a passageway through to the other blocks. I lived in block 12. I knew there was a block 25, but how many there were in total I had no idea.

Long ago a neighbor had told me you could walk for several blocks along the passageways without having to go outside. Damned house. Why the hell had it been built like that?

One day I went out for a stroll and ended up walking for forty minutes before I realized I was lost. I couldn't find the way back, but I saw a door in an otherwise dead-end corridor, and when I opened it, I found myself outside, in a place I didn't recognize at all. I had to walk for ages along the outside of the anthill before I was back in familiar surroundings.

Quite frankly, it was a terrifying thought how many zombies might be roaming the building right now. The system had warned that they reacted to living people and tried to get closer to them. And there should have been loads of survivors in the house. Or maybe not many already. What did it matter?

I was standing by the door like an idiot, waiting for zombies and asking myself irrelevant questions.

Okay, I would go take a slow walk around the corridor on my floor. I did not want to go up to the fourth floor, because if anything happened down here, at least I could get home quickly.

So off I went.

My apartment was situated in a dead end at the side of the building, by the stairwell, so it was rare for strangers to be snooping around. But I was now heading for the central staircase, where there were many more apartments and, of course, zombies.

The first zombie I came across was at the beginning of the corridor, just standing there, staring at the wall and growling dully.

In invisible mode, I took its head off. I'd like to describe the event more colorfully, but all I did was stab it with my spear. I couldn't believe my own strength. I'm not one for grandstanding, but an average spear strike to the head was quite the thing.

As I passed the elevator, I could hear scratching sounds, quite disturbing ones. I did not envy anyone trapped in an elevator with a zombie, for they would not have the slightest chance of remaining alive. If that was the situation here, they were bang out of luck.

The corridors I walked along were straight out of a horror film, the walls smeared with blood in places, and the bloody prints of bare feet decorating floor. The apocalypse had caught many people in their beds. Most of the doors were closed, although not all, and my attention was caught by a scarcely audible noise coming from one door, or rather from the apartment behind it.

Entering someone else's apartment was certainly a great risk, but he who did not risk did not increase his level. And I had invisibility, which would help me in case something happened, and a spear in my hands. I entered the apartment very slowly, to allow my eyes to adjust to the half-light. The curtains at the windows were drawn and everywhere was dark.

I worked my way gingerly towards a strange knocking sound, and soon I saw the guest of honor.

A zombie with shoulder-length hair was handcuffed to a radiator. Next to it was a bed on which lay the corpse of a young girl. The girl showed no bite marks, only a smooshed head, while the man had been bitten all over. The bite marks did not look particularly nice, black and puffy, with evidence of corruption. One hell of a stink on him too.

I could only assume the wife had already turned but the husband hadn't. He managed to smash her head in, and she to get her teeth into him. Then he probably handcuffed himself to the radiator, not desiring to become a brainless zombie. Hmm, I wondered who he was, a policeman or a sex-shop customer. If he was a cop, it was worth scouring the place for weapons and ammunition. I didn't really need them, but they would be useful for trading should I came across any sane survivors.

I glanced at the man again, and a hilarious thought came to me. Usually chicks messed up men's heads, but this dreamboat had messed up her head, literally. And rightly so. What was she doing biting him?

No weapons or bullets were to be found in the place, but there was some food, which would come in handy, so a pack of bottles of water and two bunches of oranges went into my inventory. In the kitchen I found a juicer. Shame there was no electricity. I couldn't remember the last time I'd drunk real juice. Probably before I became a beggar. Although come to think of it, I'd always been a beggar.

The apartment was much better than mine. I thought about occupying it myself, but then I thought twice. Mine was somehow cozier and more familiar, perhaps, and the number of zombies I'd killed there... wow!

Now then, this will definitely come in handy, I thought to myself, noticing the mop. Just the thing for clearing up scraps of zombie in the apartment.

While I was combing the apartment for anything useful, I heard shuffling footsteps. Invisible, and bow in hand, I stepped out onto the landing. A zombie walked past. What, were they sending out patrols now? Without hesitating for too long, I retrieved an arrow from my inventory and pierced the zombie's decaying skull.

Unfortunately, no loot dropped from it, which was a bummer. I was used to getting stuff for free.

I gathered a few bits and bobs from the apartment, such as kitchen knives — again, I didn't know why — and in a broom closet I found a machete.

All that remained now was to find someone to flog all this trash to. Except the machete, which I would keep for myself. Although letting a zombie come too close was an enormous risk.

Finding nothing else of interest, I went out onto the landing. While I'd been busy in the apartment, the landing had become crowded with zombies, so I methodically began to pick them off. It might have been cheaper with the spear, but my bow was safer.

Crossing to another apartment block, I saw a throng of zombies crowding around a scratched and dented red iron door. Nothing out of the ordinary, had it not been for one detail. One of the zombies contrasted sharply with his comrades, the difference being the length of its claws. They were very long, and sharp as knives, and I seriously didn't want to get involved with them, so without a moment's hesitation, I shot it in the head, disposing of an unfamiliar enemy. The remaining eight zombies met similar fates.

One box and one trinket casket dropped from them, but I didn't hurry to collect the loot. Only now did I notice the dead zombies lying on the floor, their brains splattered over the walls by gunshot. There was no loot, which meant someone had already gathered it. I was pretty sure ten corpses would have dropped at least some loot.

Hmm, so there might be survivors around. With nothing to be afraid of in invisibility mode, I decided to wait and see what would happen next.

Ten minutes. Nothing. I came to the conclusion there was nothing to get worked up about and I should collect my loot, but not waste time doing so. I would run over, grab the boxes, put them straight in my inventory and quickly skip back three meters.

My gut instinct did not let me down. No sooner had the boxes disappeared than two unshaven gun-toting mugs jumped out from behind a door and looked feverishly up and down the corridor, their guns following their gazes.

"What the fuck, Dmitri? Where the fuck did the boxes go?" They couldn't understand what had just happened. Hearing somebody kill their deadmen, they had lain in wait for their unfortunate assistant.

"How do I know? Someone else must have picked them up," the puzzled Dmitri said, looking around.

"No way. We opened the door as soon as they disappeared. Was I wasting my time looking through the peephole for so long?"

"Dammit. I didn't think trophies could disappear," said Dmitri disappointedly. "I was already dreaming about increasing my inventory capacity for free."

"Hey, it's my turn. You slammed the last chick," his friend said indignantly. "And that's not all you did to her, hahaha," he added, guffawing like a donkey.

"I killed her. But you slammed her before that, and more than once too," Dmitri corrected him and burst out laughing.

"True enough," the friend said with a smile. "We slammed her together, and not just the once. Anyway, since trophies from deadmen can be sold, maybe we should leave them here out in the open and wait for someone to take the bait?"

"Could do... Aaaaaagh!" An arrow piercing his arm made Dmitri stop midsentence and drop his gun. His cry was soon accompanied by that of his friend, whose arm was almost simultaneously struck by its own arrow. It was clear I had stumbled across a pair of carrion feeders who were planning to level up quickly and were not above killing survivors. To their huge chagrin, I didn't give a toss about people either.

Two arrows, two pierced arms, two dropped weapons. Everything worked out just as I'd planned. Then I shot them in the leg. Their howls intensified. Zombies would be along soon.

I could, of course, have killed them straight away without wasting arrows, but I wanted them to behold their killer.

Exiting invisibility mode, I approached them with a smile and my spear in my hand.

"Booty out of your league, huh, guys?" All by itself my mouth spread into a wide smile, which to any onlookers might have looked a tad deranged.

"Who the hell are you?" Dmitri roared, trying to pick up his gun with his unstricken hand.

"Your death." My spear entered his neck, and blood sprayed out to the side like a fountain. Then I turned my gaze on his companion.

"Any last words?" I asked, taking a look into his frightened eyes.

"You don't have to do this," he begged through his tears.

"Oh, but I do," I replied, jabbing my spear into his eye and twisting it.

Then came the notifications.

You have killed a survivor.

The capacity of your inventory is increased by 7.5 kg.

You have killed a survivor.

The capacity of your inventory is increased by 4.5 kg.

I see. So that means the more people I kill, the more my inventory grows. Or that's what it seemed to me, at any rate.

As a result, my inventory would now hold twenty kilograms, and that could not fail to delight.

Foot stomping from behind.

Damn, my head was now bait for the walking dead.

I about turned and began to fire. There weren't so many of them, just a dozen, which was good, since my supply of arrows was running very low. I gathered up my new trophies and decided to have a peek into these bastards' apartment.

Approaching the doorway where the two dead losers lay, I spotted a yellow trinket casket. I hadn't seen a yellow one before. Scratching my head, I inspected it from all angles.

Now this might be interesting.

As I stepped into the apartment, my olfactory senses were immediately struck by a lingering smell of booze.

I had taken the trinket casket and the guys' guns, and retrieved my arrows, so I could confidently close the door.

The apartment had three rooms, and its owner appeared to be a hunter and fisherman. All the walls were hung with photographs of a man and his trophies, yet he looked nothing like either of the two guys in the corridor. They'd probably taken over his home and availed themselves of his weapons. In the bedroom was an empty safe, and on a table were two opened boxes of hunting-rifle ammunition, as well as five unopened. They went straight into my inventory.

The pickings in this apartment were much richer than in the previous ones, I understood as I surveyed a small mountain of food. Canned foods, pasta, water, and a couple of bottles of vodka. A bunch of empty booze bottles lay on the floor. It hadn't even occurred to these swine to throw them out of the window. They'd been counting on trashing this place and then looking for a new one.

The sight of a stock of toilet paper and jars of cocoa was a pleasant one. My last cocoa had been with grandma. I collected all the worthwhile stuff and threw it in my inventory. Then I continued my search of the apartment, which was clearly going to last until evening. I would have a bite to eat and a rest here, and then return to my own lair.

CHAPTER 4

I RETURNED HOME TOWARDS evening, as planned. I decided to walk past any zombies in invisibility mode, and it worked. They didn't even notice me when I passed by very close.

I was beginning to understand there must be a reason for the level-10 invisibility add-on.

I had eaten "out," so there was nothing to stop me crashing straightaway. I pulled off my dirty clothes and went to bed. Exhaustion had taken its toll and it didn't even occur to me to take a shower.

The morning began hectically.

I was awakened by wild shouts outside the window, followed by gunshots, more shouting, and the sound of glass smashing.

"What the hell is going on out there?" I skipped sleepily out of bed and ran to the balcony. "Shit, should have stayed in bed."

The end of the world was apparently nigh.

Down on the street, humans were battling flying beasties that were just like humans, only with wings. They had very thin bodies and looked like bats.

The beasties produced abominable sounds that made me want to block my ears and hide. Jeez, were they attacking with ultrasound?

And where had so many of them come from? Surely they hadn't mutated into these monsters from regular zombies? I observed as the beasts smashed against the windows of buildings in their attempts to break in. Some were successful, and from inside came people's shouts for help. I watched a guy from the next building hang out of his window and slash at one beast with a sword, slicing off its wings. But another swooped down on him from above and pulled him out of the window, before dropping him to the ground, where he died on impact. The beastie then collected its loot and flew off.

My brain was trying quickly to figure out a course of action. The best thing seemed to be to wait until they flew away, then barricade the windows. Or even better, board them up.

As I was taking in all this horror, the beasties' numbers grew and grew. I decided to take a risk and picked up my bow. Screw trophies. I had to kill as many bats as I could before they noticed me.

Shooting flying targets was not the easiest of tasks, since it took several seconds to take aim each time, and it was impossible to get them in the head, because they flew so quickly. The idea was to graze them at the very least. My first flier, I have no clue how, I struck in a wing bone, making it crash like a stone to the ground.

"Fuck!" The beastie fell from the fourth floor and was still alive, floundering helplessly on the ground. Not wanting to waste arrows, I didn't finish it off, and it was harmless now anyway. From paratrooper to wounded infantrymen in one fell swoop.

Looking for further targets, I continued my firing mission. Twenty arrows later, ten flying beasts had become pedestrians. Arrows, however, were not the only thing I was losing, as my self-esteem was also taking a fall. Ten misses. WTF?

I decided to put it down to the light trembling in my arms. There were already noticeably fewer beasties, yet it was another question that was of greater interest to me, namely, why were they not attacking me?

No sooner had I asked myself the question than I answered it for myself. I'd forgotten to deactivate invisibility yesterday, and this was the sole reason I hadn't been eaten asleep.

It seemed I had come up trumps with this ability.

I had almost no arrows left, but to spare them at this point we would be totally stupid. *The more of these beasties we kill, the more people will be able to survive in this meat grinder.* I was no good samaritan, but this was a good way to clear my conscience. I downed another seven fliers and left it at that, with just three arrows left.

I closed the window and went to fix some food. I had done everything I could for now, and I needed a break from the emotional strain of battle watching. What was the point if I couldn't do anything? I decided not to deactivate invisibility, in order to check whether it could be active all the time.

Today was pasta-and-mince day, using mineral water to boil the pasta. Then I had a can of pineapple, and I washed it all down with hot chocolate. There were oranges for dessert.

As I was peeling my third orange, I remembered there was loot left from yesterday that I hadn't yet opened. It wasn't much, but there was the odd thing of interest. Pity there were no red trinket caskets.

Settling myself more comfortably into my armchair, I got busy with the trophies.

The white box went straight into the inventory, unopened. The second one I picked up.

"May I get lucky," I said aloud, while mentally giving the command to open.

You have received: a skill book, evaluation level 1.

Hmm, I do in fact seem to have gotten lucky.

I quickly studied the evaluation, and if I understood correctly, it would open my eyes to many things.

I went into *Status*, focused on *Evaluation*, and said, "Evaluation."

Skill - for 1 level, evaluation provides the opportunity to learn more information.

Which was all very well, but evaluation didn't provide much information about me. It turned out that level was way more important than I'd originally supposed.

I had no idea how to level up, but I did have an inkling it would be a good idea to collect as many fact cards as possible.

Then I decided to find out what my invisibility was all about.

The Invisibility skill shields you from the eyes of others. The higher your level of skill, the less mana used and the harder it is to find you. The higher levels conceal scent, heat, and other clues that lead to discovery.

A creature whose Invisibility level is higher than yours will be able to see you. This also works the other way around.

Now that was interesting. The system was hinting that other people existed — and not only people — with the same skill. Which meant that were I to come across someone whose skill was level 11, they would be able to see me.

That was a game changer. I would have to be more cautious.

On the other hand, I would also be able to see invisibles. Which, I had to say, was freaking wicked. I was sure there were very few folk with level-10 skills in the city right now. The great system had given it to me for First Kill. And I had not yet come across anything at even level 2. And anyway, there weren't that many system items with levels.

Besides, the system had given me an open characteristic. Possibly because my skill was level 10 and it would take quite a lot of explaining.

If I understood everything correctly, then I was okay with it. It was now practically impossible for loners to survive in this world, as evidenced by today's beastie incursion. The problem was that I wasn't overflowing with desire to join forces with other people. My skill was perfect for a loner. It didn't give me much, mind you, and I had to kill zombies not in their tens, but in their hundreds. I needed more skills and more system items.

I hope I can get a skill which works on mana. This is the second, and no mana yet.

Although, hang on, how can it work without mana? It's clearly written here that it uses mana, albeit less and less with each level. What if it stops depending on mana at level 10? That would be most advantageous. So, I must not reveal my skill level to anyone, or they'll definitely shoot me.

If I didn't shoot them first, that is. I desperately needed protection. I might get lucky with a useful skill. A protection dome or invincibility wouldn't go amiss. What about anti-impudence tablets? Ah...

I ought to check my spear while I'm at it.

Short iron-bamboo spear: a good-quality weapon.

I was pleased the evaluation was not a laconic "Weapon, spear." *Thank you for that, system.*

Okay, let's continue the check.

Tent: a bad-quality terrestrial tent.

What Chinese basement had the system pinched it from? And why did it not say, "Made in China" in the description?

While I was pondering what to check next, I heard a noise coming from the door. My first thought was zombies, but then I remembered I was invisible and they could not have sensed me.

Damn, what a bad time to be down to three arrows. I retrieved my spear from my inventory and went on a recce. Out in the hallway, I realized the noise was somebody tugging the handle on the other side.

WTF? Was someone trying to burgle me? Were there not enough empty apartments around?

Shoot, what to do? If I opened the door, invisibility wasn't going to stop me taking a bullet. It remained only to wait and see what would happen.

Five minutes of silence. Nothing. Until the sudden sound of glass smashing. It came from my bedroom, where the balcony was.

Fuck. Why hadn't it occurred to me that since it was so easy for me to break into someone else's apartment, then it wouldn't be difficult for someone else to break into mine?

Moving as quietly as I could, I went to deal with my uninvited guests, narrowly missing one of them in the hallway. Thankfully, I managed to press myself up against the wall before the stranger ran past, pistol in hand.

They're definitely looking for me.

There were only two of them, and the second

was lagging behind his partner. He looked like he weighed about a 130 kg, so an obstacle like the balcony would be a true obstacle for him.

"Fuck, where is he?" barked the faster man, who had entered the apartment first.

"He can't have had time to hide, the louse," the fat man said, spitting on my carpet in frustration.

"Pity to let such a juicy fellow get away. He must have loads of loot. I watched him throwing corpses off his neighbor's balcony."

"Maybe we could wait?" suggested fatboy as he headed for the kitchen. "Great, there's chow in here. Just what we need."

"Tolyan, we've got loads of food already, we need to find other stuff," his friend said, not sharing Tolyan's joy, but beginning instead to ransack the living room.

"Wow, look what I've found!" he soon said, joyous now as he beheld my unopened boxes of loot.

Now this was a challenge. They wanted to take my stuff, and I seriously didn't like it when other people touched my possessions. I really deadly seriously didn't like it.

"At least we won't be going back with empty hands. The boss wouldn't understand that." Now it was his turn to share his joy and good fortune with fatboy. What he didn't know was that fatboy already had an arrow in his eye.

When fatboy crashed down onto my kitchen table, I thought the walls shuddered, but his friend didn't react. Maybe it was normal for them to hear a friend making a racket in the kitchen.

Without wasting time, I dashed to the living room, getting there just in time. The man's hands were reaching out for my boxes, ready to put them in his inventory. In my anger, I pulled my bowstring back so hard the bow creaked.

I did not have time to aim accurately, so the arrow only got him in the temple. A short squelching sound, and the guy was dead.

"The fuckwits wanted to rip me off." I was seething.

Only now did it occur to me what had happened and what I'd done.

Fuck, I killed two people. In my apartment. That's a stain on the apartment. I've ruined its aura. What am I going to do? I don't want to live in an apartment where I killed two people.

Okay, let's see what the system has to say.

You have killed a survivor.

The capacity of your inventory is increased by 2 kg.

You have killed a survivor.

The capacity of your inventory is increased by 1 kg.

Not exactly a lot. The most interesting thing was that the guy with the pistol hadn't killed anyone yet, while fatboy, despite his goody-goody appearance, evidently had skeletons in his closet.

They may have wanted to kill me, but to some extent I was grateful to them for increasing my inventory by three kilograms for nothing.

Ideally, I needed at least a hundred kilograms, and half of that weight should be arrows.

Now I had no worries carrying the spear, bow, and all the other bits and pieces. That said, if any other useful loot turned up, I would again have problems with storage space. I could, of course, use a backpack, but that would be silly, making me slower and less maneuverable, and I might even snag a zombie on it. As it was, I could easily avoid zombies by weaving in and out between them.

All said and done, however, this was very bad timing, I thought to myself as I looked at the stiffs. Their conversation had made it clear I'd been spotted on my balcony and they'd been sent to deal with me. People were organizing themselves into gangs faster than I'd thought, and it was now a problem for me. I had to urgently think of a way to protect myself. It was time to move house.

Pity. I'd grown accustomed to my apartment.

Or maybe I should stay? I took another glance at the corpse in the living room.

Not an option, I thought with a heavy sigh. My windows were busted out, as was the balcony door. It would be drafty at night. What if I caught a chill? Fuck that shit. I was better off finding myself new lodgings.

I figured I still had an hour to spare before the guys' absence was noticed and the gang became concerned enough to send out a search party. *Aha, now that's an idea!*

I ran to the door and unlocked it. Now anyone could enter at any time. I dragged the corpses out to the balcony and hoisted them over the edge, putting their weapons in my inventory and realizing just how little space was left.

Screw it. If my guess was correct, when the search party arrived, my inventory would increase again.

Sure enough, an hour later, the search party arrived. I heard the front door squeak.

The bow was already in my hands, an arrow loaded and the bowstring drawn in readiness.

A swordsman crept stealthily along the hallway and into the kitchen, throwing a quick glance into the living room on the way. He was followed by another man, with a pistol and shield held out in front. Idiots. The one with the shield should have gone first.

After these, surprisingly, came a tall girl with a crossbow in her hands. A dumb weapon for the apocalypse. She'd be killed while she was reloading, if not eaten alive and raped to boot. There was nothing better than a longbow. Although, no, I lie. There was nothing better than a longbow with a supply of arrows.

"Gera, somebody's definitely been snuffed here," the man shouted from the kitchen, "there's blood everywhere. Can't see a corpse though."

"All clear this end," came Gera's voice from the bedroom.

"No corpses means they weren't deadmen."

"What have you got, Puma?"

Evidently Puma was the girl. She was currently checking out the living room, where I squatted silently in an empty corner.

"Nothing here either, except blood, lots of blood," she replied hoarsely.

"D'you reckon he snuffed these two cretins and legged it?"

"Probably," said the girl with a nod when they gathered in the living room.

I wondered if I might be able to kill all three of them. They would spot where the arrows were coming from and put a cap in my ass.

Obviously I would have to fell the guy with the shield first. But before that I had to split them up. It so happened that I had the wherewithal to do just that. I produced from my inventory a tennis ball, which had magically found its way into my home, and threw it behind them into the hallway.

The first to react was the shield bearer, who turned sharply towards the door and raised his shield to defend himself.

Teamwork was clearly their weak point. Without a word, the guy with the sword ran out into the hallway, while the chick surprised me again. Her crossbow in one hand, the other was clenched into a fist which emitted a radiance that quickly grew into a shimmering shield to cover the girl. I had no clue what was going on. Clearly protection and skill, possibly a magic shield. She now posed the most danger to me, and it was unclear what other surprises she might have up her sleeve.

While the girl aimed at the doorway, holding her magic shield, the guys investigated the origin of the noise.

My arrow entered her neck at just the moment she moved her arm slightly and the shield momentarily ceased to protect that part of her body. Her finger automatically pulled the trigger of her crossbow, and a bolt — yes, that's what crossbow ammunition is called — penetrated the wooden door right up to the fletching.

Without a second's thought, I threw myself over to the other corner of the room to get a better view of the door.

First to react to the shot, the shield-bearing fool came running. Fool for thinking his shield would save him when his head had nothing to cover it. My arrow landed slap bang in the middle of his forehead.

I was already prepared to kill the swordsman, but my plan failed. Since he was standing behind the guy with the shield, he was able to see Puma lying on the floor, and he caught the moment the arrow struck his friend. I figured he'd launch himself into the room berserker-style and start waving his toothpick around, but instead he behaved like a military commander, simply beating a hasty retreat, and so quickly that I didn't have time to bring him down.

And now it was my turn to flee as quickly as possible.

But first I would have to get my good mood back.

You have killed a survivor.

The capacity of your inventory is increased by 2 kg.

You have killed a survivor.

The capacity of your inventory is increased by 4 kg.

I wasn't exactly seeking people out with a desire to kill them. This was them seeking me out. What was wrong with just sitting at home? Sit at home, kill zombies, level up, and become stronger. I did not understand the need to level up at the expense of other survivors.

I doubted it was only me who would have been able to kill them so easily. Without invisibility, I would have found another means to kill them. You could always think of something.

People were losing their minds. So shaken by the apocalypse were they, that they'd begun to lose their human aspect. Although perhaps the problem was not so much loot as fear of strong survivors who might visit more problems on gangs in the future.

If that was the case, they were right. At present, I was by far not the weakest opponent, and we were only four days in. I could still remember naked people being thrown from the top floors. The person I'd killed suffered a fall, and in doing so made a good contribution to my inventory. I don't think he was level 1, which is what allowed him not to die straightaway but to survive the drop, albeit not for long. If that was the case, then with level 10 it might be possible to jump down easily from any floor.

But none of this was for certain.

Anyway, it was time to gather my things and look for a new home.

CHAPTER 5

GERASIM WAS FRIGHTENED. He ran up those cursed stairs to the seventh floor, where he lived, without looking where he was putting his feet, resulting in him falling over a number of times.

They'd been sent out on a rather simple errand, which involved finding two of the group, who had disappeared, and helping them if they had any problems. They had information that the apartment was inhabited by one person with a fair zombie kill tally. Meaning he was a hardened lone wolf with plenty of supplies and perhaps some interesting gear.

When the end of the world had arrived, their floor did not suffer overly, what with being home to several armed ex-cons. They had cleared the floor at once, gathered everybody together, and organized themselves into a group.

The first two days were good to them. Then

they ran out of ammo and food. Dropped crates were rare and insufficient, but then everything changed when one of the leaders took the guys on a reconnaissance mission and returned in the evening with five boxes. He said they'd found them in the fifth-floor apartment of a loner who'd managed to off a dozen deadmen.

This was how they realized that dropped loot went more often to lone zombie killers than to those who went around in crowds. When a certain sortie gifted one of the guys a dropped fact card, they finally understood there were many rules that the people were yet to discover.

They had later decided to increase the membership of the group, compelling people to join them, but also making them surrender their possessions to the collective fund, and simply killing anyone who was against the idea. And the killings became all the more frequent when they learned how to increase the capacity of their inventories.

Each of them wanted to become the strongest.

Things were going superbly for them, the group was dressed and armed, and Puma got the skill of Barrier, which could withstand several shots fired simultaneously.

But when Gerasim saw how lightening quick his compadres had been killed, he was frightened for the first time in ages, at long last realizing he wasn't the only one who could hunt. The worst thing was he hadn't seen who'd done it, and so his survival instinct kicked in: run!

Never mind, thought Gera, *I'll go see the management, and they can decide what to do.* He had no doubt there would be a hunt for the murderer. The loner was strong, perhaps even very strong, and Gera would start a rumor that hunting him might even bump your inventory up by fifty kilograms. A host of candidates would immediately rock up and go in search of him, eventually finding and killing him. Everybody on the seventh floor knew about this method of inventory expansion, and the larger the killed person's inventory, the more kilograms you would receive in reward.

* * *

Leaving my own apartment forever was very sad for the one simple reason that it was mine. I had been left no choice, however, and not even by zombies, but by the most terrifying opponent in this reality: humans.

Altogether my collected trophies filled a backpack and two other bags. Not everything fitted into the inventory, and I did not want to leave anything; they were my trophies and I would take them with me! I had previously received some trading coins, and if they allowed me to trade, then possibly I could swap some useless stuff for arrows and something else from the system. I just had to puzzle out how they worked.

One foot out of the apartment, I realized I'd forgotten one crucial thing. Returning to my living room, I activated evaluation on the dead shield bearer.

Name: Dmitri Shvetsov.

Status: Dead.

Level: 2.

Skills: inaccessible; evaluation level too low.

I urgently had to find out how to increase my skills, and I wanted more information about my enemies.

I'd had the enormous urge to check them the second they entered, but I was worried they might get a notification and the element of surprise would be gone.

Anyway, slinging my backpack and bags over my shoulder, I plodded off in search of new accommodation.

I selected the first floor, figuring everyone down there must have been long dead due to the high density of zombies per square meter.

I was right. On my way down there, I came across more and more zombies, and I did not like their appearance one bit. If in the first few days they'd looked like diseased people, they now looked one hundred percent like deadmen, their skin now very pale, and with sanious patches and lesions aplenty. Over time, their bodies had begun to decay, but their flesh was still clinging tenaciously to their bones. The sight was most unflattering and I hoped they would not become skeletons, for then it would be harder to hit them with my bow.

On the way, I came across a cretin of a zombie who had gotten his head trapped between the banister railings and was flouncing feebly in his attempt to free it.

My hands were full, but I could not resist jumping feetfirst onto the deadman's unprotected neck. An ear-pleasing crunch of bones was heard, upon which the system immediately calculated the true value of the deed.

You have gained level 4.

Your body has become stronger. Your skin and bones are stronger.

I was right. The system made people stronger with each new level. At the moment I received my level, I felt a light itching in my skin. It was gone a second later, leaving me thinking I'd imagined it.

If the itch was anything to do with the fortification of the skin covering, then it was worth revising my view of levels, and reviewing my attitude to the killing of zombies, or more precisely, to the number of zombies I killed. By increasing my level, I hoped I would become not only stronger, but also faster, tougher, and smarter, which meant I needed to level up, and the sooner the better.

When I reached the ground floor, I discovered one disadvantage of living there, and that was the stench coming from the beasties, of whom there were hordes.

But all said and done, it was quite suitable for my defense purposes. There were so many zombies down here that on occasion I couldn't even pass through the crowd. I was forced to make a noise off to the side, to distract them and give myself a chance to run through.

I'd had a specific apartment in mind since first conceiving the idea. A rich dude had once bought two apartments here and knocked them through into one big one. He'd decorated it at great expense, installed a load of household appliances, and moved his lover in there so he could rendezvous with her unbeknownst to his wife.

Apartments on the lower floors were much cheaper compared to those higher up above the twentieth. That's where the truly well-to-do folk lived.

The thing was that when the building was being built, the construction company had problems with its documentation. The authorities' answer was to obligate the company to set aside five floors for the poor, which was a colossal amount of money in this very expensive housing block. However, the developers found their own answer to this new problem, which was to economize by not decorating the apartments or furnishing them with expensive gadgets. To begin with, everything was on the level and they housed common folk here, giving them discounts on apartments. Then later they created terrible living conditions, and for varying reasons the inhabitants sold these same apartments back to the same company for next to nothing.

It was no secret to us residents that the agreement with the government would end this year, at which point they planned to take their apartments back, spruce them up, and create an elite apartment building, which had been the plan in the first place. In order to understand the disdain for the common folk, it was worth remembering that each stairwell had several entrances, but only one was open to the common people inhabiting the apartments on the first ten floors. If someone wanted to walk up the stairs, there was security everywhere that permitted entry only upon production of a special pass.

The elevator was also programmed to work with the use of cards, without which the denizens of the lower floors could not ascend to the elite. Cards were issued once only, and if you lost yours, you weren't getting a replacement.

The upper floors were now filled with society zombies and society people who couldn't give a toss about the common folk. They had even fewer morals than the zombies, and if those silver-spooners were to knock together their own group, the common folk would be their servants, their entertainment, their expendable materials, and so on.

This was why I had to strengthen up as soon as possible. While I hoped everyone had been eaten up there, the unfortunate truth was that this was wishful thinking. The sounds of gunshot from there were very frequent and I'd also noticed that zombies were always crawling up that way: zombies that were drawn to people.

None of those people, however, had the

advantage I had of free access to the street. If the shit really hit the fan, I could escape.

I had no trouble finding the apartment, and on seeing the massive iron door, I nodded my appreciation. Right now a strong door was just the ticket.

The only downer was that it was locked. I was not one to give up, however, and I certainly wasn't going to here. I decided to enter from the other side. The door to the neighboring apartment was wide open. And smeared with fresh blood.

I entered and saw zombies, so I quickly had to deal with them. The apartment was very small, twenty square meters at most, making it quite difficult to wield my spear. Pity I only had one arrow left.

I skewered one zombie's forehead with the spear. His brethren were none too pleased and immediately began scurrying around the apartment, stooped over, sniffing, and flailing their very long claws. I found myself having to dodge and repel. The zombies could not see me, but they clearly sensed something and slashed at the air, trying to grab hold of whoever was killing them. Five zombies died like heroes, gifting me just one blue trinket casket.

The last zombie actually looked at me and attacked. Apparently, killing zombies in invisibility mode did not always work out. It worked without a hitch only when I didn't actively attack them, but when I began to move, they would get wise to the situation and the skill would weaken.

"Come on, surprise me." I decided not to shelve the trinket casket for later but to open it straightaway.

You receive fact card №51: for the first month following infection, infecteds have no level, but while this does not affect their strength, mutation and evolution are accessible to them. With time, new kinds will appear.

Well, nobody said it was going to be easy. I shrugged my shoulders and moved over to the window.

I dropped all my stuff by the window and climbed out of it. The racket made by an old window being opened was a nightmare, a fact that zombies were only too glad of. Two of them wandered into the room while I was in the process of trying to open the window, so I had to stop to kill them.

Good job I had a spear.

I had definitely gotten lucky with my new apartment. The window was open a crack for ventilation, and the window ledges I crawled along to reach it were wide. If the worst came to the worst, I would not be afraid to fall off, since it was only a three-meter drop. That said, I wasn't wildly inclined to try it.

I crawled over to the window and tried to break the mechanism by knocking out the glass, but failed. It cracked in completely the wrong place for my needs, but then I produced my sword, and things instantly became easier. A sword could occasionally serve as a crowbar, and I used it to shift the window sufficiently to the side that something snapped inside the locking mechanism.

The apartment was quite cozy. I jumped down onto a fluffy white carpet, which did not remain white for long due to my red footprints.

The decor was swank, the walls hung with trendy pictures and posters, and the floor was parqueted.

"Yes, it would be great to live in an apartment like this," I said, a smile crawling onto my face all by itself.

Giving the apartment a look over, I was very glad to find neither people nor zombies. Using the same route I'd just come by, I shifted my belongings into the apartment in two trips, and I could now say coolheadedly: I am home.

Home had another small but pleasant surprise for me. In the hallway hung a key box containing two keys, one a car key, the second for the front door.

The car key prompted me towards an interesting thought. Just outside the main door downstairs was a parking lot full of parked cars. I took the electronic key over to the window and pressed a button on it to discover which ride was mine.

"Ugh, a red beetle," I said, disappointed to behold the unpleasantness. Even without this zombie apocalypse, you would never catch me behind the wheel of a car like that. Added to which, the number plate read: *Honey Bunny.*

However, I needed the car for something completely different. I pressed a button on the side of the key, and the alarm went off loudly enough for the entire neighborhood to hear. Excellent. The zombies scattered and now nobody would hang around beneath my windows, although the car did get a fair bashing from the irate zombies before they fled.

I could now breathe easy. I shut the window and went in search of the kitchen. The window shut okay, but I wouldn't be able to open it to air the apartment anymore, though there was no point doing that anyway, what with hordes of zombies roaming about down there wafting their fetid stink around.

Cleaning the apartment took all day and well into the night. I made the place look shipshape, dumping clothes and other stuff in the apartment next door and installing my own order.

The most pleasant find came before bedtime, when I decided to take a bath, and just for a moment got a jacuzzi. Without electricity there were no bubbles, but simply being able to lie there with my legs stretched out was intensely pleasurable.

After the bath, I crashed out with a blissful smile on my face.

My sleep was pleasant but not long. In the middle of the night I was awoken by such a forceful explosion I thought the city had met its end. My first thought was that we'd had a nuclear warhead dropped on us.

However, I seemed, thankfully, to be alive, which meant my version of events had not come to pass.

The building shook spectacularly, though the windows staunchly withstood the blow, which delighted me.

Since I was alive and it appeared to have passed, I decided to go back to bed, but my sleep was broken by frequent explosions and shots, albeit not so powerful as the first one.

It was probably the military stepping into the fray. It was a shame they wouldn't be able to cope. Of that I was sure. We didn't have enough troops for such an enormous number of zombies, on top of which, those that had turned into zombies were now an order of magnitude more powerful than the living ones.

Ah, who cares?

* * *

Early morning, strolling around the park, killing zombies with my spear and embracing life.

Only in moments such as these did I begin to understand just how lucky I was with the skill I'd gained.

I'd awoken early, eaten, exercised, and washed, when I thought, *Why not go out for a walk?* And so I did.

Without any impediment whatsoever, I stepped out, invisible, onto the street and headed for the recreation park, which was close by.

If I understood one thing that morning, it was that the world was fucked, totally and utterly.

Sitting at home, you didn't see it, but out on streets, destruction and death presented themselves in all their glory. Zombies everywhere. Lots of zombies. Freaking loads of zombies. Everywhere lay the bodies of dead people, their bones picked clean and masks of terror frozen on their faces. Quite possibly, those who had turned were the lucky ones, for now they did not have to stew in the hell that people were forced to live in.

That said, while there was still a choice, I would remain a human. I had never really liked just going for a walk in the park, and I was here for one simple reason. I was looking for the fairground shooting gallery, where previously you were able to shoot at targets from a bow. It probably had lots of arrows left over from those times. Ham-fisted people always managed to break them when they missed the targets, and I figured there was no way the owner didn't have a stock of spares.

It took me ten minutes to get to the gallery, then I stood there thwacking the lock with the blunt end of my spear. Each strike brought zombie noises closer. There weren't actually so many of them in the park, and naturally there were no people around, apart from myself.

After God knows how many strikes, the lock finally gave way, and after opening the squeaking door, I was able to enter the premises.

I found the arrows straightaway, seventy of

them, in a large wooden barrel. And yes, I did count them. Then I found another hundred under the counter. They were old, with blunted heads, worn-down nocks, and no fletchings. Mind you, I was still grateful, for an archer without arrows is no fighter.

Now I could relax and get on with the business of depleting the zombie population.

In the morning, on the way to the park, I had killed a couple of monsters, spending my last arrow in the process. In the same process, I'd learned the following: when I killed zombies with my spear, they began to see or sense me, whereas with a bow, this was not a problem. I figured it was a matter of distance.

Yesterday I hadn't killed enough zombies, and today I planned to climb at least one level, preferably two. My morning exercises showed that my body had indeed become stronger. A knife that slipped as I was slicing baloney had not scarred my finger or made me cuss. Actually that's not true; I did cuss, but only out of surprise.

Before starting to fell anything that moved, I decided first to get to grips with how my invisibility worked. I had to understand the basic principle of its action.

To this end, I selected small groups of zombies and skewered their skulls one by one with my spear, leaving just two or three alive.

The experiment took three hours, but it was not time wasted.

Based on personal experience, I discovered it

was only possible to kill small groups of zombies in invisibility mode, and if there were more than ten, it wasn't worth it.

After I'd killed three zombies, the others closest to them would begin to move towards me. While the fourth could not actually see me, it would slash its claws confidently in my direction, and I would become visible to those that followed, hungering for my blood and flesh.

However, after killing one group, I could calmly approach another, provided it was at least twenty yards from the first, and none of them would see me until I began to pop them off, at which point everything would repeat.

I proved myself even cooler with the bow-and-arrow part of the experiment. Sticking zombies from a distance of ten or twenty meters, I remained unnoticed, which was pleasing. Certainly the spear was still a useful implement, but the bow was many times more reliable.

And my invisibility was even better than the bow. That said, if it had been level 1, its activation would have cost me mana I didn't have, and I seriously doubted whether I would have been able to walk calmly among the zombies. To the extent I had noticed thus far, with each new level of an item or skill, or even a character's level, the system became stronger, just as I did.

The fact of my skin and bones becoming tougher gave me hope for the future.

At this point, my ponderings and experimentation ended, and a mass of zombies advanced. Singles I killed with my spear, and large groups I simply peppered with arrows, before gathering them up again along with any loot. The park suited me perfectly. A large open territory where I could simultaneously shoot and control the space around me. Total control of the vicinity: that was the key to survival. It was all too easy to get carried away and not spot enemies approaching from behind.

Enemies could not only be zombies, but people as well, and that had to be borne in mind. Bullets were faster than zombies.

Arrows flew, zombies died, and I became richer yet poorer at the same time. Barrel-loads were all very well, but arrows had a tendency to break.

By evening I'd managed to climb a level and collect a respectable amount of loot, which consisted mainly of gray boxes of food.

My dead-zombie tally was already over two hundred. If it were to continue at the same rate, I would have to destroy no fewer than a thousand infecteds in order to level up again, and that would be no mean feat.

You have gained level 5. Your body has become stronger. Your internal organs are stronger and more robust.

Another interesting thing was a yellow trinket casket, which in theory should have contained a skill card.

Taking a seat on a park bench, I took it out and, without thinking, opened it.

You receive: a skill book: critical hit, level 1.

Hmm, I instantly activated evaluation.

Skill: critical hit saturates your hand of choice with mana, and your next hit will be twice stronger than usual.

Shoot. It ate mana and provided only one hit, although in truth it was an enhanced hit. I had no problems killing zombies with my spear, and such a skill would only be useful for a close-combat fighter against armored targets.

And if I saw an armored target, I would not approach it but riddle it with arrows from a distance. Or run away.

Fine, I would leave it until later, when the whats and the hows were clear. You could never have too many skills, but I didn't want to clutter my life up with them. Perhaps there was a limit to the number of skills you could have. Who knew?

There is no limit to the number of skills a player can have. There is a limit concerning skills transferred to another sentient being. A skill may not be sold or gifted, only exchanged for another skill.

Wow. I was startled. The system had decided to speak with me.

"Thank you for deigning to speak to me. For the first time."

You have spoken out of turn. As a result, your next fact casket will be empty.

You're kidding? Well, have it your way.

Not wanting to delay, I took out the blue

trinket casket and opened it. I did not want to be in debt to the system.

Sure enough, it was empty. Then with a quiet "pop", it vanished.

"You see, now I owe you nothing," I said to the system, before smiling and moving on.

It was time to leave. I raised my head and gazed at the sky to see it was nearly evening. Wondering about at night was a dubious pleasure. I might get eaten and not know by whom.

Although, what difference did it make who ate you? Or maybe there was a difference? Either way it was interesting. I mean, what if they choked?

CHAPTER 6

RETURNING HOME VIA NARROW side streets, I took the decision not to fight any zombies along the way. There were lots of houses to the side, providing endless opportunities for concealment, and I was eminently spottable, which I did not care for. When I came out onto Peace Street, my attention was attracted by running zombies and the sound of gunshot. I wondered who might be so desperate as to start shooting with all these zombies around.

So curious was I, in fact, that I went to find out, holding my spear at the ready in case the zombies decided to rush me. Two minutes later, I saw the focus of their interest.

They had surrounded a small food store with a meter-high fence around it, to which they were now stuck, having shoved their arms through the wattling.

By the entrance to the store stood a man in military uniform with a pistol in his hand. He was methodically shooting the deadmen, but their numbers continued to increase. It could not go on indefinitely, of course, for he would run out of bullets before the zombies ran out of numbers. To begin with, his eyes darted everywhere in search of an exit, but eventually the spark of hope in his eyes was extinguished. I observed him from the side, avoiding the bullets emerging from empty zombie heads. I did not want to fall prey to a stray bullet in invisibility mode.

I wonder what he'll do next.

What happened next was seriously worth watching. He dove into an enormous backpack full of spoils, retrieved a number of metal cans, and began throwing them in various directions.

What, has he made grenades out of cans of stewed meat? I thought to myself in amazement. Ah, no, it's just regular stewed meat.

The soldier's plan was to distract the zombies. It didn't happen.

I would have thought *WTF?*, had I not known it was the living whom they were able to sense.

Perhaps I should throw a can back at him, see what he thinks of that. Then he can tell all his buddies about the boomerang can. If he survives, that is.

Now then, and what's this?

The man extended his open palm towards the zombies and spat fire at them. Once, twice, three times. Just like any other kind of damage, this did not exactly add to the bloodthirsty beasties' benignity.

I was watching magic at work. The soldier said nothing, his lips did not move, but the fire appeared pretty quickly in his palm, and was directed at its target with similar rapidity. I did not know what it was actually called, but I would call it a "fiery hot dog," for that particular sausage-and-bread-roll combo was precisely what the shape of the fire in his hand reminded me of.

I figured he had very little mana left. If he were level 10, his chances would be higher. As it was, he was pretty much done for.

Yet he did not give up. Running into the little shop, which truth be told was more like a kiosk, he emerged with a mop handle. My man! I had also had occasion to use that mighty weapon.

Producing an obviously military knife, he hastily sharpened one end and went to bag himself some zombies. After his first successful kill, however, his new weapon was shredded to splinters by sharp claws. Claws which, as I'd noticed before, seemed to be getting longer.

I produced from my inventory a piece of paper and a pencil, and wrote, "Frightened?" Using a rubber band, I fixed the note to a can of meat I found close by, which I then launched at the soldier, narrowly avoiding his head.

Make no mistake, he was a soldier. The haircut, the movements, the actions, not to mention the stripes on his shoulders. And the way he reacted like he'd been stung, skipping away from the incoming can. Good reactions.

"What the freak?" he shouted after reading my missive. "Who's there? Is this some kind of skill? Don't hold your tongue, answer me."

I waited in silence for him to verbally unburden himself. I had nothing to say to him just yet.

"Can you help me?" he asked in hope. "I'm prepared to give you all the food I found here. It's not much, about twenty cans, and there's a load of bits and bobs, nothing of any value."

Funny. He wanted to buy me with stewed meat when I had fifty boxes of food in my inventory.

Hopelessness was overcoming the man, fear and desperation creeping into his eyes.

Everyone was scared, and that was just fine, fighters were no exception.

The he said, "My daughter's here with me. I beg of you, at least save her, and my comrades-in-arms will show their gratitude if you deliver her to our communal apartment on Trade Street. She's just a child and she's very afraid. I beseech you. I'll do anything if you can help. Help! If you're a man, I'm asking you as another man. No, I'm asking you as a father, save my daughter!"

In confirmation of his claim, he went back into the store and came back out with a little girl who looked to be about seven. Her face was grimy, gaunt, and tear-stained, and one hand clutched a small doll, the other a nibbled bread roll.

Fuck, this has nothing to do with me.

Nothing!

But it was a child.

I did not like people, that was the truth.

But children were not people. If I left now, how would I feel later? On the other hand, I couldn't save everyone, could I? Although, I wasn't saving everyone, just the ones I could. And right now, that was within my power.

Fuck.

The man held the girl by the hand, the one she was clutching the doll with.

I cursed. I exhaled. I drew my bow.

The idiot had attracted a lot of attention with his shots, and there were too many zombies to count, easily over a hundred.

I was forced to pop off the zombies mechanically — to the open-mouthed astonishment of the military man — my mind being on other things. *Dammit, how can I get him and the child out of there and to safety.*

I could always just walk away, but then he would die, and it wouldn't exactly help his daughter. Am I putting all this effort in for nothing? I've got to see this thing through.

I continued to mechanically pop off zombies from my position behind them. I soon tired of shooting and was saddened to watch my arrows breaking on impact with their targets. One didn't even make it as far as the zombie head it was intended for, disintegrating in midair.

The arrows I was using had been used multiple times before, and that wasn't helping anyone, as I would soon be fresh out of ammo.

After clearing half the zombies nearest to me, I quickly gathered the trophies they dropped. No small thing for my survival.

The crates and trinket caskets warmed the soul, while the ever-newly-arriving zombies only maddened me. At this rate the bowstring would soon snap and I'd be left not only arrowless, but also bowless.

Still a reasonable distance from the zombies, I risked opening one red trinket casket. *I mean, what if I get lucky?*

You receive: magic snare, 1 pc.

A magic snare is able to restrain even the wild razorback Saur.

I knew what wild meant. Razorback likewise. But Saur? I couldn't even imagine what that was.

I must say, the system had bunged me a useful weapon.

The snare looked like any other snare, a regular bear trap, only it was decorated with runes.

But I had to get back to killing zombies. I reduced their number to five using arrows, before finishing them off with my spear and retreating.

And not before time. The fence holding the zombies at bay would not last much longer. It was at a fair tilt under their weight as it was, and the man was preparing to retreat into the store with the feeble plastic door. Which would certainly be no hindrance to the zombies.

These bastards need finishing off ASAP.

They're making noise and attracting more bastards. A constant flow of bastards, you might say. No matter how many I killed, they were instantly replaced by new bastards drawn to the din.

When I killed the last zombie, I felt I needed a drink. Or a good cry, I hadn't decided yet. My stock of arrows was way low.

The exit was clear, but the man was in no hurry to emerge from his refuge.

I reckoned he understood from the arrows and boxes disappearing into thin air that I was very busy, and he did not disturb me. Clever man.

For some reason, I felt awkward about exiting invisibility, as though I would appear naked in front of him. And there was the child to think about.

"Tell me, what kind of parent takes a child out onto the street at such a frolicsome time?" It was me who broke the silence, while he eyed me warily.

"Andrei Shatunov." In response to my question, he introduced himself. "And who might you be?"

"Call me Varg, Mr. parent of the year," I sighed. "Let's go, get your brain in gear."

He did not argue, but came out, holding tight to daughter's hand while simultaneously donning his backpack.

"Thank you for the assistance, Varg," the man said with all his heart. "If it wasn't for you, we'd be dead by now. I'm not concerned for myself, I'm concerned for my daughter."

"You should have thought about that before bringing her somewhere like this."

"I didn't bring her, I saved her. She was living with her mother, who turned into a zombie, although she was a nasty piece of work even before the apocalypse." The soldier allowed himself a weak smile. "My daughter locked herself in the bathroom and called me from there. I ran straight to save her."

I didn't understand where he could possibly want to run to, or why he was talking about phone calls, there was no electricity anywhere. I did not like being lied to, and I told him as much.

"Why are you lying to me? Obviously I don't really care, I'm just interested."

"What are you talking about?" asked the man, surprised.

"The city's electricity went down almost straightaway," I said, pointing out his mistake.

"You must be mistaken. They didn't turn it off, we have it, and we're using it just as we always did." He was still surprised. He couldn't understand whether I was just an idiot or I'd been holed up in my den for too long. Just then I was struck by a simple thought which made me feel like a proper idiot. And I was sure I was right.

"I'll kill them, those fuckers," I hissed when I realized the motherfuckers living on the upper floors had turned the electricity off for those on the lower floors. Top-down management in my anthill.

The man did not stop me swearing, though he did cover the girl's ears. What an idiot I was. They had simply decided to reduce the chances of saving the common people. Jeez, all this time I'd been sitting in my apartment with no news, no Internet, and no light, at the whim of those idiots. No, I was not the only idiot here, but I was a spiteful and vindictive idiot.

"Nice toy you've got there, quiet," said the man in evaluation of my bow. His own weapon attracted a lot of attention and was only useful from behind a barricade.

"Better than a firearm." I could only agree with him.

"Well, not better, but quieter, that's for sure."

Not wanting to continue the argument, I fell silent, but the man could only manage ten minutes.

"Have you got any arrows left? It's just that there might be a lot of zombies in front of the dorm."

"Courtesy of you, I'm nearly out, so I'll have to do some spear waving." I saw no reason not to have a dig at him.

"Sorry again," said the man, realizing how precious ammunition was. "I'll return your arrows just as soon as we get there."

I almost tripped over in surprise at such an announcement.

"What do you mean? You've got arrows?" My astonishment was utter.

"We have. What we haven't got is people who can use them," he replied, checking about him to see everything was okay. "I'll tell you something else as well, we've even got a system bow."

It was the sort of news that made the day seem not so bad after all.

"You got a bow from the zombies? You're kidding."

"We did indeed."

Andrei was pleased with my reaction of joy at the mention of a system bow.

"There are lots of us there, we just got back from a hotspot. It's a pity we all handed in our weapons. We've only got personals with us and it's not enough."

"What? You've got a bow but not enough firearms, right?"

"Right."

"And you've also got arrows?"

"Right."

"Fuck. What haven't you got, since you've got everything?" That was annoying. I'd destroyed a whole bunch of zombies, but I still wasn't getting a bow or any arrows from the system, while a bunch of military guys had them.

"We've got no bullets or firearms and very little system stuff. And the worst thing is we've got no food. The dorm is full of people with families and there's catastrophically not enough to go around. That's why I popped into the store on the way, to look for food. But don't you worry, I remember my promise to pay you back for saving us," said the man sadly.

I had to think. If there were lots of them and they had loot that was useless to them, I could exchange it for food, of which I had more than plenty.

I didn't understand how there could not be enough food when it was dropped so regularly. Actually, that's a lie, I did understand. A family of three would need a minimum of two boxes a day, and that was without eating their fill. It was likely that only a man could kill a zombie, and not everybody would find it as easy as me. And there were bound to be mothers who had lost their husbands. And brothers-in-arms certainly did not abandon the struggling families of their fallen brothers.

"Well since there's not enough food, we must start killing zombies. A lot of zombies."

"We call them infecteds," the man said with a chuckle.

"It doesn't matter what you call them, it doesn't change anything. And it doesn't make them less dangerous," I noted, not looking at him.

"We're nearly there."

"I know."

We continued in complete silence, meeting ever-increasing numbers of zombies and having to run and hide. Sometimes we had to distract one with a noise, by finding objects lying around and throwing them away to the side.

How resentful Andrei was when he had to discard a can of meat in order to distract a horde of zombies suddenly blocking our path.

I don't know how long it took, but we eventually made it to the military dorm. How many times a day did I curse the moment I had to overcome my emotions and help? It was tortuous walking around the city uninvisible. More than once did I want to disappear from view and walk slowly, killing zombies. My temporary partner, on the other hand, was like a snake, slithering noiselessly between obstacles and crawling nimbly up walls which otherwise required walking around. And all this with a child in tow.

Eventually we got to where we were going.

"And how are you planning to get in there?" I asked.

We hunkered down behind a burned-out car not far from the building. From there we observed the crowd of zombies surrounding the dorm in a solid ring. A six-story building, the windows of the first two floors boarded-up and barricaded, and a ton of garbage piled up at the bottom, preventing the zombies getting right up close to the building.

"I'm going to call my guys," the man said, recovering his wits. "Combat will think of something."

"He'll call you a helicopter," I quipped, not hiding my attitude to him.

I mean, with the sound of their own guns, the soldiers had gathered a whole army of zombies and were now stuck here like idiots with their backs to the wall.

Meanwhile, having said he would call, Andrei exchanged messages with his guys. At last he understood that making a load of noise was not the best idea.

"Listen, Shatun, how are we going to get inside if the windows and doors are closed? Please tell me you haven't barricaded the door?" I asked. If he mentioned a rope ladder, I would start swearing in front of the child.

Right now I wanted to leave them and go home. After all, I had seen them as far as the dorm. I understood, however, that without me they might not stand a chance.

"How do you know my call sign?" asked the man in surprise. Then he waved it away. "Ah, never mind, it's not important. Look, there's the main entrance, very sturdy doors, installed by a quartermaster from his old stocks. In his words, that door will outlive the building."

The quartermaster was right. The look of the door inspired confidence. No doubt a bunker somewhere was missing a door. The only thing was, how did they open it?

I soon became bored of waiting for I didn't know what, and the main reason was the little girl, trembling like a leaf from cold and fear and biting hard on the hem of her coat so her teeth wouldn't chatter.

Cautiously, I touched her shoulder.

"Shatun, look, can you see us?" I asked.

He turned towards me and froze. "What the f...?"

"Be quiet," I hissed, before returning my visibility. "What does Combat have to say?"

While he was recovering his senses, I decided to check how my invisibility would work on others.

It had concealed the child, and that was good.

The military man was still frowning, and I didn't like that.

"What's up?"

"Bad news. In order to save my daughter, they gave me nearly all their food reserves, and they haven't managed to find any more.

"I see. Not good. Do you run fast? Can you get to the door and inside before the zombies get there?" Just in case, I decided to check before acting.

"I could do it alone, but otherwise no," said the soldier, realizing what I was getting at and scratching his head.

He grew thoughtful again, but I was tired of hanging around and decided to do something.

"Write to Combat to open the door for us."

He didn't understand what I wanted to do, but he didn't argue, evidently in thanks for being saved.

"Combat says they're ready, he even sent a photo. The guys are ready to cover us," he said, showing me the picture on his phone.

The photograph made me smile. Hard-looking men with forbidding faces, armed to the teeth and standing next to the main door. One enormous chap looked particularly comical, like a bear with a length of banister in his hands. Were he to suddenly become a zombie, people would never get away, you wouldn't be able to take him down.

Oh, how I didn't want to risk it, but it wasn't just my conscience at play here. My need for pragmatism had also kicked in. If they had a bow and arrows, the arrows weren't important because the bow was system. These past days, I'd been in a constant state of panic that my bowstring would snap, and here there was a whole new bow.

Should Shatun be taken down by zombies, I would have no hope of a normal trade deal. This was why I had to take the risk. Or rather, it was because of the girl *and* the bow. The bow was important. The girl too.

I produced a pistol and eight rounds from my inventory and handed them to the surprised Andrei.

"Check the barrel's in working order and load it for me," I commanded, hoping it wouldn't enter his head to shoot me.

He began fussing around with the barrel, checking, pulling, hemming, shoving rounds in the clip. I watched, trying to commit to memory what he was doing. Why, I don't know. Jeez, he worked quickly. I couldn't remember any of it.

"The barrel is dirty and loose, but it can be fired. It's just not worth using it now, we don't need any excess noise. I put the safety catch on, this catch here." He showed me, thinking I could use a gun.

"Thank you. Now listen carefully, I'm going to take up another position. As soon as you hear my signal, run like hell for the door. It'll be your only chance, believe me." I really wanted him to do everything as I asked and not die by his own stupidity.

"What about you?"

"I'm a freaking invisible, had you forgotten?" I tried a smile to show everything was okay. In actual fact, I was not at all convinced by my plan.

I would switch on invisibility and walk away from him in the opposite direction to the entrance.

"I hope I can run faster now," I said to myself, firing into the air. The zombies immediately turned in my direction, doubtless bored of standing beneath the windows and trying to grab hold of survivors. They turned sharply, as one, and ran towards me. It would have been a treat to watch, but I wasn't watching, I was running. Running fast. Running very fast.

In order to get away from the beasties, I had to run all the way up the street and back down to the dorm, where my bow was waiting for me.

As I ran, I gave myself a pat on the back for leveling up. The old me would have been eaten half way. My metrics for speed, stamina, and even agility, it seemed, had increased. The adroitness and lightning speed with which I leaped over an upturned car would not have looked out of place in the movie *Yamakasi*.

I needed urgently to gain one more level, that went without saying. It was well worth being able to race like that without being short of breath. And I'd outrun death! It was a good job zombies were sluggish and not hard to escape. Just keep running and don't look back.

CHAPTER 7

SHATUN COULD NOT BELIEVE he'd survived and that everything had worked out okay. After sprinting into the building, he could eventually breathe a sigh of relief. He handed his daughter over to his brother, who let out a roar of delight, then plonked himself down on the steps.

"How are you, brother?" asked his brother, Clubfoot.

"Better now, brother, better now. I got way lucky today," Shatun said, wincing to remember the basket case he'd come across by the store.

He was very grateful to the strange man who'd called himself Varg, and he felt terribly disheartened that he hadn't been able to return to help the guy, but had instead kept running. Were it not for his daughter, he would of course have hurried back to help, not even suspecting it would have been the last thing he ever did.

He could only hope the guy knew what he'd gotten tangled up in. If he was being honest, the guy had not looked like the sort to take risks on account of others. As they chatted on the way here, he'd been surprised the guy had helped him at all. He'd seemed unsociable, marching to his own drum, although happy to kill zombies without the slightest hesitation, as if they hadn't been people but a few days ago.

"What are you doing causing all this brouhaha, Shatun?" said Combat, a gray-haired man who now entered. "I'm very glad you and Lera are okay," he said, offering his hand and embracing Shatun tightly.

"Very little of the credit is mine, Combat," Shatun admitted honestly. "Some guy helped us to get home."

The silver-haired man became thoughtful. "The one who fired those shots?" he asked.

"That's right, he distracted the zombies so Lera and I would have time to run back here, but I couldn't help him in return to his home," Shatun said despairingly.

"He must have been a good guy, he chose a worthy way to die," Combat said, appraising the act.

"I don't think he died. He was too strange for that," Shatun said, squeezing out a smile.

"Okay, let's go. You can tell me the finer details in a few minutes. There's no point sitting around here," Combat said, beckoning with a hand.

All the soldiers gathered in a room that now served as command control, eager to hear about Shatun's foray.

He was poured a large anti-stress double from the emergency supplies, and everyone listened attentively. He held nothing back, recalling all the specifics of the chaos happening in the city, and how he had stupidly shot two zombies, as a result of which two hundred more came running. But the audience were most interested in the guy who had destroyed the zombies and helped their battle buddy to safety.

"Shame he perished. We could use a guy like that," Clubfoot said in a deep bass. "I would personally throw a party for him for saving my brother."

"He's not dead," Shatun said, trying to believe his own words." I told you, he's too streetwise and strange for that. If we feel in our element at war, then he was literally created for the apocalypse. That was the impression I got."

"He may have been strange, but he did help you," said a middle-aged man with graying temples.

"He just felt sorry for Lera."

"That's what I mean: a good guy," boomed Clubfoot. "There's no time for civility in war. It's not a children's game."

A dismal silence hung in the room as everyone thought their own thoughts.

"What are you going to do with the food?" Combat asked out of the blue.

"Give it back to the guy, if he shows his face. I promised to return it to him for saving us." Shatun was firm in his intentions.

"Well, since you promised, you must follow up on it. It is mildly unfortunate, of course, what with our people going hungry, and we have to think of something urgently."

"All the stores in the vicinity have been looted," said somebody. On the very first day, marauders had twigged what was going on and stripped everywhere of everything.

This was not exactly big news for the fighters, for they all had telephones, and friends in the city with whom they exchanged information.

"Mikhailich, how many days' food have we got left?" Combat asked of his friend.

"Call me Quartermaster, since we're at war. Well, if we cut the women's and children's rations a bit more, then a day, two at the outside."

The fighters began to argue. Despite everyone understanding it was the right decision, they were not happy with the scenario. A man could not afford to go hungry if he needed his strength to find food and ammo in a war.

"This is not good. We cannot starve our own people to death. We shall have to go on a raid in the morning and hope we can find at least a couple of boxes of food."

"Haven't you used my bow for firewood yet?" A new voice came unexpectedly from the open window.

Everyone turned in that direction and saw a

strange man sitting on the windowsill and calmly eating an apple.

"Who the hell are you?" asked Combat, flabbergasted at the man's behavior.

"You survived, you badass!" said Shatun with a wide smile.

* * *

The crowd of zombies by the dorm had noticeably thinned, which meant that my game of chase had made the soldiers' lives slightly easier. At least now they could leave the building.

I had come right up to the dorm, picking my way through rotten-smelling zombie corpses, to the necessary part of the building, i.e. where there was a window wide open on the fourth floor.

Of course I was no mountaineer or rock climber, but scrambling up the wall would present me no problem. And should anything happen, the fall would not be far.

My body was now so strong I could afford not to worry about my strength failing me before I reached the window.

This may have been what I thought, but I still got a fair sweat on. The bars on the windows helped enormously in the climb, and here I was, five minutes later, sitting on the windowsill and listening to their conversation.

What were the chances that of all the windows, the one I chose would be the one I needed? And that my new acquaintance would be telling everyone about me right now? Too much attention for my modest self.

The office they sat in was huge. I'd been expecting the same pigsty you found in all dorms, but here was cleanliness and orderliness. The fighters obviously shunned disorder in everything. If only they'd cleared away the bodies in the street as well. The stench down there was just terrible.

I'd soon grown bored of sitting on the windowsill and selected the right moment to make my presence known. It was seriously amusing to behold their astonished expressions when they clocked me appearing out of nowhere.

I had to give them their due, mind, for they did not immediately panic, merely tensing slightly and preparing to leap into action and break my neck should the need arise. The tension in the room was diffused by my new friend Shatun.

"Well say something then. How's my bow?" I asked with a grin.

"Combat, I told the guy about the bow and promised to give it back as a reward for helping us."

"Well since you promised, that means we must give it back," the gray-haired man said with a nod. "Quartermaster, give orders to have it brought here."

I was beginning to like these soldiers more and more.

"Perhaps you'd like some tea?" the same gray-haired man inquired.

"I wouldn't say no. Black with lemon."

"We've got no lemons, only tea and sugar," he said, shooting down my request.

"Catch," I said, throwing him a lemon, which he caught dexterously.

I was given a seat at the table, and pandemonium let loose. While we were waiting for tea, I was interrogated about all the minutiae.

Evidently, I was not the only tea lover around. A woman of about thirty-five entered the room bearing an enormous tray laden with a teapot and cups.

"Great, you have electricity," I said enviously as I watched the steam curling from the electric kettle.

"Where do you live? Why haven't you got any electricity?" Combat asked.

They posed their questions very carefully, trying to avoid putting the screws on, and after so many days of solitude, I was happy to talk with people who weren't trying to kill me for the enlargement of their inventories.

We chatted for about an hour over tea. I told them where I lived and why there wasn't any electricity there, and I shared information that I thought of minor importance but which was news to them.

When the first round of tea had been drunk and the second poured, Combat asked a question that was clearly important to him.

"You're an agile chap and you've no doubt hacked no few zombies to pieces, so you must have a fair few trophies, I would imagine?" he began as calmly and good-humoredly as possible. He did not want to frighten me and give me the wrong idea.

"Not as many as I'd like," I replied, pulling a face. "If I understand correctly, you're alluding to your need for food, right? The question is, how are you going to get it? Trade? Or might you just gang up on me now and try to take it by force?"

I was under no illusion here. These guys were soldiers, their bodies decorated with battle scars received in real battles where they had killed people. Killing me for the sake of their own kind would be no sweat for them.

The only ace up my sleeve was a grenade I'd gained just before climbing up to the window. I had decided to open a couple of boxes in the hope of receiving something interesting, and I hit the jackpot.

"We are not bandits. We're not going to rob someone who saved my brother," boomed an enormous man sitting next to Shatun, who would have had little difficulty snapping a tank gun in half.

"I give you my word as an officer, nobody here will do you any harm," Combat added. "Most of us are combat officers, not vagrant riffraff."

My words had ruffled everyone's feathers, but I had to ask so I could be sure of their attitude towards me.

"I meant no offense, I just wanted confirmation," I said with a shrug. "You understand the world has changed, and not for the better."

"But people have not ceased to be people," came the retort.

"Did you know you can expand your inventory by killing people?" I asked them.

The men exchanged glances and nods.

"The capacity of my inventory is currently twenty-nine kilograms. I have never been the initiator of an attack, and all those people I had to kill because they were trying to kill me. Or because they were persecuting innocent people."

You should have seen their faces when they realized how many people had been killed by a regular guy like me.

"And... you haven't killed any common folk?" Combat aimed his piercing stare at me.

"Why would I want to do that?" I asked in surprise. "I would have been happy not to kill the ones I did, but they attacked me."

Despite not giving a toss about the people I'd killed, I was still concerned about one thing: if I killed too often, I might go mental. And I still didn't understand how it would affect me. Likely not at all, but who knew what might happen in the future? Before all the chaos, I'd read stories about the lives of maniacs, and they were said to change with time. Perhaps it would be the same with me.

"If you had a weak psyche, then First Kill would show as much. Believe me, I've seen a lot and I know what I'm talking about," a man chuckled, thinking aloud.

I wanted to shout, "at last," when I saw a lad

enter the room with my bow in his hands.

"Here's the bow you were promised. And in the corner is Shatun's backpack full of food. It's missing two cans of stewed meat. Sorry about that," he said guiltily.

"You can keep the food for yourselves," I replied, brushing the matter aside, "but give me the bow, soldier," I barked, trying to copy the speech style of the officer standing before me.

"I see you are fearless," Combat said with a smile.

"What do I have to fear?" I replied, concealing my fear behind bravado.

"Well for example, Savva might not understand your joke and quickly break your neck. At the age of just twenty, he has been through two hotspots and killed enemies with ease," Quartermaster said.

"I have invisibility," I said, activating it. "And this as well." Deactivating invisibility, I displayed the grenade in my hand.

I thought they would all scatter, or at least be worried, but they merely burst out laughing.

"What's so funny?"

"Do you know how to use it? Do you know you might die if it goes off?" Combat was beginning to like reckless ol' me more and more.

"Yeah, I've seen it in the movies. You've got to pull something here and lob it. As for me, I hope I'd to be able to dive through a window, and the zombies would manage to catch me, like diehard fans." Everything suddenly seemed very funny and

I began to laugh. Maybe they'd put something in my tea?

"Hey, that's not a freaking children's toy."

"Well if the zombies don't want to play with me, who am I going to have my fun with?"

I was surprised by my own behavior. I was being too calm and relaxed. The events of recent days were catching up with me, probably a hangover from everything I'd been through.

I might not have suffered any failure of nerves or emotional stress before, but the change of perspective would definitely have manifested itself in me somehow. The world had previously been normal, but now it was a catastrophe.

My bow was handed to me, and at last I could take a look at my beauty.

Evaluation.

The Archer of Arkhavar's short bow, level 1.

The bow has a range of 100 meters.

Here it is, my precious.

I immediately began to study the bow from all angles, even fitting an arrow to it and drawing the bowstring. The tension was good, although not as light as that of my old bow. It would have better stopping power. *Excellent. I think we'll make a good team.*

"A good bow," I said plainly to the assembled crowd.

"I'm glad you like it. And thank you for the food," Combat said with a smile.

While I was lost in my examination of the

bow, my cup was refilled with fresh tea and the company continued their discussion among themselves.

"Varg, what might you be interested in as an exchange? Perhaps we could help each other?"

Shatun slapped his forehead and said, "Oops, that's right, I promised him some arrows as well."

"Well, since you promised, that means we must give him some," Combat said with a sigh.

I was taking more and more of a shine to Combat. He was a man of honor. Someone like him would definitely never stab you in the back. But you wouldn't want him as an enemy either. As a rule, enemies didn't live long around wolves like him. Or they ran around with one paw missing.

"In exchange, I can offer food and ammunition. What I need is arrows, equipment, blue trinket caskets, yellow trinket caskets, and any other interesting system items."

"Fine, the arrows will be brought to you now, and as for the rest, we can offer you two fact caskets," Combat said, arousing my interest.

Fact caskets were interesting and would always come in handy.

"We can offer you no system weapons, since we don't have enough ourselves. In fact all we have is a small number of bladed weapons," Combat continued, in a somewhat complaining tone.

Savva came back into the room five minutes later with some arrows and two blue trinket caskets for me.

"How much do you want for the caskets?"

"Four food boxes each," he said, watching me closely to gauge my reaction, before adding, "blue trinket caskets are dropped less frequently."

"But they're not as essential as food," I retorted, adding my two cents' worth.

It actually seemed a fair offer, I just felt like saying something for appearances' sake. I had nowhere else to offload the gray boxes, and they would take up space. Added to which, it was dangerous to leave them in my apartment, for I had weapons there which I feared might be stolen at any moment.

Without another word, I produced eight boxes and put them on the table in front of the delighted Combat.

"Quartermaster, see to it right away that anybody who has not been fed today gets fed."

Quartermaster could not do anything without objecting. Such was his character apparently.

"It would be better to feed those who didn't eat yesterday or the day before first," he muttered, despite the glint of joy in his eyes. It was painful for him to look at hungry people. He had served as quartermaster for twenty years and was accustomed to always taking care of his people, and now he found himself with a catastrophic scarcity of resources.

While they busied themselves with opening the boxes and distributing the food under Quartermaster's watchful eye, I counted the arrows.

Evaluation.

Regular sharpened arrow.

I was happy enough with the quality, which meant they would be good enough for the zombies as well. But there were only thirty-two of them, which was not enough.

"Is this all you've got? A couple of thousand wouldn't go amiss," I said, dreaming aloud.

"Unfortunately, that's it. We have very few arms for killing zombies, and we lost another person on our last sortie." After this reminder, everyone fell silent and reminisced about Tartarian.

"You need to kill more zombies if you're going to survive."

"If only we had the means to do so."

"What would you say to me giving you credit?" I offered, unexpectedly even for me.

"What sort of credit are you talking about?" Quartermaster was immediately interested. "And how would we pay it back?"

Without a word, I unloaded all the bullets I had. To me they were just excess baggage, while someone else could use them to kill a hundred zombies.

I did keep lots of red boxes in my inventory just in case, however. They would come in handy later.

Then I laid on the table the simple sword I'd taken from the guy I killed.

I also had something interesting in reserve for Clubfoot.

Card: guardian's shield.

Evaluation.

Heavy full-length shield, capable of withstanding over a thousand strikes.

"What do we owe you for all this?" Combat asked nervously, while Quartermaster carefully counted the bullets.

"I don't know, but the main thing is arrows. Let's do it like this: you can settle your account when you find something I need."

I absolutely did not want them to die stupidly from zombie bites. These were the first normal people I'd met in recent times.

"And this shield card will do for Clubfoot. I reckon he doesn't even need a weapon, he can just batter enemies with the shield."

Combat nodded his approval, took the card, and activated it.

Wow. I was shocked. The shield looked very impressive. It was forged of iron and massive, as tall as the giant himself.

"Have you ever broken a tank gun, Clubfoot?" I asked jokingly.

"How do you know that?" he replied, his mouth agape in surprise. Then, slow on the uptake, he turned his gaze on his brother. "Shatun, brother, was it you who told him that? What the hell? I didn't break it deliberately, it snapped off by itself," the fighter said, puckering his offended brow.

In my turn, I applied no little effort to stop my own jaw from dropping and revealing my astonishment.

He actually broke a tank gun, rattled around my head.

Just in case, I made a mental note not to annoy him under any circumstance. No level would save me from those gigantic paws clamped around my neck. I would burst like a frog.

"Look, Combat, we've got fifty 9-mm rounds, forty-one 5.56 mm, and another half hundred for..."

At this point I stopped listening. I simply wasn't interested.

"It is my understanding that you are people of your word, so you can pay me back when you consider it necessary. There's no hurry. I trust you not to cheat me or sell me short."

"I accept," Combat said, extending his hand to seal the deal. Then they set about planning a task for the following day. This was of no interest to me, and I began to yawn, wondering how I might break the news that it was time for me to leave.

"Varg, please be our guest and overnight with us, and tomorrow you can leave to go about your business." Having seen me yawn and look out of the window, Combat was offering me a bunk.

"I don't feel at home sleeping in a large group of people. You might consider me paranoid."

"Don't be so silly," he barked. "You're pooped out after today, and it's dark outside. It isn't safe wondering around the town alone at this time. There are more and more flying beasties about during the night."

If I was being honest, I really couldn't be

bothered to go anywhere. I was exhausted.

"Have you got hot water?"

"We have," Combat said, pleased. "Shatun will show you the way."

"Comrade Combat, where exactly will Shatun show him the way to?" asked Shatun.

"Quartermaster, where do we have free bunks? Free bunks with no attendant problems," Combat asked, turning to Quartermaster, who was still busy with the new stock take.

"I'll have to think about that. I remember there is definitely an empty bed in room 32."

"Is that with Polina?"

"Yes sir."

"Hey, that's not what we agreed. What freaking Polina?" I asked angrily. "I want a separate room."

"Keep your cool. Not all the apartments here have been tidied up yet. Come back in two or three days, and then we'll be able to give you a separate room," Combat said.

"I've got my own apartment, I don't need your accommodation. Maybe you could make me up a bed in some box room?" *Hope springs eternal.*

"What, are you scared of a chick?" Combat asked, raising a surprised eyebrow, before bursting out laughing. "You're right to be scared. Our Polina is a feisty girl."

It was a good thing she wasn't a granny.

Why the hell did I agree? It was certainly difficult to oppose Combat. His look alone was enough to frighten anybody. I just figured it wasn't worth getting cranky like a small child and arguing with soldiers over a such a trifle. The world had ended, I had been provided a safe haven, and here I was, like an idiot, being pigheaded and laying down conditions.

Perhaps with a different group of people I might have followed through with my exhortations, but not with these. I did not want to lose face with officers I had yet to trade with. I assessed the situation soberly and understood everything had changed. And I was still concerned about the red boxes. They were of little value to me, but it would be a pity to ditch them.

I did not want to learn to use a firearm. I was convinced the system had good reason not to provide them in the red trinket caskets. They would soon become less useful than the level-four sword.

In the meantime, we approached the place where I was to spend the night. Along the way, I observed the residents of the dorm with curiosity. They all had a despondent and burned-out look to them, although I saw no hysteria, which was probably the officers' influence. The worst thing was their hunger and exhaustion, given away by their red eyes.

If the fighters were in no condition to do decent battle with beasties, then they were in for very hard times. Although I didn't think they would survive long as it was. New kinds of mutant zombie would soon be appearing, and even I wasn't exactly burning with desire to run into a mutant, for it was sure to be a true horror show.

Damn, there are so many children here. A small crowd ran gaily down the corridor, laughing loudly. I pitied the children. While I considered myself a sociopath, I would never do anything to harm a child.

If the soldiers were on their own, they might be able to survive. But since they had a host of hungry mouths to feed, which they could not abandon, they would probably perish. If I joined them, the question of sustenance would be partially solved, but then I would have to carry out their orders, and I hated the thought of doing that. I hated people too. People were dumb douchebags; I had never seen any good come of being a person.

"We're here," announced my nominal escort as he stopped in front of an unremarkable door.

"Listen, Shatun, you and I are almost friends, yeah? Maybe I can sleep in your room?" I asked hopefully.

He laughed jovially and knocked on the door.

Maybe I'll get lucky and there'll be nobody home, I thought.

The door flew open as my hopes were dashed.

"Andrei? Hi, good to see you. Is everything okay with Lera?" a woman asked, hugging him as a sister hugs a brother. "And who's this with you? He's not one of ours. Is he a survivor or something?"

"Um..." My throat had gone dry. "I... I was just passing, but it's time for me to go." I about turned and took my first step back in the direction we'd come, but Shatun grabbed me by the scruff of the neck with his large paw and turned me back around.

"Pol, I'd like you to meet my new friend. He saved us from the zombies. He's not a local boy here, but it's too late for him to go home and it's a long way. Perhaps he could spend the night with you?" he asked, mostly for the sake of decency, since I knew she wouldn't refuse him. To him she was like a sister whom he had sworn to take care of since an incident a year ago on a task that had killed her husband as he took a bullet meant for Shatun.

She gave me an x-ray look and nodded.

"Well, good luck, brother," Shatun said, shoving me through the door and slamming it shut. The louse.

I tried the handle, but he was obviously holding it on the other side.

I turned around and found myself being examined intently by two pairs of curious eyes.

"Um, hello," was all I could squeeze out. I wanted the ground to swallow me up.

The eyes gazing steadily at me belonged to a girl of about seven and her mother, a beautiful redhead. The last thing I could possibly have dreamed of just then was to spend time in the same room as this beauty. The sociopath was caught in a cage. The girl jumped down from her chair and approached me slowly with a smile that to me seemed sinister.

CHAPTER 8

"HI, LET'S PLAY." The girl came at me head-on, right out of the blocks. "Why aren't you saying anything? Are you afraid? Of us? Maybe of the zombies? Is it true you helped Lera? What's it like outside? Scary? What are we going to play? Will you tell me a story? What stories do you know? Have you ever seen a dragon? Let me tell you a story then, since you don't know any. Or do you?"

To say I was afraid would be putting it mildly.

She talked and talked, and I stood there at a loss what to do. Her mother merely looked on, making absolutely no effort to stop her daughter tearing her new victim into tiny pieces with her psychological attack.

"Why do you need to know so much?" I eventually asked, cracking under the flood of questions eroding my consciousness.

"Ooh, so you're not deaf after all. That's good.

I was beginning to get worried for you," said the girl joyously. I realized I'd made another silly mistake.

"Save me," I whispered in the mother's direction, my lips scarcely moving.

She did not hide her delighted smile. "Liza, have you done your homework?" The woman asked, deciding to take pity on the strange man.

"What are you talking about, mom?" the girl asked, agog with horror. "Homework in the zombie apocalypse? Homework is toast, school is toast, the whole world is toast. NO HOMEWORK!" the girl announced, adopting a proud pose and looking belligerently at her mom.

"What if I go find a belt?" the lady threatened.

"What if you don't?" The girl picked up the gauntlet, not wishing to capitulate.

And thus they stood, glaring at each other, each waiting for the other to climb down first.

"Can I go now?" I was so tired."

"Go where?" Polina asked, turning sharply towards me.

"Go where?" the girl asked, mirroring her mother's movement.

"To shoot myself, probably."

"Oh, how vulnerable we are," the mother said with a smile.

I didn't manage to utter another word before I was taken by both hands and led to the table in the lounge. Polina went to the kitchen, and the little one sat down next to me and fixed me with a thoughtful stare, as though she'd found herself an interesting new small animal and was contemplating what might be the best thing to do with it.

"Liza, help me lay the table," Polina shouted from the kitchen.

"Just a second, mom." The girl ran out in a flash.

Left in solitude, I was able to have a proper look at where the gods, or the system, had dumped me. A small apartment, not like a communal apartment, two rooms, tiny kitchen. On the wall hung a television, small, but flatscreen. Windows double glazed, which was good; at least you wouldn't be able to hear zombie noises. Howlings and rattlings were definitely not the best music for children's ears.

The wallpaper portrayed various amusing cartoon heroes. The woman or girl — God knows how old the mother was — had obviously put it up for her daughter. The furniture was not new, but it was of decent quality, and on the whole the apartment was clean and tidy. A woman's touch was in evidence, and in this particular case, two women's.

To my surprise, Liza really did bring food and put it on the table. If a couple of gingerbread cookies and half a loaf of bread could be called food, that is.

Then Polina came back with a pot of hot tea, and we all sat down at the table.

"Help yourself, don't be shy," Polina said, nodding towards the cookies. They did not touch them, instead going for the bread. Bread on its own, plain bread, not even any butter. And this at a time when you could get a smorgasbord in a box dropped by a zombie.

"Yef, ftake a mcookie, they're fyummy."

"Liza, how many times have I told you not to speak with your mouth full," Polina said, her brows knit.

"It's Polina, right? How old are you?" I asked. The girl choked on her bread and her mother gave me a strange look. What was the problem? It was a simple question. Was it bad form to ask someone their age? Stupid traditions. How else could I find out?

"I'm twenty-five, as if it's any concern of yours. Are you asking awkward questions to break the ice? So it's my turn now, yes? Can I ask you about—"

"Wait a minute." I interrupted her, my face reddening. "I meant no offense. I just don't know how to address you."

"What do you mean?" She still didn't get it. Dummy.

"Well, can I call you Pol, or is it strictly Polina?"

"He's funny," Liza said, smiling. "Only he won't last long in the big wide world if he behaves like that. Can we keep him, Mom? It would be too bad if he got eaten."

"Can't you tell?" asked the mother through a sweet toothy smile, her head aslant and her eyes ablaze. Was it just me, or was there inside them a little devil bashing its paws against the glass and yelling, "RUN! I'LL HOLD HER DOWN!"?

"Well, at first I thought you were eighteen." I lied.

"Uh-huh. You're lying."

"I'm lying." I gave a sad sigh.

"Why do you need to know?" she asked, considering retaliation.

How should I reply? Only with the truth. Otherwise I'm afraid she'll set her daughter on me.

"I don't know how to address you in my thoughts, understand?"

"No."

"I don't understand either sometimes," I said, my sigh even sadder now. "It's hard for me to interact with people. Zombies are much simpler and more intelligible."

Now they were both looking at me like I was a weirdo. Nothing new there, then.

"How on earth did you survive the streets?" She was truly amazed how a guy like me had not yet been killed. I was strange, yet seemingly harmless.

"By twisting and turning."

The conversation reached a dead end, and Polina decided to change the subject. She told me about people's lives in the dorm, what recent news there had been, and much more besides, after which my head began to hurt.

Ye gods, does this woman ever shut up? She speaks and smiles and she knows I don't like it. Is she taking the piss? Aha, I get it, she's taking revenge. Women are fearful creatures. Much more fearful than zombies.

That said, a zombie woman could literally eat your head, while a living one could merely mess with it. Yes, living ones were more fearful, that was for sure.

"Mom, how come a man who hasn't even told us his name yet isn't eating?" Liza, silent for a while until now, asked.

"Maybe he hasn't got a name? And maybe he's embarrassed to accept food from two girls?" Polina said mockingly, with an insidious look in my direction.

I give up. I simply give up. How hard it was to resist them.

"My name is Varg."

"What about the food?"

"The food sucks."

"Where are you going to find better?"

I did not care much for the irony in her voice. "Here," I said, handing her a gray box.

At last I managed to knock her off her stride and shut her up. She sat there, gawking and not understanding what was going on, pride and curiosity battling inside her. They were hungry and had nothing to eat but bread. I was an idiot for not thinking. I could have treated them earlier.

"It's not worth it, take it back," she said, returning the box to me. "Food is too dear right now to waste it on strangers."

I thought I was impossible to surprise. Turned out I was wrong. What was all this? Pride or pity?

Either she pitied me, or her upbringing did not allow her to accept anything from an outsider.

"Take it," I said, pushing the box back.

Silly girl. Nothing to feed her daughter with, yet here she was, acting like who knew what. *Maybe she'd wise up if I put an arrow in her knee?*

"You mustn't waste your food on absolute strangers," she retorted, not touching the box.

Pride, it would seem. Doesn't want to accept help from a stranger.

"*I* decide what to do with my property," I said, beginning to simmer. Well, maybe not simmer, but throw a tantrum inwardly. Although my facial expression did not change, apart from possibly a mild twitch in one eye.

"What's up with your eye?" the little one asked immediately on seeing my eye twitch.

Shoot, it's a twitch, I'm not imagining it.

"What's in the box?" Her childish curiosity could not be contained.

"Food."

"What kind of food?"

"I don't know."

"Who knows?"

"The system."

"No one else?"

"I don't know."

"Maybe..."

"Just take the box and give the mental command "Open," I said testily as I shoved the box back into her hand.

How difficult it was to be among people. I'd gotten used to solitude in the last six months, and now this. I was having it thrown back in my face.

In two shakes of a lamb's tail, the girl had done as I said, and she now began removing the food from the box, her face pure astonishment. Hmm, it seemed the system had not shortchanged her. The first thing she produced was a packet of candies, followed by butter, pâté, and sausage.

"A fantastic box, thank you very much," she exclaimed in delight, rushing to embrace me. I tried to keep her at arm's length, like an annoying kitten, carefully and good-naturedly. "It's a pity there's nothing to drink and no fruit. Sneaky boy."

So that's her game, is it?

"Here." I handed her a bunch of oranges and several bottles of juice.

Now it was Polina's turn to be surprised. "Where did you get so much of everything?"

She could not resist expressing interest.

"I kill zombies," I said with a shrug, as though it was no big deal. "A lot of zombies."

"You? Hmm, sorry, but you don't look like someone who kills a lot of zombies. People perhaps, but not zombies."

Well, you seem to know better." I shrugged my shoulders again. "I've also had to kill people."

Liza enthusiastically shared the food with her mom, even offering me some, nattering away as she did so. We remained sitting at the table for another hour before going to bed.

The apartment had one bedroom; an

excruciating prospect. I was frightened to even imagine sleeping in the same room with other people. I said I'd sleep on the floor in the lounge, but there was no way they were going to accept that.

The bedroom was furnished with two beds. Liza was forced to sleep with her mother, and I got a whole bed to myself. Before getting into it, I took a shower. I did not want to make someone else's bed all sweaty, and I'd done my fair share of running that day.

Sleep evaded me and I tossed and turned for a long time. When I eventually drifted off, I was immediately awakened by a child's loud sobs. Liza's.

Her sobs were not the only sound, for distant shots could be heard, along with cries I understood to be those of flying beasties.

"What happened?" I asked sleepily of Polina. She had also awoken and was now hugging her daughter to her chest, comforting her and gently stroking her head.

"I think we're under attack," she said, alarm in her voice. "Sorry. Liza got scared and woke you up."

"It's nothing to worry about."

I peered out of the dark window but could see next to nothing, only the flickering silhouettes of flying beasties. They were flying at the neighboring windows in an attempt to break in, but were so far being fended off with gunfire.

Not good. They might come crashing in

through our window, and we had a child with us.

"Why isn't your window boarded up like the others?" I did not understand such lack of forethought.

"I haven't gotten around to it. Too much work, not enough hands," Polina replied calmly. She did not seem particularly resentful of the situation.

I figured the first people to board up their windows would have been families with husbands present.

"You didn't have the materials for it?"

"Uh-huh."

Shit.

Why was I getting wound up about this? It was only for a second, mind, but I did not like the situation at all.

Just then, my contemplations were interrupted by a thunderous squall and a dull thump.

One of the winged beasts had noticed us and decided to crash through our window. Almost successfully. The freak got stuck halfway through, lacerating it body on the sharp sides, but nonetheless continued to work its way forward.

The girls screeched in unison, deafening me, and also attracting more attention.

Fuck, I could see more and more monsters flying our way. They must have realized there was an entrance here. Smart creatures.

"Take Liza and get out of here," I said, ushering them forcefully from the room. I could see a beastie scratching the window in the lounge.

"Run, fast, I'll hold them off."

"Where to? What about you?" She was so frightened she didn't know what to do or where to run.

"Run!" I barked, Combat-like. It worked. She took her daughter by the hand and ran from the apartment.

Now I didn't have to worry about them.

This was seriously bad. Why did all this nonsense have to happen to me?

The lounge window was already plastered with flying beasties and they would soon break through. The one stuck in the bedroom window was almost through as well, but then came my arrow. Invisibility would not help me here, and that was also seriously bad. I should probably have fled myself, but as ill luck would have it, strange thoughts kept whirling inside my head. There were lots of women and children in the building, and if these monsters managed to break through, there would be rich and bloody pickings for them.

Why did this apartment have an especially weak door? It would be a pile of shavings in no time.

I don't know what I was thinking, but I decided to stay and hold off the zombies until backup arrived.

Jeez, who was I kidding? What backup? Everyone had plenty of problems of their own and were shooting zombies elsewhere. The shots did not cease, and the locals weren't exactly up to their ears in bullets. I was clearly going to remain alone here with these monsters.

The first one I killed with my old bow, out of habit, but it was cumbersome and inconvenient for indoors. I took out my new precious and sunk an arrow into the head of the beastie fumbling in the window.

Yes, not bad at all. I appraised the ease with which the arrow entered its skull. The stopping power was greater than that of my old bow, and this one was short. What, then, would a system long bow be like? It was a terrifying thought, though it didn't stop me wanting one. If I survived, that is.

One of the beasties decided to attack at speed, widening the hole in the window.

I launched an arrow but missed my target, and rather than piercing his head, I struck it through the chest, pinning it to the wall. *Hmm, the walls here are not very strong.*

I heard the sound of glass smashing in the other room. Without a thought I ran there, drawing my spear on the way. A beastie had put its foot through the window and was caught, as in a trap. With a single powerful strike, I sliced off the foot, before quickly thrusting the spear into its chest. I didn't kill it but rammed it against the cornice, and it dropped like a stone, no longer my problem.

I ran back to the beastie nailed to the wall by my arrow, and took its head off with a swipe of my spear. I don't remember how long I spent beating off zombies, but the room was no longer habitable. I would not have been surprised if the blood here, now ankle-deep, began to drip through the floor, and from the ceiling onto the heads of the people in the apartment below.

I fell into a kind of trance, shooting, chopping, and spiking on autopilot. My head was empty and light, all extraneous thoughts evaporated, leaving only the call to kill.

Then suddenly it was all over. Though when exactly, I didn't know. I simply became aware of myself standing among piles of corpses, caked in blood and disgusting green slurry, which to all appearances I'd been bathing in. The spear was a veritable museum of brains, many small chunks stuck to it.

Nearly sapped of all my strength, I checked the onslaught was over and headed out into the corridor.

Opening the apartment door, I beheld weapons pointed at me.

"Stop!" came Polina and Shatun's shouts at once. "That's Varg. He's one of the living."

The soldiers were in no special hurry to unshoulder their weapons, and I had no energy left for these games.

"Don't lower your weapons, I'll just chop off the hands holding them," I said, for some reason convinced I would be able to do so.

"You think you've got the strength for that?" sneered a short-cropped lad with a dagger in his hand.

"I've got a new offer especially for you," I replied wearily. "If you don't lower your dagger, it's going to end up in your ass."

The lad wanted to add something, but Shatun grabbed him by the scruff of the neck and dragged him away. Then we all heard the sound of ears being boxed.

The small crowd looked at me strangely.

"Are you intact? No bites or scratches?" The perfectly reasonable question came from Polina, who was standing behind the group of lads.

"The eagle is intact, alive, and in need of a shower and a feed."

"Everyone needs a feed," came voices from all around.

"He who does not kill zombies does not get fed," I growled. I didn't give a damn about them.

I was not released until Combat came running and requested I wait a little longer. He said I needed to wash off all the muck so I could be checked for possible bites and scratches. They would not risk having a potential zombie inside the dorm.

While Combat gave orders, I exchanged a few words with the lads.

The flying beasties had decided to take the building by storm from the air. Breaches had occurred not only in my room, but also in two other places, and this had been the people's call to arms.

Six people had been lost among the soldiers and civilians. They had been very lucky I'd provided them bullets. They had not risked entering my room, presuming me dead, and the time they figured it would take me to be eaten was spent reinforcing positions. The soldiers had barricaded the corridor, readying themselves to do battle with the monsters there, rather than in the apartments, where it would be inconvenient.

"Comrade Colonel, you ought to see this," said a ghostly pale lad running out of my temporary apartment.

"What is it? I'm coming."

Soldiers cursed professionally. They were always able to produce such elusive words that the average person would not even suspect of their existence.

I now became witness to just such a monologue.

Combat exited the room mildly whey-faced and immediately shook my hand.

"What happened in there?"

"What's in there?"

"What's the situation in there?"

There was no quieting the curious crowd.

"Varg turned the place into a slaughterhouse." The answer came from a man who had seen all sorts, but was obviously seeing the likes of this for the first time. "Zombies, lots and lots of zombies, killed by one person. It wasn't him shut in a room with lots of zombies, but lots of zombies shut in a room with him."

Polina gave me a quizzical look and decided to check for herself. She entered the apartment with some other people, before quickly skipping out again, also pale.

"I have no apartment anymore," she announced sadly, staring off into the distance.

I felt uneasy. I had, it seemed, yet again been the reason for someone else's grief. Where were she and her daughter going to live now? Would they be given a new apartment or housed in a storeroom? She had no husband and breadwinner, which meant she wasn't much use to the community. Unless she went to bed with someone, in which case she would be considered a whore.

"Comrade Colonel, I counted no fewer than thirty corpses in there, but no trophies," a shifty fellow piped up.

"Of course there aren't any trophies, I took them," I said, unable to understand his dismay.

"There were a lot of boxes, weren't there?" he asked, squinting at me.

"Loads," I replied with a grin.

"Then you must share them out, since you are now living on our premises." The man clearly did not like me, nor the fact that all the trophies had gone to me. Why should his family go hungry, eating just once a day?

"Come and get them, then." I summoned a box into my hand to deliberately provoke him.

"AS YOU WERE!" The shout made me want to stand to attention and salute, and with both hands at that. Combat could be most convincing.

"Yes, sir!" cried the frightened man.

"Vasilenko, we will speak tomorrow about your behavior with our guest. He single-handedly repelled a monster attack, while you were clenching your butt cheeks in the utility room. You are now on the list for the next foray, understand?" Combat was angry at such an embarrassment in front of a guest. He had given me his word as an officer, and this desk jockey had tried to bully me, in doing so putting the management in an awkward situation. After all, the combat officers had taken control of everything in the dorm right at the start.

Eventually I was shown the way to the communal shower room, where I had a decent wash, before being examined and released, my hosts satisfied I was free of infection.

The clock said 02:00, and again I wanted to sleep, exhausted and drained of adrenaline.

But the dorm was buzzing like a beehive, people scurrying about and fulfilling Combat's orders. Furniture was deconstructed into planks and used, along with sheets of metal that were brought, to board up the broken windows.

Chapter 9

WE WERE REHOUSED, together again, only this time in a small storage closet with two folding beds.

"I don't like it here, I want to go home. My apartment has three rooms and no zombies," I informed my new acquaintance before we went to sleep.

"Since the beginning of the apocalypse, the dorm has been undergoing a transition, including the introduction of new rules. The best apartments are given to those who are of the most use to our community. The same goes for food. The families with combat-capable men are fed more and better," she replied.

"And I see you have a deficit of accommodation."

"We have a deficit of time. The management still hasn't decided who's going to sleep where.

There's VIP accommodation on the sixth floor, where visiting generals used to stay, and there's a real battle for it. Wives are nagging their husbands to get it for them."

"What fun."

"Except that's not going to happen. Those apartments will go to the most useful and faithful, to keep up their fighting spirit."

This woman was pretty smart, and her mental health was in order. Many others in her position would be in hysterics, or on the contrary, totally downcast, but this one was doing okay, hanging in there.

Or perhaps she wasn't. Perhaps she was putting up a front. Who knew?

The morning did not begin with coffee. Rather it began with a search for the bathroom to do my toilet. The night had passed quietly, without gunshot, affording me a decent night's sleep, so this morning I was bright-eyed and bushy-tailed.

Passersby told me where I could find the bathroom and even escorted me there. People had begun to recognize me, and I wondered if everyone had been told about me.

Some were well-disposed towards me, but there were also those who would scowl and darken and upon catching sight of me. The reason was, as I understood, the loot I had gained yesterday, no doubt mingled with a general distrust of outsiders. Here they lived as one big family, and along comes a stranger, whom everyone is talking about and who has lots of food but isn't sharing it. I wouldn't have been surprised to learn that my being robbed had been suggested.

Unfortunately for them, if they were to kill me, they would not get anything anyway. I had killed people and already knew that nothing dropped from their inventories. Except for skill books, of which I had received one.

After finishing in the bathroom, it occurred to me to go in search of Combat's office. I wanted to leave, and to say goodbye properly. It would also be good to see Shatun.

Shouts were coming from the office, and one of the voices I recognized as Polina's.

Apparently she was less than happy about something.

There was no guard by the door, in fact there was no one there at all, so I did not enter immediately, deciding instead to do a spot of eavesdropping.

"You're suggesting my daughter and I live in a room with only two folding beds? In a dirty store cupboard? Fine, in that case I shall clean up my own apartment by myself, I don't need your help!" the girl said at top volume.

Things were not going her way.

"I've told you a hundred times, your apartment is temporarily assigned to you anyway." Combat did not shout, but responded calmly, although he was clearly struggling to do so. He did not like doing this, but he had no choice. "You know what we agreed. All girls without a man in the family move to smaller accommodation. We need some way to motivate our fighters, and right now we have people living here who've lost their homes and decided to join us. I've got to find space for them as well."

"So you decided to put me and my daughter in a filthy closet, as though we're useless," Polina said with a bitter smile, tears in her eyes. She understood the situation. "So, what, do I have to lie on my back beneath a lonely soldier for somewhere to live, is that what you're hinting at?"

"I'm not hinting at anything. I will, however, repeat one more time that there are fewer and fewer singles around, while there are more and more families every day demanding accommodation. We haven't got enough materials to fortify all the apartments, and as yesterday's incident showed, unfortified apartments are dangerous to live in. One more break-in like that and we might all be done for."

I was bored of listening to all this, so I stepped into the office, without knocking, to see Polina looking hornet-mad and the silent Liza clinging to her hand.

"Ah, Varg, good morning, how did you sleep?" Combat said, changing the subject.

"Like a rat shoved into a dirty storeroom," I said, not standing on ceremony. "I held the line of defense yesterday, and I haven't been given an apartment."

"Please forgive me, but we have no free accommodation at the moment. In fact we have a waiting list for it. People might not understand if I

give an apartment to a new arrival just like that—
"

"I don't give a toss, if I'm honest," I said, interrupting him. "I'll be brief. I've got to go, but I'll be back soon with boxes to trade with, and if by then there's an apartment assigned to me as the owner, you'll never see me again. I can find other survivors who will only be glad to trade for food and ammunition."

"Okay, I'll have a think what can be done," the man replied seriously.

"While you're having a think, I've already had a thought. I want to buy an apartment on the sixth floor, a general's apartment."

"Pkhe..." Combat choked on his tea.

"Do you see a problem with that, Combat? Your people are starving, you'll soon be throwing stones at zombies, and you're too mean to buy yourself a few days grace in this game of survival?"

He gave me a severe and reproachful look from beneath his puckered brow, but I couldn't have cared less. I was not a military man and I wasn't about to bow to him.

"There are four apartments, one with three rooms, one with four rooms, and two with five rooms. Which one do you want? And what can you offer me for it?" He had realized the truth of my words. They needed at least a day's respite, and that would be enough time to stock up on supplies.

"I give you forty boxes of food, and that apartment is mine forever, accessible only to those with my personal permission. I can leave my belongings in there, but if so much as one thing goes missing, I shall be very angry."

"And what will you do, angry boy?" another man, silent until now, asked with a smile.

"What's the highest level any of your people has?" I asked of the speaker, turning towards him.

"What's that got to do with you? Maybe you're a spy?" he said distrustfully.

"Three," Combat replied, looking me closely in the eye.

"I'm level five," I said, dumbfounding them. "Do I need to tell you that each new level makes you stronger? I'm not going to tell you about my skills, but what do you think someone with a whole bunch of skills you know nothing about can do when they're invisible?" It was, of course, a cruel lie about the skills, but who would know?

The man bared his teeth and disappeared. Well, he thought he'd disappeared, yet he remained vaguely transparent in my eyes. And by the reaction of the other people in the room, I understood they could also see him, although maybe not quite so distinctly.

"Don't you dare, Fedya," barked Combat.

"Don't worry, I'm just going to teach him a lesson," he said, approaching me with an amused grin.

I showed no sign of being able to see him, merely turning my head every which way. He came up very close to me and aimed a blow at my jaw.

He probably thought he'd hit the target, but I

dodged his fist and responded with a counterpunch. Previously, I wouldn't even have made him step back, but now his feet became sharply disconnected with the floor and the man's solid body crashed into the wall, upon which he became visible once more.

"That's your first lesson, Fedya. Level one is only the first stage of invisibility, and anyone whose level is higher can also see you. Add to that the fact that I'm stronger, and your head would implode like a watermelon."

Combat was surprised. Polina was surprised. Liza was delighted and gave me the thumbs up.

While Fedya was trying to regain his senses, I looked back at Combat.

"So, what do you say to my proposal?" Should he refuse, it would be the end of our dealings. I was not going to continue sleeping in a kennel.

"I need to speak with Quartermaster first," he replied, producing his telephone to write a message. "He'll be along shortly."

Quartermaster came flying into the room. Combat began to put him in the picture, while he shifted his gaze between me and the colonel.

"Fifty gray boxes, and the apartment is yours. We accept your terms, but fortification will come at an extra charge. The place has six windows and they all need reinforcing with metal, agreed? The sixth floor is high up, so it needs securing from flying beasties."

"How much?"

"Fifteen red boxes, and we'll get busy with the

fortification today. I happen to have a little plywood left over for something like this," Quartermaster said with a smile. He loved to haggle and he was going to squeeze as much out of me as he could. He was sure I didn't actually have so much of everything and was waiting for me to backpedal.

I silently approached an empty part of the room and began to unload food boxes. Followed by red boxes.

"Are you going to count them?" I asked with a smirk.

"I already have. It's all there," Quartermaster said, amazed. All he could think about now was how many zombies this weakling had killed. Compared to me, everyone here was a snot-nosed little girl trembling at the sight of each box.

It was not only Quartermaster who thought this, but also Fedya, who had come to after being struck.

"I shall show you your new apartment myself," the colonel said, rising and heading for the door. "Come with me. Quartermaster can clear this lot away."

"Uh-huh, I'll do everything," quartermaster replied with a nod.

"Polina," are you coming or staying here?" Already at the door, I turned back to the girl, who was still trying to figure out what had just happened. She still looked very downhearted.

"Me?" she asked, lost.

"You" — I smiled — "and her," I said, pointing

at the little one.

The girls did not disappoint, following us without a word.

We took the stairs up to the last floor, where the luxury (by their standards) apartments were situated.

Even the corridor up there looked snazzier than the lower floors, and it was immediately obvious no paupers lived here.

"This apartment was assigned to General Gubin," said Combat, leading us inside.

"I see Gubin knew which side his bread was buttered," I said, whistling at what I saw. The only thing missing for complete comfort was freshly cut flowers, although there were empty vases.

Liza's mother was too slow to stop her daughter being first to go and check out the rooms. She didn't even suspect why we'd brought them along with us.

"So, now it's yours," said Combat, congratulating me as though on some great honor. "I shall give full instructions later today."

"Good. The first thing to do is fortify the windows." Without wasting time, I began dictating what needed doing and how. Then turning to Polina I said, "You are now going to be living here, while I'm not around. Just leave me one room."

"Why are you doing this?" Her face displayed no joy. Quite the opposite, in fact, only suspicion and despondency at the inevitable.

Looking at her, I realized she had dreamed up a bunch of horrors. Meanwhile, Combat could only grin into his whiskers.

"Listen, I don't feel comfortable among people. I'm already a touch more used to you than to others, but I don't want to see anyone else. You're going to live here and keep the apartment in order. On top of that, goods are going to be delivered here for me, about which you will send me a text message, when I find a phone, and I will come to collect them. Nothing of an intimate or terrible nature. You will simply be a housewife and secretary rolled into one."

"Good choice," Combat said approvingly. "Pol is a good and responsible girl."

It seemed to me he was playing the matchmaker, a thought that made me shudder.

"You bring her any goods meant for me, and in the future I will leave her my goods for exchange." Realizing what trouble I was putting her to, I decided to set things straight right away. "If I find out anything's happened to her to make her suffer, and any of my boxes go missing" — I stared Combat in the eye — "everyone will suffer."

"I understand." The man nodded. He respected me, aware that not everyone would be able to survive on the street at such a time, and that what I'd done when the zombies attacked the room was evidence of what I was capable of. Furthermore, I was a very strange one. Someone like me could harbor a grievance for a long time, making revenge his raison d'être.

"It's good that we've come to an agreement. And now, if you have no objections, I would like a chat with Polina." I nodded the colonel towards the exit.

"On that, I shall leave you," he said with a wave of his hand as he left the apartment.

In the living room stood a large round table that would seat eight. I sat down at it, gesturing for Polina to sit opposite me. Then Liza came running.

"Why are you doing this?" Polina asked, breaking the silence

"I don't know. Because I'm strange, because the bats in my belfry occasionally demand strange actions of me." I chuckled cheerfully and produced a number of boxes.

I was starving, so I kept opening boxes until there was enough food on the table.

Eight boxes in total, but it was well worth it. The table was spread with various delicacies, and the girls' bellies began to rumble as they feasted their wide eyes on the abundance.

"Why did you give up so much food for this apartment? Don't you understand how much that is?" Polina asked, her gaze continuing to bore through me.

"It might be a lot for you and them, but not for me."

"Is it so difficult to level up?"

"From level 2 to level 3 it's probably two hundred zombies." I shrugged, since I didn't know exactly what it depended on.

"You just carry out these minor instructions for me, and everything will be okay. By the way, have you got a telephone?" I suddenly remembered the most important detail.

"No."

"Could you somehow find two decent phones?" What if I got lucky and she said yes?

"I can in exchange for food," she said with a nod.

"Excellent" — I was delighted — "that makes the task at hand a bunch easier.

I unloaded thirty boxes of food and two pistols. Then I produced red boxes and opened them. I only had fifteen left, of which I opened ten.

"Here's fifty rounds for the pistols. Do you know how to use them?" I asked tardily.

"I do," she said, looking at me dazed.

"Then you can work it out. It's for your personal protection. And now, can you knock us up something to eat, please? And find those phones as soon as you can. I have to leave soon, I have lots to do in town."

We ate, and I had the chance to assess her cooking. It sure beat mine. I was more of a microwave-dinner kind of guy, while here was she, frying onions and potatoes and slicing an assortment of meats.

"Delicious, thank you." I had not forgotten my manners.

"Thank you for the food. And the apartment. And for saving us yesterday." Her voice trembled ever so slightly.

"I did what I wanted, no more no less, as I always do" I said, not giving her time to start with the hysterics. I was not one for sympathizing and listening.

"Thank you from me as well, it was very yummy. You're the best," said Liza, rubbing her tummy with joy. I hoped it wouldn't burst.

"Ten boxes of food are yours to do with as you wish. The rest are to be exchanged. When Quartermaster shows up with the goods, send me a text with the price, then go ahead with the exchange."

"I understand. It will be done," she said, nodding confidently. I guessed she wanted to ask or say something, but I didn't give her the chance, instead rising and making a beeline for the shower.

As I stood there in the shower, I couldn't understand what was happening to me. What the hell was I playing at? Why did I need an apartment? Why did I want to help them? Why had I helped Polina and her daughter? Nothing like this had ever happened to me before, and now I was fearful of such changes. Perhaps it was the system affecting my mind, manipulating me?

The old me would never have gotten tangled up in this, by which I mean the person I was before the apocalypse.

And where had this feeling of guilt come from? Why did I feel responsible for the devastation in their apartment. I hadn't invited the zombies, they'd by arrived themselves. And the fact of them being turfed out was their problem, not mine.

It was easier being a loner. A loner had no need for rules and laws. I was a law unto myself. I could do anything I wanted, and that suited me just fine.

I very much hoped the trade idea would work out. These numbskulls had to learn to kill a lot of zombies, and then a lot of loot would drop, which they basically didn't need, apart from the gray boxes.

My reason for going to the shower was not exclusively that I wanted to wash off yesterday's dirt again. Yesterday I had received a yellow trinket casket, and I did not want anybody to see me with it and discover its contents. My skills were my secret weapon, and they had to remain secret from everybody else. Although obviously it wasn't all that easy with invisibility, for it was difficult to hide.

I opened the trinket box and read the notification.

You receive: skill: X-ray vision, level 1.

You are able to see through any obstacle at a distance of up to 25 m.

Attention! In the first few hours after studying this skill, you may experience a mild headache. You will be taught to use the skill intuitively.

Ignoring the possible consequential headache, I immediately gave the mental command to study the skill.

It really was something. My head felt a mild tingle, but that would be of little concern when I could see what was occurring in Combat's office.

True, it was a strange picture, a naked lad spying on men, but still.

Knowledge of how to use the skill was an added bonus. I could scan through one or two walls, and even select the required radius. *Why didn't my invisibility skill come with an instruction manual?* Perhaps it had taken the system a while to figure out that people were dumb and needed everything explaining to them.

Suppose there were people sitting right now in their dark rooms, quivering with fear, and not knowing how to activate *Death To All Zombies*. I imagined the system's surprise at the stupidity of stupid people, and my mood immediately brightened. *Okay, that's enough fantasizing, it's time to get busy.*

CHAPTER 10

I LEFT THE DORM with mixed feelings. I was happy to eventually get away from the place, yet for reasons I did not understand, a hint of sadness would not leave me in peace.

Before leaving, I sought out Shatun and gave him five gray boxes for him and his daughter. We had a brief chat and I hinted that I needed information.

Being a kind soul, he naturally shared it, and now I knew at least a little of what was happening in the city. Most importantly, he warned me of places best avoided due to their being under the control of bandits and other scum.

Shatun did not even suspect that an excursion to such places was precisely my reason for asking.

Sitting there with them, I came across a problem: my inventory was too small for any more boxes. Were this to continue, I would be forced to look for separate storage space or create a cache, which might be robbed, and that would be most inconvenient for me.

As I learned from Shatun, banditry was rife in the city. The streetwise had not slouched, taking stock of the situation quickly and switching their hunting attentions from zombies to people. As it transpired, the opportunity really was there to gain a skill from human, even if it was nothing particularly useful. And then there was your inventory. If it was large enough, you did not have to kill zombies, instead simply raiding shops without breaking sweat.

The conversation also revealed one more important fact I hadn't previously thought about. Things in your inventory did not spoil, which meant you could stock up on large quantities of meat and it would not go off because of the heat or absence of a refrigerator.

The soldiers had a lot of friends throughout the city and had already begun to unfurl their web, which was being successfully woven by Fedya. They had not, however, come across, nor even heard mention of, my tower block. A plethora of small bands were forming, numbering anywhere from twenty to a hundred members. There was also a large group of people in the upmarket area of the city. The affluent had their own security teams, weapons, and fortress-like homes, and right now they were consolidating their power and, according to Shatun, could well become a force to be reckoned with. Among them was one general, who had invited my new acquaintances to be part of his team. Or to be more precise, he had not so much as invited as ordered them to leave their families and report to him at once. He was told in no uncertain terms where to get off.

I left the dorm and headed for the nearest school. I didn't know why, but today I decided to kill all the zombie children. Not that it would not be easy, mind.

Yesterday I'd wondered what would have happened if I'd fled the room and the zombies had broken through. There were lots of women and children in the dorm, and I really wanted to see some infected tots. For some reason you didn't come across them so often in the city, and so I decided to go to the school today and free their souls, gifting them an easy death.

It did not befit children to go running about the city eating people.

The school was not large, about three hundred pupils, so it shouldn't be difficult.

I reached it without incident in invisibility mode, managing along the way to kill a couple of particularly audacious zombies that hampered my passage. I also ran across the funniest zombie to date: a middle-aged man, wondering along the road, wheezing protractedly, his only clothes a pair of loose-fitting boxers adorned with yellow ducks, worn down at his knees. A poor excuse for a zombie, though amusing, and I felt compelled to let him rest in peace.

At the entrance to the school I took a quick look around. Where were all the children? The schoolyard was empty.

As I approached the doors, I saw them to be closed.

Then the penny dropped. The zombie apocalypse had broken out on Saturday, and at God knows what time, perhaps even during the night.

What a dunderhead!

It all has to do with people. They have a bad effect on me.

I had not known such disappointment in a long time.

I urgently wanted to kill someone, and it may even make me feel better, so I set off to prowl the side streets in search of zombies.

After ten minutes of slow meandering, during which I killed a number of zombies, I saw some people.

A guy and a girl with heavy bags in their hands were running furtively down a narrow street. Focusing in on the bags they carried, I saw food and various other bits and bobs.

The guy was obviously nervous, checking constantly around, and the girl was puffing with the exhaustion of hauling her bags.

As they approached the next crossroads, I saw zombies up ahead.

The couple could not see them, but they clocked that I'd seen something.

I accelerated to catch them up. I wanted to be

closer.

The couple emerged from behind the last building and into the zombies' field of vision. The zombies roused themselves, began to growl, and set off in pursuit of the pair of marauders.

When she saw the zombies, the girl tripped over and fell flat on her face on the tarmac. As she did so her cap fell off, and I saw she was a blonde of about eighteen. She looked back in terror at the beasties.

You feckless bumblers, I cursed them silently and produced my bow.

As I was popping off the first five zombies, the two fools just kept on running, not even looking around now. Strange though it may seem, the guy did not disappear into the distance, but helped his lady accomplice to her feet and even relieved her of her bags. Then they ran off again.

It's easy to shoot targets that cannot see you and are not chasing you, and it's even easier to hunt when you know you aren't being watched. I discovered this as I cast an eye over the nearest buildings.

I continued to fire at the zombies until I was sure the couple had run far enough to be out of danger. That's the kind of bizarre invisible hero I was, to act like that out of sheer boredom.

I gathered my loot, which was not much to write home about, two gray boxes and one red one.

Still, I'd had a warm up, and now it was time to go kill some people.

* * *

Crunching an apple, I sat on the curb opposite a gas station that looked like a small bunker. The window blinds were rolled down and impressive in their thickness. I wasn't convinced even a car would have been able to penetrate such armor plating.

But I had not come here to admire the gas station. An extremist gang, as Shatun had put it, had taken up residence there.

I did not know whether they'd been a gang before all this shit kicked off, or whether they'd formed since, but either way I did not like the look of them.

Too brazen-face and unguarded, vicious-looking as well. People with weapons and bottles of booze in their hands wandered to and fro up on the roof, their merry laughter constant and their shouts attracting ever more zombies.

Six naked men hung upside down from the roof. They did not look like zombies, at least not by the condition of their skin, which was not pale and covered with bloody spots and blue patches. Their fingernails had not grown into claws, and their eyes were not grown over with a cloudy film but simply rolled back.

A quick once-over of the gas station told me everything I needed to know. Twenty-seven people, half of them asleep, the remainder killing zombies for fun.

They had their wits about them too. I saw them take down three zombies without letting the gray boxes slip through their fingers.

Their method was quite interesting. One of them would keep throwing a lasso at a zombie until the noose landed around its neck, then they would hoist it up onto the roof and kill it, before throwing the body back down. It was certainly not a bad method, but it would soon create a mountain of corpses growing up the wall of the gas station, which would allow the rest of the monsters to climb up.

As I chewed my apple, one of the men felt the urge to go to the toilet. Without thinking, he relieved himself on the zombies below, guffawing as he did so.

In the mood to make his life difficult, I drew my bow, affixed an arrow to it, took aim, and let fly. The man was very drunk, staggering, and about fifty paces away, and the arrow meant for his heart struck him in the belly.

At first he couldn't understand what had happened. Then he began to wail in agony. I sat back down on the curbstone, smiled, and resumed my apple munching. The man fell flat on his back on the roof, where his comrades immediately rushed to his side and looked in non-comprehension first at the arrow and then at him, while he could find nothing meaningful to say. Well, what could he possibly have to say?

Then one of the gang, a man wearing camouflage fatigues, crawled carefully to the edge and looked over in search of the archer. In vain.

Evaluation.

Hmm, nothing's happening. Shame. It worked on the one I killed before.

The guy in fatigues took his rifle in his hands and searched for something to aim at. What though? I wasn't there. I wasn't there either, or there.

Perhaps I should bung them a grenade, make their day? No, that's boring.

Another man ran downstairs to where the bedroom was and woke someone up. He received a slap around the face for his trouble, but the man rose, cursing (if I read his lips correctly) and went up onto the roof.

I get it, this guy's got a skill. Standing on the roof, he raised one hand, and from it a number of spheres flew off in different directions. What was this? Had he decided to make the day brighter?

Then I had a thought which should have occurred to me earlier.

Evaluation!

Search For Life sphere. Attracted to the living.

The spheres could not see me, and that was a fact. They didn't even come anywhere near me, which meant they were useless and not a patch on my invisibility.

Ha! With the spheres not finding anyone, the bandits relaxed, figuring I'd left the scene. They rose from their squatting positions by the dead man and scanned the vicinity, talking and cursing. I could not hear what they were talking about, only catching snippets of swearwords.

You have killed a survivor.

The capacity of your inventory is increased by 4 kg.

Ooh, so he died after all. At last. I'd gotten tired of waiting and wondering if they were going to treat his belly wound with antiseptic.

I was bored of sitting in the same place for so long, but just then one of the men struck a convenient pose, so I shot him.

You have killed a survivor.

The capacity of your inventory is increased by 5 kg.

Fuck. He managed to cry out and attract the others' attention, leaving me no time to lose. I quickly began to shower them with arrows, without taking particular aim.

In response, they began firing randomly all over the place. *It's so difficult to hit your target when you can't see it.*

You have killed a survivor.

The capacity of your inventory is increased by 2 kg.

You have killed a survivor.

The capacity of your inventory is increased by 1.5 kg.

You have killed a survivor.

The capacity of your inventory is increased by 6 kg.

You have killed a survivor.

The capacity of your inventory is increased by 2.5 kg.

The system only showered me with messages when I'd finished shooting and the remaining survivors had legged it down from the roof and slammed the door behind them. How jittery they were. I'd only killed a couple of them, yet they all fled.

By now my inventory was fifty kilograms, but frankly it was still too little. Too damned little. I wanted at least five hundred, if not a whole ton. Something told me that would not be a problem in this new world.

Shit. They weren't exactly burning with desire to come out and meet me. They had even barricaded the exit to the roof, and clearly no one was going to be sleeping up there anymore. They were all tearing about, shouting.

Fine, I'll sit here and wait for thirty minutes. While I was waiting, I opened a couple of trinket caskets, of which I had collected a fair number.

I did not want to be seen with them in the dorm, nor did I want to have to answer a bunch of bothersome questions, and there was little enough space left in my inventory. If something heavy was dropped, I would have to leave it there.

I took a blue casket, hoping it would produce something useful.

You receive fact card №117.

The assortment of rewards increases with time, just like danger in this world.

Nothing much really, although it was useful to know.

You receive fact card №456.

On the trading platform, it is impossible to buy or sell skill books. You may only exchange them for other skills.

That was more like it. Although I didn't know where to find the trading platform.

I guessed the trading coin might be able to help me, but I hadn't gotten around to evaluating it yet.

You receive fact card №25.

Killing with a firearm gives 80% less experience and drastically reduces the chance of a reward dropping. Kill your enemies with a system weapon, and you will know what happiness is.

That was pretty much what I'd supposed. Firearms were way undervalued by the system, and so far I had not met any soldiers higher than level 3. The news gave me an enormous advantage, thanks to my bow. And until people discovered this, I would have the opportunity to sell weapons that were useless to me.

It was just a pity the soldiers received fewer rewards, so they didn't have many goods they could exchange. On the other hand, there were loads of them, and there was only one of me, so they ought to be able to provide me with arrows and other gear.

It was now time for the last fact box.

You receive fact card №31.

Large groups of survivors attract far more zombies than individual survivors. They will attempt to kill people by any available means.

Another advantage of being a loner.

I now understood why zombies attacked the soldiers so often and why the ones in my anthill always ran up to the upper floors.

I looked up from the facts and focused my attention once more on the gas station. Nothing had changed and the bandits were still arguing and waving their arms. At that rate they would soon be knocking one another down.

Shatun said a friend of his had seen them shooting from the roof, killing other survivors unlucky enough to be walking past the station. I wanted to kill as many of them as I could from where I was, since it was currently impossible to get inside the station, and I was weak in enclosed spaces. Fine, I would wait, and in the meantime open a couple of red trinket boxes.

You receive a card: curved sword.

You receive a card: disposable crossbow, loaded with a cold-explosive bolt.

You receive a card: the Glaive of Hopsh, level 2.

You receive a card: crystal-tipped arrows, 15 pcs.

You receive: warrior's flail, level 1.

You receive a card: regular bolts, 32 pcs.

You receive: long spear.

You receive a card: iron-tipped arrow, reinforced, 88 pcs.

Seeing the capacity of my inventory shrink, I did not dare open the remainder of the trinket boxes. The long spear and the warrior's flail would take up at least fifteen kilograms. Fuck.

And as if to spite me, those bastards did not want to emerge from their shelter.

Fine, I would wait some more, and to pass the time, I would see what I'd received.

I activated the arrow card immediately, and in my hand appeared fifteen arrows with crystal, though not fragile, arrowheads.

Evaluation.

In terms of arrowhead strength, crystal was in no way inferior to iron, but at the moment of impact with a body, it broke up into small particles, and without losing speed.

It was scary to even imagine such an arrow entering an enemy's body. It was not a weapon for zombies, but rather geared towards the elimination of sentient beings.

I decided not to produce the glaive, since it was fairly heavy, instead confining myself to admiring the picture of it. I did not especially need it, but its level-two status commanded respect.

The crossbow was interesting and no less dangerous. Upon striking its target, the bolt would explode and produce a chill or a serious freeze, I had no idea which. I thought it might freeze a small area, which meant it would be ideal against enemies packed into a narrow space. I hoped I wouldn't get killed by an explosion of ice shards.

I was pleased with the reinforced arrows, which were made using ancient technology, had rhomboid heads, and were decorated with unusual runes. I hoped they wouldn't break gradually with each strike.

That killed another hour, by which time I was seriously bored. I was even entertaining the thought of lobbing a grenade at them or letting loose with the crossbow. *Okay, I'll wait just a little longer.*

I took out the coin and examined it again, but still saw nothing. Then suddenly I got it.

Evaluation!

A trading coin which permits 24 hours' access to the trading platform.

To activate the coin, you must toss it. You do not have to catch it.

Bingo! So that was it. And there was me, rubbing it, biting it, even begging it to activate.

And what's all this "you do not have to catch it" all about? Does the system have so little faith in me?

Anyway, I held the coin in my hand and ran through everything once more in my head. I looked at the gas station, which was quiet now, and made my decision. The coin flew up, fell back down, and...

Trading platform activated. Time remaining: 23 hours 59 minutes.

Great Scott! Now that was something!

An interface opened in front of my eyes, like in an old game. It was a real gaming panel for people to sell their wares.

My eyes immediately lit upon an interesting item: apple of control.

I clicked on it and a new message appeared.

You have not chosen a new name or nickname. Old names have no meaning here.

In order to use the trading platform, choose a new name.

What did this mean? The system was being belligerent. Why the hell did it want to change people's names?

Although since it was saying I had to change my name, who was I to argue?

I didn't know how to change my name, so I simply said, "I want to choose the name Varg."

A window popped up with a response: New name accepted. From now on your name is Varg.

You receive 1 trading coin.

Wicked! Probably.

The coin would definitely come in handy, but right now I was more concerned with the trading platform, the operation of which I intended to get to grips with, while not forgetting to keep one eye on the gas station.

It took me an hour to understand how it worked. The first and most important thing was that only items on cards could be exchanged, which meant that all the other weapons were useless to me and would need palming off on the soldiers.

Next I figured out how to use all of this. You could put any item up for exchange and name the price you were willing to exchange it for. There was no money involved, or maybe I just hadn't found the relevant information yet. You could also write exactly what you were looking for.

And so I completed my first purchase, which was immediately deposited in my inventory.

Someone had posted a card saying, "Basic arrows, 55 pcs. Will exchange for a box of food."

I offered three boxes and they were accepted immediately. There were many surprises, not least the number of goods I didn't recognize, and which bore no description. In fact none of them bore a description, and if you hadn't come across something before, you wouldn't know what you were buying. The only thing that would help you was logic.

The main currency here was boxes of food and bullets. It seemed people had become used to this useless — in my opinion — weapon after all, choosing effectiveness over quality.

A firearm truly was a killer bit of kit, I couldn't deny it, but I also couldn't ignore its disadvantages. You had to be able to use such a weapon properly. And what about the scarcity of ammunition? What if it jammed at an inconvenient moment? Who would be able to restore its battle-readiness quickly? This was not to mention the shooter's ability and accuracy. You could fire off a dozen or so rounds, and even hit your target, but that would not necessarily fell a zombie.

I found another interesting item and wondered if it was worth splashing out on.

Light leather armor, level 1.

The seller was asking twenty boxes of food. Checking the rest of the platform, I found nothing else like it, or at least nothing that wasn't too bizarre-looking. There was heavy armor, but the idea of an archer in a suit of armor was nothing short of comical.

Screw it, I thought, and sent the seller twenty-five boxes.

I waited. *Exchange cancelled.* WTF, man? Or maybe not man?

The cancellation was accompanied by a notification.

The armor costs thirty boxes.

Fuck. He'd realized I really needed the armor and decided to haggle.

I wanted to send him packing and move on, but... shoot, I really needed that armor.

I weighed up the pros and cons for ten minutes, coming to the conclusion that nobody was exempt from a random bite and it was worth being prepared for such a situation.

Very well, you greedy bastard, thirty it is. And I sent him the boxes.

You were given a minute's thinking time, which was fine by me, because you wouldn't have to wait God knows how long merely to be informed of cancellation.

The exchange went through successfully.

The system tinkled, and my inventory was credited with an armor card, while the boxes disappeared. I unpacked it straightaway to see what I'd received.

I examined the armor thoroughly. It really was light, and made of tough yet flexible leather, which would not restrict my movements. But even such an ignoramus as I understood it was not complete, covering only the chest and back, without even a hint of protection for the shoulders or legs.

Of course it was entirely possible that here, just as in the game, it was never going to be a complete set, and the rest would need to be sought separately, my protection becoming more comprehensive as I rose God knows how many levels.

The armor was easy to don, with the exception of the unusual bindings down the left side, which required pulling tightly.

I did not, however, don it right away. Not because of the zombies wandering around and the people in the gas station, but because of my doubts concerning its quality.

First I hung it on a wall, stepped back twenty yards, and took out my bow to conduct an experiment. I fitted an arrow, drew the bowstring — not tight, but enough to kill — and let loose.

The arrow struck the middle of the armor, pretty much where the heart would be, and did not pierce it, leaving only a small scratch.

The evidence suggested that the armor, or protection, had passed the test. I was not, of course, going to repeat the experiment with my pistol, for it was clear you would stand little chance.

When I managed to get hold of a second set, then I would conduct a ballistics test.

It took five minutes to squeeze myself into the armor, over a T-shirt so it would not rub. All I had to do was remove my light jacket.

I ran, I jumped, I did push-ups. The armor fitted me nicely and, sure enough, did not restrict my movements. For the final test, I shot a couple of zombies. Everything went excellently and the protection did not hinder my shooting.

I hoped it wouldn't be hot to wear, but only time would tell.

I spent another half an hour scrolling through the shop, and realized it was not all good news. There was certainly a lot on offer, but nearly everything demanded a box of food in exchange, and I only had ten gray and five red boxes left. That meant it was time for me to go to the farm, as the players said. But this was no game, as I was going to be killing zombies. If I could.

Chapter 11

WHEN I OPENED the trading platform, I was dumbstruck to the very core of my bizarre and avaricious soul. There were such unbelievable quantities of stuff I needed that I wanted to buy everything at once.

Only now did I understand just how weak I was, wallowing in my little swamp, deluded that invisibility would save me in my hour of need, and that I'd be invincible if only I had a hundred arrows in reserve. Right now, in front of my very eyes, someone sold five hundred arrows, and I didn't even get to see the price he sold them for. Holy crap, five hundred! That meant that somewhere in the world was an asshole archer who did not have to dig around in stinking zombie brains for arrows to clean and reuse like me, instead killing zombies with volleys of them, no hassle.

I also realized how naïve I was. Level 5, pah!

Without wasting time on gathering my spent arrows, but instead with the aid of the trading platform, I could be leveling up without stressing it.

I only managed to buy two hundred arrows, at which point I ran out of food boxes. And that was after taking down zombies in the gas station in order to reap more food boxes to trade with.

Fuck, that sucked big time. I was losing the race against time in this new world.

On top of my inventory woes, others were now piling up.

The gas-station hoodlums eventually decided to send someone out to reconnoiter the situation. He crawled to the edge of the roof and looked cautiously down. My mood by now was so wretched that an arrow immediately got him right in the eye. However, even that did not cheer me up, so it was clearly time to skedaddle. The system sent me notification of, and a reward for, my killing of a person I did not care about.

You have killed a survivor.

The capacity of your inventory is increased by 2 kg.

I swatted the notification away with my hand, like a pestilent fly. What with twenty-two hours left on my trading licence, I had more important things to do than shepherd these jackasses.

* * *

I walked swiftly and surely towards my new target. I wouldn't be able to get to sleep if I wasted the time allotted to me for trading on the platform, so I briskly marched two blocks down from the gas station and found a building I liked the look of, which had a convenient balcony on the second floor. Climbing up to it was a piece of cake, as was scouring the vicinity for signs of people. The building contained four apartments devoid of people, and one with two zombies clattering about behind its locked doors. They were so eager to break out that they were shredding the door with their claws. *Dumb ass zombies; it's quicker through the window.*

The building was situated on a narrow street more or less empty of zombies. I knew how to fix that. The balcony door was old, plastic, and easily opened by a hefty shoulder shove. I was in. The first thing I saw was a sideboard full of crockery. Excellent. I opened it and unloaded everything into my inventory.

I returned to the balcony and began throwing the crockery down from it in all directions. Sure enough, upon hearing the ring of plates smashing, zombies began to move in my direction. I found more crockery in the kitchen and threw that down as well, attracting even more zombies.

When a largeish crowd was gathered beneath the balcony, I drew my bow.

Let's get to work!

What could be better than shooting zombies? Correct. Killing a plethora of zombies.

The first twenty arrows all hit their targets, leaving my boxes lying down there all lonesome. After fifty arrows, their ranks began to thin, and those that remained began to wander off in various directions. When I cast off my invisibility, they turned around and came back to get me.

Shooting. Shooting. The only thing I really loved in this world was shooting from a bow. Maybe I'd died and gone to heaven? Or hell?

Here was a slow moving zombie in a plaid shirt with a name tag. He'd probably been a store clerk before the chaos began, but now he was plodding towards me to receive an arrow to the head.

Here was a zippy one, an old lady, and here came a girl who ought to have been adorning the front pages of fashion magazines, but was instead lying with an arrow protruding from her forehead.

The system was merciless and did not choose who should remain alive and who should become a soulless beast. My eyes were drawn to a child with its cheek chewed out, seriously unlucky to have been eaten alive.

The supply of zombies ran dry approximately two hours later, and I went down to collect my rewards. Gray boxes alone numbered fifty, and there were other colors besides, which I did not count but threw directly into my inventory. *Later, I'll count it all later, no time now.*

My new problem was the lack of zombies, but any intelligent human must be vaguely resourceful, and I was ready to do anything to fulfill my desires.

I returned to the second floor, to the same apartment. Finding a music center, I put it by an open window and switched it on at top volume.

Any remaining survivors in the area would probably be wondering who the idiot was, entertaining himself like that. I didn't care, I was fine, and I expected a fresh wave of zombies to be along shortly.

I spent another hour killing zombies in calm concentration, nothing to stop me. Well, almost nothing.

I was standing there, having just let fly with yet another arrow, when suddenly I heard a gentle whistle, and slightly to my left I noticed a movement, which was accompanied by a dull thud.

Slowly, like in a cheap Hollywood film, I turned my head and saw a large needle, made of bone, ten centimeters long, and sticking in the wall right in front of my eyes. The son of a bitch had whizzed right past my ear, only by some miracle missing my already not exactly smartass head. My reaction was instinctive. I hit the deck and switched on invisibility, which I'd forgotten to do earlier.

Head down, I crawled back into the apartment. Only then did I draw breath. And only then did I realize how close I'd been to death. I certainly wasn't afraid of death, but I didn't want it to happen right at the start of this global pandemonium. I'd only just begun to enjoy living in this new world, and for everything to end now? No, that would not do.

Cautiously, through the window in the other room, I looked to see who it might have been. I soon spotted a vile zombie. Protruding eyes which might fly out of their sockets at any moment, and raised arms that ended in hands with gaping holes right through them. This must have been the fucker who shot at me, yet I could not understand how. There couldn't possibly have be supply of needles under his skin. Or could there? Of course there could, what was I thinking? Anything was possible in this world now.

I won't be at all surprised to see spaceships full of aliens zipping across the sky in the fairly near future.

Words would not accurately describe the maliciousness with which I launched my arrow at the zombie. I reckon the bow sensed my rage and supercharged the arrow, making it pass right through the dumb head, before the beastie collapsed to the ground.

There was no way I could work without invisibility now. Damn. The system had hinted not long ago that the zombies would evolve over time.

I sat down on the bed and got out a box of food. I rejected the buckwheat offhand, but the Snickers was just what the doctor ordered, and I also found a can of beer. Sweet chocolate and bitter beer, just what was required after a bout of stress like that.

I hadn't yet finished the beer when the system decided I hadn't had enough adventure for one day.

Attention! You are offered the chance to take part in a special test. You will have to fight against other survivors who have also accepted the offer.

You may refuse the offer, but if you do so, you will lose one level.

What? There was no way I was going to lose a level.

Of course I accept! System, I accept!

It was immediately obvious that the fight would involve only those who accepted.

Which meant it would involve a lot of amoral characters like me who were only too happy to level up at the expense of others.

You will be transferred to the battlefield in 5...4...3...2...1

The world darkened and span, and I found myself standing in some kind of forest and... barfing.

A superb means of transportation! Why don't you just go ahead and shove me in a box, tape it up, and bung me in the mail? Perhaps in twenty years' time, or thereabouts, you'll be sending me as a mummy?

After my head stopped spinning, I fished out a bottle of water and drained it in one go. I held out a hand, looked at it, and nodded, satisfied it wasn't shaking so badly anymore.

Does everyone get all giddy like that, or is it just me?

Attention! Attention! The test has begun. It will last for one hour. At the end of the test, any survivors will be transported back to where they came from, and those with the highest number of kills will receive a reward.

Who the hell is this woman? Why did she have to go talking about rewards? Now I'm not going to leave the other players a single chance.

Invisibility settled down smoothly over me, I drew my bow and arrow, and I was ready.

I stepped a few paces away from where I'd vomited, and began scanning the area. *Trees, more trees, ooh, there's a man, aged about forty, sitting on his butt and wagging his head fitfully.* A minute later I was by him and without compunction loosing an arrow right into his heart. One down. Hmm, no loot. No messages concerning inventory augmentation either. Not good.

Not far away, I heard gunshots. New clients; I couldn't not go. Wasting no time, I hightailed it in that direction, keeping a good look out all around on the way.

When I got to where the noise was coming from, an interesting picture met my eyes: two people shooting at each other from behind trees.

One of them, a ginger lad wearing a bandanna that did nothing to conceal the color of his hair, stood with his back to me. An easy target, a no-stress kill. The redhead did not even have time to understand what had killed him before he dropped down dead on the ground. His opponent did not notice his death, and continued to fire in the hope of a hit.

Absolutely not in the mood to take a stray bullet, I flanked him in a wide arc and sank two arrows into him. The first got him in the neck, where it stuck but didn't kill him. The man fell to his knees and grabbed his throat, clueless as to how it had happened. I could have left it at that and moved on, but then I realized somebody else might finish him off and claim the victory for themselves, and I wasn't going to let that happen. The second arrow got him in the head, and he was still.

It was a pity they didn't help to enlarge my inventory. And just when I needed it as well. I figured it was too dangerous and long a process to collect their weapons, and why did I want to clutter up my already overfilled inventory?

I moved on into the forest in search of new victims. I had absolutely no qualms about killing people here, since they'd chosen the rules of the game themselves. It was doubtful anyone had ended up here by mistake. The system had given a distinct choice: either you fight, or you lose a level. There was also the reward I wanted to receive, and would receive, I had no doubt about that.

The most important thing was not to relax, otherwise I'd get a cap in my ass, which was a sad and final prospect. Even a wounded arm or leg was out of the question. An archer with a wounded arm would be a pitiful sight.

Three minutes later I came across my next two opponents, engaged in a more serious battle. A bullet hit one guy and immediately bounced off him, courtesy of a hastily manifested barrier. The other was not only shooting, but also throwing stones. What was he, some kind of commander of the rocks?

I wasn't even sure if it was worth getting involved. People with skills were far more dangerous than common folk with weapons. The chances of an accident were too high; I might screw up.

The two antagonists had thrown all caution to the wind and ceased to notice the situation around them. One was flinging rocks, while the second deflected them with his shield and took shots whenever possible, and the engagement had attracted not only me, but also other carrion feeders. It turned out vision was a good skill; it allowed you to be aware of your surroundings.

Now then. What's this weirdo doing here?

I noticed a familiar face who still thought no one could see him in invisibility mode. Surely Fedya hadn't decided to risk such a venture? How had he persuaded Combat to let him go?

Fedya came closer and hid behind a wide tree, where he dropped to the ground and lay surveying the battlefield. I had just decided he was a total idiot trying to edge his way into someone else's contest, when he stood back up and trotted away again, having probably decided to find himself an easier opponent.

The trouble was, I wasn't the only one observing him. Twenty yards from the tree was the figure of a lad standing so camouflaged and unmoving by another tree that I didn't notice him at first. Evidently he also had a skill, probably something to do with chameleons. Chameleon, as I christened him in my thoughts, moved off after Fedya, dagger in hand and ready to attack.

"Now then, my friend, you can't go around slicing up my friends, there aren't so many of them left," I said with a bloodthirsty snort as I stuck Chameleon with an arrow and pinned him to the tree.

That's fate for you. He had hidden himself so cunningly among the trees, and it was a tree he found himself pinned to. Just in case, I let him have another three arrows, and only then did I approach him. I was interested in his dagger, its form was interesting, and I might get lucky and get something unusual.

Dagger of the occult, level 2.

Nothing special then, and a creepy name to boot. My first job when I got home would be to sell it for a good price.

I checked again that Chameleon was actually dead, before returning to the two lads.

As I stepped into the clearing where they were still fighting, I realized I had been right to wait. The stones had stopped flying, and the guy with the shield now had a wounded arm. It seemed they'd run out of either strength or mana.

I finished off the wounded bird first, although my arrow pierced his skull when all I actually wanted to do was stick him in the eye.

Oops. I'd killed a person right in front of his opponent, and the latter immediately began firing at me from his hiding place behind the fat tree trunk.

I was forced to waste time crawling in a wide circle around him in order to approach him from the rear.

What the fuck? I wanted to shout at the top of my voice, but I made myself keep the curse inside my head.

As I was crawling, some slanty-eyed bitch cut my loot with her curved machete.

The chick was taking my booty! My mind exploded, and in my ire I drew a crystal-tipped arrow. She was so engrossed in killing the man that she wasn't keeping an eye out around her, and I would be able to kill her quickly and easily. But she had to be made aware of her mistake before she died.

My arrow flew straight into her lower back. The shaft, being useless now, immediately broke off on contact with her body, while the crystal was disbursed around all her insides, making her screech wildly and roll about on the ground from the intense pain in her belly.

"Oops, I seem to have gone a bit overboard," I said to myself. Her cries only intensified with the pain of her internal injuries.

Figuring she had probably been sufficiently

punished already, I produced a new arrow and put her out of her misery.

I sat down on a tree stump for a minute to catch my breath, and pondered just how exhilarating the hour, or however much of it remained, would be. Killing people was not quite so simple as I had originally thought, but there was no choice. Only one law was at work here: kill or be killed.

The world was changing, and if I didn't change along with it, it would eat me up. I had no illusions concerning my strength: I was a simple person who had been lucky enough to gain a useful skill, and without it I would not survive here, fact. However, I couldn't even shoot a pistol.

I would have to ask Shatun to teach me just in case. It might come in handy in the future. On the other hand, the system might take offense and stop treating me favorably.

The dead chick was bleeding so profusely I didn't want to go anywhere her. She'd also caused such a ruckus that she was doubtless being observed from a distance.

Perhaps it was worth me observing her too? I stood to the side and waited. I had time, and I hoped I'd amassed enough points for victory.

Three minutes later, a young lad of about eighteen ran out of the bushes and approached her body. His face was covered with blood and his right hand was missing a finger. The poor thing had been mauled. More importantly, though, he had no weapons with him at all.

He made a dash for the girl's body, next to which lay her blade. After giving her torso a kick, in a most un-gentlemanly fashion, he picked up the machete. The next instant, one of my arrows was sticking out of his mouth.

I saw no point in waiting any longer. I'd had a short rest and I could move on.

I decided to head in the direction Fedya had run. I might catch him raping someone, which would give me good reason to shoot him.

I caught up with him quite soon, and not before time. He was shooting to defend himself from three people at once, who were, in their turn, trying to surround him.

Hmm, they had joined forces; a good tactic for survival, but not for victory.

If they'd had firearms, Fedya would already be dead. As it was, they were armed with shields, swords, and spears, and Fedya appeared to be almost out of ammunition. Had it not occurred to the idiot to take a bladed weapon with him?

No sooner had I wondered this, than he threw his pistol into his inventory and produced a knife instead. Clearly not a system knife, probably military.

There wasn't a whiff of invisibility about him and his chances were running low. He may have been a trained fighter, but there were three of them and they had more weapons. On top of which, he'd used up all his invisibility charge, and he was now in serious trouble.

What was I to do? Walk on by? Help him? Kill

them all?

There was no time for long contemplation, for Fedya was about to have sex without his consent, and rough sex at that.

One of his attackers threw a spear and Fedya barely managed to dodge it.

Shoot, it was a pity I had no popcorn. Watching this might have been very entertaining.

I drew an arrow and took out the guy with the shield. Actually, that was a lie.

As it transpired, he was wearing chain mail beneath his clothes. He turned sharply in my direction, and only then did he die, from a second arrow entering his forehead.

I did not like it when my arrows failed to find their target. The scumbag thought his chain mail would save him, but he'd forgotten to wear a helmet. Although judging by the number of trinket boxes dropping, that was not surprising. Not a single one dropped for me. That said, I could buy one for food. As I understood, food was much more valuable than weapons right now. You could not feed a family on weapons and armor.

"Kill him, he's killed Shield," shouted the lad who had thrown the spear. He now drew a sword and rushed at Fedya.

They thought it was him who had killed their friend. *I've said it before and I'll say it again: invisibility is a fantastic thing.*

The guy with the sword was five meters further away than the spear thrower, but he ran to his friend's aid at full tilt, for his friend was already tangling with Fedya.

Okay, I would help with this one as well, I decided, and loosed an arrow directly into the runner's heart. Now Fedya was one on one with his opponent.

Now it would be a fair fight, I noted, before wandering off, satisfied. I was not going to help him with the last one as well. If he couldn't handle him, it was his problem, I wasn't his nanny. If he died, it meant he was weak. And if his opponent was, say, level 5, he would definitely die.

While I was walking through the forest in search of my next victim, I noticed something. I was leaving footprints behind me, and that was not good. If that continued, winter would be the end of me.

"System, do you have any footwear that doesn't leave footprints? If you do, I'll buy two... no three pairs right now." I addressed the system in a whisper, and as was its wont, the system switched on its ignore function. "Well yes, screw me, I get it."

Lost in ruminations concerning my footprints and what could be done about them, I nearly bumped into a black man on a stakeout.

Pumba-Yumba, what are you doing here? I wanted to shout out in surprise.

Instead of this, I took out my spear and thrust it into his chest. In the process, I nearly lost my head when he, reflexively and with his last ounce of strength, span around and swung his hatchet towards my head.

I scarcely managed to jump out of the way, and I was forced to leave my spear behind. He was nigh butt-naked, wearing only a loincloth. I wondered what the system had promised him for taking part in the test? A pair of pants?

I retrieved my spear from his chest and looked at his weapon.

Recurved blade of Mataburai.

Basically a hatchet, but the system felt it needed to be called a blade.

Actually, I thought this was not only the system's doing. Gnawing away at me were worms of doubt that this loot was of another world which also had its own system.

If that was the case, I would need to look for elven weapons, if they existed. Elves were masters of the bow.

Daydreaming of elven bows, I wanted to laugh out loud. Uh-huh, great masters of the bow, if our earthly books and movies were to be believed. In reality, however, they were probably all old perverts who fought with weapons unacceptable to men, yet here was me wanting to emulate them. That would be a real hoot.

Time to end of test: 30 mins.

Attention! Infecteds will be introduced to the test zone for the next stage.

Shoot, half an hour gone already, and I haven't even whacked a hundred yet.

I must get a wiggle on!

Wait, what? What next stage?

CHAPTER 12

I HEARD THE ARRIVAL of the new zombies immediately. In fact, the whole forest heard their frenzied howls.

The howls came from all around, which made me tense a little. I cast a quick eye around and was shocked by what I saw. It was very unpleasant to realize that the sweet kind little zombies' center-stage position was being usurped.

The forest was now being flooded with real monsters that only vaguely resembled zombies. Among them I saw winged mutants, my old zombie friend who could shoot needles from his hands, and beasts more terrible still.

One of the zombies wandered in my direction, breaking and brushing aside, with a single kick, a small tree blocking its path. Three meters tall, it had a body of monstrous bulging muscles, above which was an ugly mug with a deformed jaw.

Brutal. All people were fucked; nobody would survive if these monsters made it to the city.

I decided that since the opportunity had presented itself, I had to at least try to fell the hulk. I shot an arrow right into the center of its chest, but it didn't penetrate deeply at all. The monster didn't give a shit about the pathetic little splinter and paid it no heed, merely continuing to march on its chosen target, the corpse of an old man in rags whom I had not previously noticed.

The hulk picked up the corpse like it was a feather and began to greedily chow down on it. Twenty seconds later, nothing was left of the old man. The monster's teeth were so sharp that even his clothes were no hindrance.

Most disgusting was the way it chewed the head until it burst like an overripe watermelon.

Such a beast must not be allowed to live, I decided, beginning to thwack it with arrow after arrow. The first arrow sank firmly into its head, but the beast merely bent over slightly and drew air into its nostrils in an attempt to sniff out the location of the food source causing it pain. Only my fifth arrow managed to down the monster, and it was a devilish sight to behold.

I hoped such beasts were not going to frequent my path too often. On the other hand, a beast like that ought to drop valuable goodies, which would be fantastic. Unfortunately, I would not be getting anything this time, because this was only a test.

Then the situation changed dramatically, as I

stopped playing the hunter and began doing my best to survive. Even though the zombies could not see me, too many of them had appeared in the forest, and the chances of accidentally bumping into one had profoundly increased. I now found myself doing precious little but trying to avoid them.

With roughly ten minutes to the end of the test, I was tired of running, and clambered up the nearest tree for a breather.

By this time, I'd managed to kill four more survivors, although in truth, two of them I didn't really kill, rather gifting them an easier death than being eaten alive by monsters.

The forest now recalled a slaughterhouse. The system had totally lost his mind and sent freaking loads of zombies, some of them occasionally crashing into my temporary sanctuary and receiving a swift arrow the head.

What the hell are you doing touching my safe haven!

I discovered another kind of zombie I had not come across before. I called it a "jumper" since it was a thin beast with large legs, like a grasshopper, which enabled it to jump several meters. Right in front of my eyes, in one powerful leap, it caught up with an unlucky creature trying to run away, and made dinner of it. And so fast that I didn't have time to relieve its suffering.

The only name I could possibly give this test was the "Forest of Death," although I did like it. Bored of hunting down gormless city zombies, I felt alive to find myself among powerful predators. I wasn't worried about not getting lucky or being killed at any moment. There were always bigger fish to find, which in my case was somebody with stronger skills.

Test finished. Congratulations, you have survived. You will be transported back in 3...2...1

Once again the world flickered momentarily and returned just as fast as it had disappeared. My head thrummed and my stomach rejected the last food I'd eaten.

Shoot, I ruined a clean carpet, but a satisfied smile crept onto my face, for I had survived and been able to return. My body was still shuddering slightly from the journey back.

My reverie was interrupted by the system.

Congratulations from the system, Varg. You killed the most survivors and take first place.

As a reward you receive:

Yellow trinket casket, 1 pc.

Gray trinket casket, 1 pc.

A choice: 1 of 3 mastery stones:

Mastery stone: the Thief of Guvengr.

Important note: Irno Shtorf began his career as a thief 20 years ago and plied his trade right up until his death at age 30. He was executed by hanging on the Royal Square of Guvengr.

Mastery stone: the Paladin of Tarfion.

Important note: from a young age, Silvo Ivares, a paladin of the god Argas, learned to use a sword and shield. He preached the word of his god until his death at age 24. He died of unrequited love when he found his sweetheart in bed with another. After killing them both, he took his own life by skewering his heart on his sword.

Mastery stone: Kallt Nurn.

Important note: Kallt Nurn was a rank-and-file archer in the service of the city of Ersavi. He learned his trade on the job in battle for a whole seven years. He died during the siege of his native city of Ersavi, when a stray enemy arrow pierced an artery in his neck.

You have 60 seconds to make your choice.

Attention! An additional reward has been sent to all surviving participants according to merit.

The capacity of your inventory is increased by 62 kg.

The system baffled and delighted me simultaneously.

I didn't know where to begin. Inventory: extremely cool!

But what were these mastery stones? Since the system had informed me of all these people's professions and how long they'd spent studying their trades, that meant they must be books of some sort.

"System, I choose number three, the archer." The paladin was also not a bad choice, if his achievements were anything to go by, but an idiot paladin was something I definitely did not need. It might be a disciple coming to serve me.

You have made your choice and your reward has been transferred to your inventory.

I was lost for words. I didn't know what to

think or what to grasp at. Jeez, my inventory was now 114 kg. Not in vain had I felled so many people, though I could have felled more.

I wonder if Fedya survived. And if he got a reward. Or do they only give them for first place?

Anyway, I picked up the gray trinket casket and turned it over in my hands.

Evaluation.

Gray trinket casket provides food with special properties.

I opened it and saw another notification.

You receive a Dark Pear.

What kind of fruit is this?

Evaluation.

A Dark Pear enhances your night vision.

I saw no point in keeping it on ice, so I ate it. My eyes became teary, my vision blurry, and my nerves stressed. I hoped the pear would not do me any harm.

In a couple of minutes, my vision corrected itself, but I perceived no difference from before. I would have to check it at night.

Then the mastery stone made its way into my hand. A regular small stone, similar to an emerald, nothing special, and giving off no terrible vibes.

Evaluation.

A mastery stone transfers the abilities harnessed in it to whoever activates it.

I wanted a drink. I seriously wanted a drink. My hands began to shake. Had I seriously gotten so lucky as to receive the archery skills of a person from another world? Damn, that was very cool. I hoped he was a human, not some four-handed gnome whose abilities would not befit me.

In terms of personal asset, this stone was up there with my invisibility.

Without giving the potential consequences a second's thought, I activated the stone. I saw pictures, lots of pictures, so many that my head began to hurt. And the world began to ripple.

My head was already splintered, as from a thousand needles driven into it, yet the pictures did not desist. I did not know how much time passed, but it seemed like an age. My ears popped, my nose bled, I felt nauseous, but the visions did not leave me, flashing before my eyes in quick succession. A variety of shots, combinations, and firing techniques, among other things. No concrete faces or names, just a bow and other archery paraphernalia.

My muscles hurt, and terribly so. It seemed they were swollen and threatening to tear my skin and leap out. Then suddenly everything stopped. When I snapped out of my reverie, I was on my bed, my breathing labored, a dull ache throughout my body. It was a mystery how I'd managed to make it as far as the bed.

I lay there and smiled. Ye gods, words could not describe how bad I felt. I had previously considered myself a good archer; now I wasn't worthy of being called an archer at all.

As I gleaned from the description, the archer Kallt Nurn was a rank-and-file guardsman, but his marksmanship was simply cosmic. Shooting through obstacles, in the dark, his reflexes, his reaction to sound, and that was to say nothing of his marching fire. He would make mincemeat of our very finest bowmen with one eye closed and one arm behind his back.

And the best thing was that all his abilities had now become mine, and all that he had been able to do, I was now able to do.

Evidently strength came not from skills, but from stones such as this. It would be good to find the stone of a champion archer with two hundred years' training behind him.

I smiled bitterly at the thought.

Shoot, give me a stone like that now and my head would just burst. First I needed to level up. I could think about stones later; right now it was too dangerous.

Speaking of levels, the system was holding back with my next one. It might at least give it for the sake of appearances.

My body hurt awfully, and I understood why. It was absolutely not prepared for the skills that Kallt Nurn had possessed. He had trained his body every day, year upon year, and participated in dozens of battles. I felt that any bowshot might tear the shit out of my ligaments, and there was no way of knowing how long they would take to recover.

I urgently needed to get home, to chill and get some sleep. It was also worth opening a skill casket. Not wanting to put it off, I picked one up and opened it.

You receive a skill: regeneration, level 2.

If this is a gift, then thank you very much, system. Just what I need, and very useful for the future. I had no time whatsoever to treat my various cuts and grazes, and this skill would help me enormously.

Evaluation.

The skill of regeneration will help your body heal its wounds and recover the integrity of its skin covering. At higher levels, someone with this skill is very hard to kill.

Excellent, just what I needed. In fact, just what anyone would need. On this note, I left the dorm and headed home to my apartment.

On the way, I killed approximately seventy zombies, perhaps more, gaining the next level, which the system had kept from me.

You have gained level 6. Your body has become stronger and your eyesight keener.

I only killed the zombies with my spear, trying to take out the loners that stood in my way. Now it was painful to hold the spear in my hands, let alone shoot my bow. I could not shoot for the time being, my head still hurt, and as if that wasn't bad enough, I was seeing double.

By the time I got back to the anthill it was dark. Solitary gunshots could be heard, and even more corpses littered the yard.

Ye gods, how painful it was to walk up the stairs. On reaching my apartment, I stopped in my tracks. It had been broken into, the door smashed wide open.

Entering was risky, but what was I to do? My curiosity and desire to rip out the throat of whoever had burgled me outweighed the risk.

I entered cautiously, trying not to make excess noise. The entire apartment was parqueted, so the floor didn't squeak like floorboards would, which was a good thing right now. My invisibility also concealed sound, but I was not yet one hundred percent *au fait* with its properties.

My spear I held at the ready, to spike the barefaced intruders at any moment, but it turned out surplus to requirements, as did my disposable crossbow, which I would have used without compunction.

You will pay for the murder of our brother, you bastard! declared a sign daubed on the wall in red spray paint.

So, they were looking expressly for me, how lucky. How did they know I'd killed somebody's brother, if I didn't even know myself who I'd killed? It went without saying the weapons I'd left were gone, the weapons of a shield bearer killed in my apartment. I could also conclude they knew my identity from documents they would have found. Damn, my passport and a pile of personal effects; the bastards had taken everything.

What was I going to do now? Where was I to rest my weary bones? I was dead on my feet as it was, and it was now pitch black outside. Which reminded me, my night vision had improved massively, that was for sure. Excellent, the pear had turned out to be particularly useful.

It was risky to remain in the building, since they might come back during the night. And what if they had kick-ass skills? I was in no state to fight off anyone right now.

Go back to the soldiers? Somehow I didn't want to go wandering around a dangerous city at night. Although...

I logged on to the trading platform and entered in the filter: dark pear.

It was quite a rare item, sold by just two people. One charged 120 gray boxes per pear, the second a system weapon higher than level 1.

As far as I was concerned, they were both idiots if they were exchanging such a dope item for such chump change.

Okay, let's see what I have.

The glaive was the only thing I could give away, which was a pity, as it looked pretty good. Never mind, screw it, night vision was more important than a weapon I might never use.

I responded to the offer with my *Glaive of Hopsh, level 2* card and waited.

I was made to wait a whole fifty seconds. The seller was probably in two minds whether to accept or not, but in the end the glaive went to him and the pear to me.

I chuffed the pear on the spot and got a new notification.

Your night vision has improved.

The world had indeed become a tad lighter. Shoot, if my night vision were to become indistinguishable from my day vision, would I be able to get a decent night's sleep? Although, who cared? Sacrifices had to be made for the sake of strength.

I left the anthill and shuffled back in the direction of the soldiers' dorm. Zombies did not sleep, even at night, and coveys of them ran past me. I was beginning to get the impression they had begun to set up ambushes for people.

A zombie jumped up to the second floor of a building and, clinging onto a ledge with the claws of one hand, hammered the window with its free hand until it smashed. I was just thinking the end was nigh for people, when the zombie was torn to pieces by a blast from a shotgun which appeared out of the window. Then, attracted by the loud noise, more beasties came running to the building from all sides.

It wasn't too far to walk, but in the dark I occasionally had to slow down to let zombies past. It was a good job I didn't come across any giant monsters, otherwise I would have been toast.

On top of everything, I was slowed by the pain racking my body, which regeneration was scarcely coping with. I hoped to be fresh as a daisy tomorrow or the day after. Without regeneration I'd be out of the game for a good week.

As I walked I saw a toy store, and hatched a simple plan: take as many toys as I could, in order to buy my freedom from Liza. While she was torturing them, she could not be simultaneously torturing me. I was a genius.

I began loading my inventory with soft toys

and dolls of various sizes. Then I took some radio-controlled cars, except they were for me rather than Liza; I'd always wanted one. In another section I came across quadcopters, and took a dozen of the most expensive ones. It was odd they hadn't been looted already, despite evidence that zombies had been in the store.

The gaming consoles were in the farthest section. I was not overly familiar with them, since I'd always been too broke to afford one, so I took a variety, along with a hundred disks. My inventory was now over half full, and it wasn't made of rubber.

It was time to leave, otherwise I would have to create a store of children's toys in one of the rooms. And I was no idiot: if I rocked up now with piles of toys, I would have nothing to keep Liza off my back later. You always had to have a plan B.

It was another twenty minutes to the dorm, and I decided to take a small detour. Long ago, before the apocalypse, I'd once visited a hardware store in this area to check out renovation materials, but on seeing the prices, I decided I wasn't a renovation kind of guy after all.

The store was shut, and shut inside was a zombie that couldn't get out. When he'd turned, the store detective had no doubt gone on a bit of a rampage, smashing up everything in sight and becoming trapped by falling metal water pipes and other heavy stuff.

I summoned my spear and smashed the window. A dozen zombies immediately came running but could not see me. Carefully, so as not to cut myself, I climbed inside and approached the store detective.

He was an elderly man in an old black uniform with a sew-on badge declaring *Security*. He wasn't making too much noise, just hissing and clacking his teeth, but his bones were all fractured, what with his being well crushed. Even as a zombie, he hadn't been able to break out of his iron trap.

A spear to the head cut his suffering short, and now I was the only survivor in the store.

I had around fifty kilograms of free space, which I intended to fill with various items.

On a rack hung some interesting tools. I snaffled five hand saws, one chainsaw, several hammers and screwdrivers, and some other bits and pieces. I also found window grilles; the very thing for my new apartment. The problem with these was their weight — not light — so I could take no more than five, which was disheartening.

Never mind, I would take what I could manage, which included a couple of packets of large-gauge nails and screws to hold the grilles firmly on the windows. As I left the store, I promised myself to come back tomorrow.

On the way to the dorm, I set to thinking. Why was I doing all this? Why was I making an apartment habitable in a place occupied by lots of people. I seriously didn't like people.

It was a question I couldn't answer. No doubt my distorted sense of justice was to blame. It always made me do strange deeds I didn't understand.

Like helping Polina and Liza, for example. Why had I done that? I didn't know.

Perhaps the answer was Liza, and I simply pitied a child who had suffered because of me. I'd created a real bloodbath in their old apartment, which, as a result, they had lost. And all because I just happened to be close by.

If only they hadn't asked so many stupid questions and constantly tried to draw me into conversation, I would feel quite at home there. Probably.

CHAPTER 13

IN THE YARD BEHIND the dorm it was peaceful and quiet. The entire area in front of the building, however, was crowded with stamping zombies, and in places the façade looked pretty weather-beaten.

The entrance was surrounded by barricades unassailable to the zombies, but a human could easily crawl under them. The soldiers had simply chucked piles of various junk everywhere.

I made it to the entrance quickly by crawling under two tables and an old bed. It was reasonably clean beneath them, but a bunch of crap lay on top.

Shoot, I've got to crawl.

Two fully armed soldiers stood sentry inside the door.

I knocked lightly and observed the guards' reactions.

They exchanged frightened glances and began whispering to each other.

When I knocked for the second time, they realized they hadn't been hearing things and eventually reacted. One scampered off somewhere, while the second addressed me.

"Who's there?" barely audibly whispered the soldier, whom I had not seen before.

"Varg."

"Varg?"

"Varg."

"You'll have to wait," he said, louder now, and getting out his telephone he began to write a message.

Okay, I would wait, it was no problem while I was invisible. I hoped they wouldn't throw a grenade at me from above. Otherwise I might return the gesture.

After five minutes I saw Combat coming down, accompanied by some fighters.

"Who's there?" the colonel snapped in a whisper.

"Varg," I snapped back similarly quietly, teasing him.

The door opened, but what I saw was machine guns pointing at me.

I was forced to deactivate invisibility so the fighters could identify me. When the zombies saw me, they immediately went apeshit.

"It's you." Combat breathed a sigh of relief, and with an invitational gesture said, "Get inside quickly."

Following his order, I entered, and my eyes immediately fell on his bandaged shoulder. He looked kind of tired.

"What's up with your shoulder?" I asked, nodding at his blood-reddened bandage. "Have you been infected?"

"Stray bullet, it's nothing." He waved it away and we set off up the stairs to the top floor. "Can you pop into my office? Or maybe you want to have a rest first? We can talk tomorrow."

"It's been a hard day, let's talk tomorrow, I want to sleep." I had no desire whatsoever to converse with anyone.

Combat cast an attentive eye over me and nodded.

"Do I look like shit?" I asked, squeezing out a crooked smile.

"You looked fresher this morning. We weren't reckoning on seeing you again this week. Has something happened?"

I could, of course, have kept my mouth shut, but was it worth it? I was trusted here, so I had to keep them in the picture concerning at least some of my business. God forbid these fighters might think I was a spy.

"My apartment in the anthill was burgled," I explained. He had not failed to spot my crooked smile. "It'll take a long time to find a new one, and I'm drained after today."

"Everyone's had a hard day today."

"You can't imagine how hard."

"Hey, show at least a little respect," hissed the

soldier walking behind me. "The person in front of you just happens to be a real colonel."

"Relax, Grisha," Combat interrupted, without giving me the chance to reply. "He may be a civilian, but he gave us a big helping hand with food and arms. He's also no weakling, so you'd do well not to be rude to him."

"Pfft, I'll... right now." I drew my dagger and brought it lightning quick to Grisha's throat.

Combat stepped in once more. "Chill out, Varg. There's no need to be so aggressive, you have no enemies here," he said, and the colonel laid a placating hand on my shoulder.

"Fine." With a grimace, I slowly put the dagger away. My entire body was hurting so badly I wanted to roar. I was sure I'd be crippled if I was forced to demonstrate my powers like that again anytime soon.

"Maybe our doc should have a look at you?" Combat suggested, staring at me with a concerned look on his face.

"No, I just need to rest. The thing is that sometimes you've got to pay for the system's gifts."

The higher we climbed, the clearer it became that something unpleasant had occurred in the dorm during my absence. On the way to my new abode, I saw injured people in the corridors, lots of them.

"What happened?"

"We were attacked," Combat replied, his tone calm, as though he were discussing a fishing trip.

"And you talk so calmly about it?"

He chuckled.

"I've fought in many wars and been subject to many attacks. I'm probably just used to it. Although it's impossible to get used to the fact that civilians are suffering in this meat grinder."

"Many?" My question sounded confused, but Combat understood well enough.

"Seven civilians died, three of them children. More than twenty were injured."

"Who was it?"

"A neighboring group, they attacked during the day, firing at the building and then throwing grenades."

Why were people attacking people? It was a question I could not answer. Those bandits attacked these soldiers for no reason. I would understand if there was a struggle for resources or territory, but apparently even the apocalypse wasn't able to fix human stupidity and avarice.

"Why?"

"Because they're thugs. And also because we've got a lot of chicks, and half of their group are ex-cons. The only thing I don't quite understand is where they got so many weapons from."

Frankly, it was a sad situation. The soldiers were losing this battle for life. The problem was weapons, and they had very few. Plus, they had to feed their families and the other civilians who had joined them since the apocalypse kicked off.

"This is where we part ways. If you need me, pop in tomorrow and will have a chat. Unfortunately we weren't able to find you any arrows or anything else of value today."

"Okay, I'll come see you tomorrow just as soon as I'm up to it." As it transpired, everybody needed rest. The mastery stone had wrecked all my plans, and now I was wasting time.

"See you tomorrow." Combat shook my hand and left with his fighters.

As I wandered in the direction of my apartment, I reflected on Combat. At first glance he seemed a regular guy offering me accommodation and help. But it was worth remembering he was a hardened wolf, and even the fact that he'd let me return to my accommodation alone said a lot, both for me and him.

If I were a spy, many people might die.

I was no fool, and I understood full well he had used the gesture to express his trust of me, and that was worth a lot. Were I in his shoes, I wouldn't even let someone like me over the threshold. I was too dodgy for them.

His attitude was certainly very pleasant, and I was in no hurry to lose his goodwill just yet.

Arriving at my destination, I knocked, and the door was opened by Polina. I couldn't help but smile at her reaction. I had managed to surprise her.

"You weren't expecting me?" The silly smile would not disappear from my face.

"I wasn't," she admitted, smiling back. "Come in quickly. Or wasn't it us you were looking for?"

"No, it was you. Well, a hot shower and a

clean bed, to be precise."

Electricity was another reason I hadn't stayed overnight in the anthill. You couldn't get a decent wash there now, to say nothing of hot tea.

"Aha, who's this then?" Liza ran out of the room. "Mama said we wouldn't see you for a few days. But I told her you'd be back today."

"What made you think I'd be back?" I asked, taking a couple of steps back and keeping my distance just in case.

"You like living with us, that's why," she said, sticking a proud finger in the air.

"I like the warm shower and the hot tea here. Although I would take them the other way around," I retorted, categorically disagreeing with her.

"Liza, leave the man alone, he's only just got back," Polina interrupted. "Will you have some dinner? Come and sit at the table. But take your overclothes off first, they stink."

For fuck's sake, it was all spleen with these women. I was so accustomed to running around among zombies that I'd ceased to pay any attention to my scent, but now I was embarrassed, because I really didn't smell great.

It occurred to me now that my armor needed washing on occasion. Unfortunately it didn't have a self-cleaning function.

Polina noticed my torment and took pity on me.

"Take your armor off and I'll wash it," she said with a smile.

Now I was even more embarrassed. I had no spare clothes left, and this also didn't go unnoticed.

"What, don't you have any other clothes?" she asked.

"Uh-uh."

Liza beamed.

"Mom, now you're tormenting our guest. I mean, the owner of the flat," the kid said, mocking me mercilessly. "Look at him blush, he doesn't know what to do with himself."

"Maybe living among zombies isn't such a bad idea," I said, sounding the thought buzzing in my head.

"What if you get bitten?" Liza would not be appeased.

"I won't get bitten."

"Come and take a seat, hero, while I go and find some new clothes for you," Polina said, interrupting our discussion.

I sat silently on a stool, like a student in an exam, waiting for my supervisor, i.e. Polina. Liza seized the opportunity to pummel me with questions and simultaneously tell me all the news.

The most noteworthy news was how frightened she and her mother had been during the attack. Her mom had produced some weapons in preparation to give battle, but she hadn't needed to since it was all over so quickly. True, a girlfriend of hers had been killed, which made her sob a couple of times in front of me, and I felt a twinge in my heart.

"Liza, listen, I've brought you something." I took the toys out of my inventory.

Liza, her mouth agape with surprise, looked on delighted as toys appeared out of thin air.

"Weeeee," she squeaked, throwing her arms around my neck. I wanted to draw back, but didn't manage in time and lost the battle. What a pest. So small, yet with a grip like a hulk.

"Thank you! Thank you! You're the best!"

We didn't notice straightaway that Polina had returned and was standing in the doorway watching us.

"Are you buying off my child? Tsk-tsk." A wide smile on her face, she wagged a jokey finger at me.

Evidently threatening fingers were a thing in their family.

"So what did you bring me?" Polina's question came like a bolt from the blue, and I nearly jumped. "What, nothing? Pfft. Surely you're not so clueless about girls? If you give a gift to one girl, you must give a gift to the other as well. You live with the two of us under one roof," Polina continued, jokingly again. Or maybe not jokingly, who knew?

I felt a panic attack coming on. I began running hot and cold and even forgot about the pain racking my body. My look became vacant, my legs wobbly.

"Mommy, don't be mean to my best friend!" Liza said, coming to the defense of poor lil' me. "See how bad he looks, like he's going to faint."

"Never mind, he'll know for next time not to

bring presents exclusively for you," Polina said, deflated. "Look how many toys you have, when I don't have anything. Maybe I'm offended?"

"You're an adult!" The little one was not giving up.

"And you're a child. So what?" Not about to back down, Polina put her hands on her hips.

"Mom, if we drive him mad now, he'll never bring us anything again." A clever thought from the little girl.

I wanted to jump out of the window. The one that had been nailed shut, after a fashion, with plywood.

Only now did I pay attention to the outrage. Patching up a window using plywood which I could punch through in one go? I used the plywood as a distraction to tear my mind away from their conversation.

It worked. For a few seconds.

"Hey! Wakey wakey, we're talking to you." The little pest tugged at me.

The adult next to her thought this was great sport, looking at me with an impish smile. What had I done to them? No good deed went unpunished, as personal experience had convinced me.

"Have you got anything to drink?" I asked Polina despairingly. "I'm gonna croak in here with you two if I don't get a large double. You mess with my head worse than the zombies. Even a real hulk would be no match for you."

"Hulk? What's that?" asked the girls in

unison.

"Do you mind if I don't answer that?" I so didn't want to talk to people right now.

"Since you started, you must tell us." Polina sat down opposite me and fixed me with a stare. "We are very interested."

Ye gods, why on earth did I mention hulks. Oh well...

"A hulk is a zombie, three meters tall and covered in unsightly swollen muscles, an enormous pie-hole with fangs capable of scarfing a person in a couple of bites, and it can snap a tree in half like a matchstick."

"Eek." Liza was petrified.

"So it's true that zombies can mutate into different kinds of monster," Polina concluded bitterly. "If that happens in the dorm, it's all over for all of us. Although hang on, if you survived an encounter with one, that means they must be pretty ham-fisted, right? Or slow? How did you get away from it?"

"I killed it. It wasn't easy, mind." I shrugged my shoulders, and Polina and Liza gaped in surprise. "Hey, what's with those looks? Don't you believe me? Tsk-tsk, very disappointing."

Liza reacted instantaneously. Flying at me like a tiny shooting star, she began to stroke my head, saying, "Of course we believe you, don't worry, we absolutely believe you, you're the strongest and most powerful, and you're also chatty and fun," she babbled, scarcely able to hold back her laughter.

I couldn't understand whether she was being serious or joking; after all she was still a child. That's right, a cunning little demon. Again my head exploded.

Turned away, her back to us, Polina was laughing quietly into her fist.

"Oh, I get it. You want to drive me insane in order to inherit the apartment," I said, proclaiming my version of their reason for taunting me.

"Our secret is out, Liza, run!" Laughing gaily, they ran to the kitchen, leaving me alone with my thoughts.

"Shit," I groaned. "What have I gotten myself into? Where did I go wrong? Is this your doing, system? Did you give them a task to drive a poor sociopath insane?"

The At least Polina had left the clean clothes she'd brought, and I knew where the bathroom was, so I headed there, grabbing the clothes on the way.

In the shower I was at last able to wash off the muck of ages, the water turning black and all the tiles now covered in sand. *Wow, I didn't think I was so dirty.* As I washed, I recalled that I'd collected most of this dirt in the forest. Shoot, and I'd entered the apartment wearing boots. I simply could not live as others did.

I was in the shower for half an hour, washing myself squeaky clean, and it dawned on me that I didn't have my own soap or washcloth. Things would have been quicker with a washcloth, and there were two hanging in the shower, but they weren't mine and I didn't want to use them. However, I was lucky enough to find an unopened bar of soap, which I just had to appropriate.

Okay, if this apartment was definitely to be my base and I didn't want to keep living like a bum, I would have to furnish it with an array of goodies.

I emerged from the bathroom in my new clothes, clean and contented. I sniffed the air. Mmm, delicious aromas wafted from the kitchen, making my mouth water.

In the living room I saw neither Liza nor the toys.

"Take a seat and I'll feed you," came Polina's voice from the kitchen.

Damn, I'd come out of the bathroom very quietly. How had she realized? Maybe some kind of skill?

She put on a fantastic spread. Fresh meat balls, a bowl of hot mushroom soup, potatoes, salted cucumbers. Yummy.

"Was all this really in those food boxes?" I asked, unable to believe my eyes.

"Of course. What did you eat when you lived by yourself?"

I absolutely did not care for the expression "by yourself." It clearly held some hidden meaning, but I couldn't make sense of it.

"Buckwheat, pasta, stewed meat." I counted on my fingers what I was in the habit of cooking for myself.

"Just as I thought, meager rations. How did

you survive on that?" Polina asked with a disapproving shake of the head.

"Look who's talking. Up until this morning, you were starving in here."

"True enough."

The yummy aroma had evidently attracted not just me, but also another little nose. Liza ran from her room and sat down at the table.

I looked at her apprehensively.

"By the way, Varg, don't you want to tell us your name? We're sitting at the same table, and we've known each other for ages, but we converse like strangers, as though we're on the front lines," said Polina.

Shoot, what does she want? What a lot of questions.

"Igor," I blurted, tucking in to the tasty meatballs on my plate.

"I'm Polina" — she smiled — "but you knew that anyway because I introduced myself straightaway."

Ouch! How could that not hurt?

"And I'm Liza, and you also know that already," the child added.

We ate, we tried to converse, despite my resistance, and at last it was time to sleep.

"Come with me, I've made you a bed up." Polina took me by the hand, and her touch was like an electric shock, rendering me incapable of defying her.

She led me to the bedroom, where there were three beds, one single and two double.

Liza jumped into the double, disrobed beneath the covers, and crawled back out dressed in pink pajamas.

I was shocked.

"What, we're going to sleep in the same room?" I uttered, scarcely able to speak.

"Of course." Polina didn't understand my concern. "It's much safer that way. We have already slept in the same room, or had you forgotten?"

Sh-shoot.

Right, you're a man, Varg, remember that. You must be strong. You're not afraid of zombies, so you shouldn't be afraid of people, especially women. Everything's going to be okay.

I pulled myself together, adopted a stone-faced expression, turned to the older girl, and asked:

"Do I have a choice?" Not a single muscle twitched on my face, and right now I was the epitome of courage and gravity. The only thing stonier than me just then was a cliff face.

"Uh-uh." A smiled response, which knocked me for six.

How can this be? I'm hardcore. I'm...

Damn it all. I accepted the inevitable and crawled into bed, turning demonstratively away from the girls to face the wall, offended.

"Poor thing," I heard Liza say pityingly, as I drifted off me.

And I thought I couldn't sink any lower.

CHAPTER 14

"I HAVE A PRESENT FOR YOU," I said, addressing all those present as I placed the quadcopters on the table.

I'd awoken this morning to find myself alone in the bedroom, and tasty smells wafting in from the living room.

Polina and Liza were laying the table, and my armor was drying in the bathroom. The clock said 9 AM. How had they managed to do so much already? Frankly, it would have been a massive hassle for me to wake up so early and get so busy. The girls were of some use after all, that was for sure.

After thanking them for a tasty breakfast, I slipped out to find Combat. I did not like rooms crowded with people, but unfortunately you didn't always get the choice.

I found him in his office, which had been

crowded since early morning, and as I entered there was a heated debate in progress.

"Thank you, Varg. Quadcopters are handy pieces of kit and will definitely be useful for reconnaissance," Combat thanked me sincerely with a nod.

"Fedya, give orders to have them stowed somewhere."

"It will be done," Fedya replied, sniggering.

"What's up with him, Combat? Why is he so chirpy at this early hour?" Considering he'd almost died very recently, I did not understand his joy.

Combat wiped his temples wearily and took a glug of tea.

"Pay no attention. Fedya expanded his inventory by ten kilograms during the test yesterday, and now he's running around all happy and telling everyone," Combat explained.

Fedya sidled up to me baring all his teeth.

"Listen, Varg, my advice to you is this: if the system gives you an invitation to a test, decline it off the bat. It's no place for someone like you."

I was fuc... I was shocked. Shocked at how pleased and proud he was of himself as he told everyone what he'd had to endure during the test.

"He's right," Combat interrupted. "I didn't have time to tell you yesterday. We have a new surprise from the system, an offer to participate in a test which is practically impossible to survive. So his advice is sound."

"Even for an experienced fighter like me it was hard, and you'll get eaten in a minute," Fedya continued with a grin. His words were not meant to disparage me, much more to impress, otherwise he would already have put his teeth away. But I had no desire to argue with the fighters, since I already had grand plans for this place.

"Fedya!" Combat struck the table with an angry fist. "Next time I hear that kind of attitude from you, you'll be scouring all the toilets in the dorm!"

"Sorry," said Fedya, standing to attention.

Combat was not satisfied with the response. "How does a fighter reply?" He was on a roll.

"Yes sir, comrade colonel, no more conversations like that!" said Fedya.

It was not enough for me, however, for the thrill of the challenge had awoken in me, and my core demanded his pride be ground to dust, and the mirthful grin be wiped from his mug.

"Fedya, it goes without saying how cool you are, but you owe me three arrows."

"Fedya, do you owe him arrows?" Combat asked. It was immediately clear he kept discipline tight.

"Absolutely not, comrade colonel! He's lying, I owe him nothing," replied Fedya, scowling at me.

No doubt he was thinking the newcomer was trying to set him up.

"What do you mean, Fedya?" I feigned surprise and theatrically grasped my head. "Don't you remember the guy with the big shield, who died, but not of old age died? And the swordsman who ran to help the black-haired guy with the dagger, who was kicking you? Surely you haven't forgotten, Fedya, your eyes darting about? And your moans of pain? Or have you forgotten how you nearly filled your pants in fright?"

His expression made it clear he was feverishly trying to understand what I was talking about, his brain cells twitching away. Then the penny dropped.

"Y-you..."

"Yes, Fedya, me. There was also someone with a chameleon skill, whom you didn't even notice as you walked past, and he followed you. He wanted to have you, Fedya, he desperately wanted to have you. And you know what kind of dagger he had?" I was enjoying watching his expression change. "This kind." I delved into my inventory for that very same dagger and showed it to Fedya.

He had nothing to say. He gasped for air, like a fish on a riverbank, and his face turned beet-red in his anger and pique. He had just been put down in front of everyone.

"Three arrows, Fedya, is precisely how much your life cost, and I could have terminated it at the drop of a hat." I could see Combat cottoning on to the truth, and I saw no reason not to continue. "I followed you and watched you doing somersaults and darting from tree to tree like Rambo."

"Fedya goofed up," said one of the men present.

"Varg, how many did you kill in there?" someone else asked. "Fedya killed three, but he didn't take first place."

"Loads more than that." Not wanting to recount any details, I dodged the question.

"Okay, let's move on," Combat said with a clap of his hands. "Varg, we wanted to ask if you had any desire to help us thin out the crowd of zombies in front of the building. We have a foray into the city planned for today, and yesterday's bastards raised such a racket it's going to take us a couple of days. You seem to like killing them."

I thought. The boxes would come in handy, and I still had five hours until the trading coin became inactive.

"Any loot is mine, deal?" I said, laying down my conditions.

"Maybe half?" The response came from behind my back, but I ignored it.

"Deal." Combat extended his hand and I shook it.

"Then I'll go try to change the situation with the zombies. Why put it off?"

"I'll give orders for you to be let out. And my people will go with you."

"Okay. It's important now for everyone to level up. Plus you seriously need food boxes."

Off I set to kill zombies. I did not know why I'd decided to help them. Perhaps I considered it would be only right. They hadn't done me any harm, and I saw no evil intent in their attitude towards me.

Even Fedya didn't really see me as an opponent, more as a competitor. We had the same skills, and it was hard for him to accept that a civilian might be better than him in some respect. It might have been mean-spirited on his part, but I accepted the rules of this game. I had my own foibles, and he his, and the main thing was that he didn't cross any lines.

Before going outside, I popped home for my armor.

"Are you going out again?" Polina asked. She was cooking again and wearing an apron. I had gotten seriously lucky in this regard.

"Uh-huh, Combat asked me to help clear the horde of zombies in front of the dorm," I said quietly. Then Liza came running and all hell let loose.

"Cool. Can I come with you?" came her voice from behind my back.

"Aren't you going to ask me first, Liza?" Polina's eyes flared with anger.

"But Igor will protect me!"

"I might just belt you now for your stupid ideas," Polina said. It occurred to me I had a good chance of being belted myself if I crossed her when her passions were running high.

Shoot, my armor was still wet.

"It hasn't had time to try," Polina shrugged as if she'd read my thoughts.

"Fine, I'll go without it," I grumbled.

"Perhaps it's worth waiting, it's dangerous out there," said Polina. Surely she wasn't worried about me?

What an idiot! I suddenly thought to myself. I had completely forgotten about the materials I'd taken from the store on the way back to the dorm yesterday.

"Polina, I need the use of a spare room."

"Follow me. There's a room where the laborers conspired to leave dirty foot marks, and I haven't cleaned them up yet."

She led me to a room covered in signs of frenzied activity in the form of dirt, dust, and wood shavings.

Under Polina's noncomprehending gaze, I unloaded everything from yesterday's shopping spree onto the floor.

"I'll leave it here for the time being and bring some more later. The windows need reinforcing. What that lot did is total crapola, just sticking pinboard on any old how, those slackers," I said, exasperated at the shoddy workmanship. "By the way, I think I already told you, but there are zombie jumpers who can easily jump up to the third floor."

"Thank you. Thank you for all your help. And there's no need to cast your eyes shiftily around the room looking for a reason for me saying that, because you won't find it." Smiling, she approached me and punched me in the shoulder.

Once more I was convinced life would be easier with zombies than people. How was I to understand what she said? I thought I understood, but apparently I was thinking about something else.

Although I had to admit I found it easier to talk to her than the others. She didn't have their look of fear or distaste.

As I stood by the entrance, Liza came running up and asked me to bend down.

What could I do? My first thought was to ignore her and just leave. I didn't like being close to people, but shoot, she was a child. What if she took offense and burst into tears?

And so I had to bend down. Liza hung on me in a tight embrace, and whispered low right in my ear.

"Mama likes drawing, and she also likes beautiful things," she whispered, before running off. I froze, stupefied to realize I was being manipulated by a child, but there was nothing I could do about it.

What a kid. I was reduced to being given advice by a child, concerning what presents to give a woman. But what was the occasion? Present a gift to one, present a gift to the other. It hadn't occurred to them that I'd simply been buying Liza off. And I was a fine one. I could have said it was a bribe, but how difficult it was to talk to people when they were so close.

Yet again I was convinced my life would be simpler and more understandable in the company of zombies.

I decided to start the zombie massacre from inside the building. A swarm of them was plastered against the barricades, and in a number of places they had managed to break through it and almost reach the main entrance. The soldiers had done well, managing to bolster their defenses, it was just a pity they weren't too effective against such a crowd of zombies. For a minute I observed the two sentries by the door, who kept looking at it nervously, weapons held at the ready.

The first and second floors of the dorm were not residential, so that civilians would not suffer in the event of a breakthrough. The zombies could easily get in here, so all available materials had been used to build barricades in the corridors of those floors. Metal sheeting had also been fixed over the windows.

I dropped in to see Quartermaster and ask for the key to an apartment where I'd earlier spotted a convenient small balcony, a prime spot for an archer.

The zombies would not be able to reach me there, while I could easily pop them off with my bow.

Before embarking on the clearing mission, I logged onto the trading platform and bought five arrow cards. I got the simplest and cheapest ones, costing from three to five gray boxes each.

I still had thirty-three arrows left from my last purchase, and I now bought another four hundred. It was enough to be going on with. The distance to my targets was not far, and even basic arrows without any frills would do, although at some point it would be good to stock up on fire and explosion arrows for future use.

All my plans had gone down the drain during the test. I wasn't complaining, mind, for it had given me something I could not have bought on the trading platform, so I was very pleased. For this alone, **level-two regeneration** had been worth it. And that was to say nothing of the mastery stone.

The way I saw it, my helping the soldiers was not such a bad idea. It was warm here, I was well fed, and I was not accosted with stupid questions. Well, with the exception of Polina and Liza's. But Polina was a good cook, meaning any sin could be forgiven her, and Liza was a child, and children were forgiven everything.

I had agreed to Combat's request not solely on account of my leveling-up and future plans. I simply needed time to be alone and ponder everything again. What I'd thought up was in large part not like me, but right now it seemed like the right decision.

The world was changing faster than I could have imagined, and I was too overwhelmed by the fact that people were uniting into groups and working collectively, something I totally did not want to be a part of. Being a cog in a well-oiled machine of human stupidity was not my thing. Whereas being at the very top of that system and reaping the benefits would be just the ticket.

At the moment, the fighters were weak against the zombies. True, they had huge battle experience, but you couldn't take on zombies with your bare hands, and they needed to procure more weapons. Aside from which, their progress was being hampered by the human factor. They had families to protect and they were trying to create normal living conditions for them. That was how they'd drawn me in, with their lack of decay which was present in others, and even in this world they would remain people.

For this reason, while they still weren't very strong, my assistance would be accepted on my terms, and I would be able to take a position in their system. I had to face the unfortunate truth that loners did not live long.

At the end of the day, I could have lived alone, but I would have to hide in various strangers' apartments or filthy basements, feeding on what I could knock together in a hurry, and being forever on my guard. Thank you, but that was not the life for me. My buckwheat now came served with liver.

The sustenance factor was of no small importance. I did not want to spend time on cooking, washing, and all the rest of it, and if I was being honest, I was too lazy anyway. And besides, Polina was an excellent cook, and didn't appear to be trying to do me any harm. My principal reason for not liking people was their treachery.

Combat was pretty switched-on, If you asked me, and he was happy with my position in their camp. While I was of some use, they would not hassle me overly. They were surrounded on all sides by enemies, from whom I was not against earning bonuses, and that was very heartening. I did not like wandering the city aimlessly, killing the peaceful population, it wasn't my cup of tea. I might not be the most balanced person in the world, but I did not want to become a maniac. That said, I had no sympathy for anyone who attacked unprovoked.

Especially where zombies were concerned. There were so many of them gathered by the dorm that my heart fluttered in anticipation. I didn't have to go searching for them in the city, I just had to sit calmly on the balcony and shoot away to my heart's content. Then I would come calmly downstairs for lunch and a rest in civilized conditions.

I surprised my first zombie as it was climbing over the barricade. It had managed to clamber over its companions and was nearly in the area by the main entrance.

The second one I killed reflexively, not even looking in its direction. After that, I let off thirty shots with only one miss. I now understood that all yesterday's ordeals and time spent on the trading platform had not been time wasted. I did not have to take precise aim, my hands automatically knowing what to do. This ability from the system was so much a part of me that I might have had it always.

Obviously, part of the reason might be that I'd been a professional archer for so many years. Back then, in archery lessons, I hadn't had to shoot running targets or magic shields in the knowledge it would slow my opponent's movement.

Of course you could spend dull ages shooting at magic shields with basic arrows, but it wouldn't bring any noteworthy results.

With these thoughts in my head, I shot zombies, and my mood tangibly improved.

Shooting was sheer pleasure. There was nothing better for me in this world, and nothing compared to it.

There were a lot of zombies, I might even say an awful lot. The bandits from the neighboring group who had attacked yesterday had put some effort in. Their explosions had attracted a colossal number of zombies to the dorm, and in doing so, trapped people in the building. The soldiers had certainly not sat idly around. They'd been killing zombies, but way too slowly, especially considering there was a good couple of thousand on the doorstep.

Half an hour later, the first people exited the dorm building, armed with whatever was to hand, and began chopping at the zombies through the barricades. By all appearances they'd been waiting for me to clear the yard of infiltrating zombies, and only then they emerged. Smart.

From my balcony, I observed as they carefully, cohesively, and without taking any risks, set about destroying zombies. They held in their hands mainly spears, knives, a couple of swords, sharp pieces of rebar, sections of pipe, and basically anything else they could lay their hands on. The biggest problem was not being able to reach their rewards.

But the main thing was that they shouldn't touch my rewards. Nothing else mattered. I hoped they wouldn't want to get on my back over such a trifle.

I thought of myself as a zombie-destroying

machine who never stopped for a minute, continually hitting his targets. From time to time and from the corner of my eye, I saw the zombie-slashing soldiers by the main entrance stop what they were doing and stare up at me in awe.

No doubt in their minds I was a curious beast that worked much better than a machine gun. By arrow number three hundred, the fire was in my belly and I had to buy more. It was a good job they were available.

While killing zombies on autopilot, I occasionally had to look out for soldiers who had failed to spot a clear danger, and I became very passionate about the engagement. Several times a zombie archer crept towards the fighters, but I made sure it didn't get too close. Another time I shot a jumper in midflight, after it had sensed easy prey and try to leave the barricade. I hoped that would help the guys understand what the new mutant monsters were all about.

With a mountain of corpses higher than the barricade, the fighters grew tired. They were constantly having to push dead zombies back in order to get a good stab at the newly approaching ones.

And I kept firing. I soon understood I would not be able to kill them all and needed to change tactic.

Activating invisibility, I went down to mingle with the crowd. With difficulty, I managed to slip through the dense ring of zombies and get behind their backs. Then began the gathering of trophies.

Boxes, trinket caskets...

Ooh, there were so many that I delighted in each one I picked up, for they could always be exchanged for something useful. Or if it came to the pinch, I could give the bullets to the soldiers, as they were seriously short on ammunition. They were of no use to me, except for exchange purposes, but ten or twenty boxes would not exactly bankrupt me.

I could not collect all my trophies straightaway, because access to some of them was obstructed by zombies' bodies, so I had to shoot them in the back in order to hustle my way through to the boxes.

I was soon tired and decided to take a break, which I used to nip to the hardware store. I did not want to lose my comfortable accommodation this time, so I planned to fortify it more securely.

I reached the store without incident, hacking to pieces only those zombies that stood in my way, while ignoring the others. With the exception, that is, of one archer monster, the likes of which I preferred to kill immediately, because they were too strong and dangerous, not only for me but also for others.

While I did not particularly sympathize with people, I was also a person, and I did not want humankind to lose to the walking dead in this game of survival. Being the top dog, if at the same time being the only dog left on the planet, was not a prospect I relished. In this new world, I would create for myself the sort of life I had always dreamed of, where I would do only those things that were to my liking. If I didn't get killed, of course.

This time I relieved the store of various sizes and thicknesses of plank, filling the remaining spare seventy kilograms of my inventory.

I returned immediately to the dorm. I did not have much time, so I decided to run back. I still had at least ten trips to make today, and I also needed to do some shopping on the trading platform.

I reentered the apartment via the balcony, the keys to which I already had. The apartment was quiet, Polina and Liza being out, which I was glad of. Despite them not arousing any unpleasant feelings in me, communication still had to be in moderation. I was surprised to find the door not locked. What if we were burgled? I would have to raise the question with Polina later. Were they all so trusting of one another that they didn't even think about potential theft?

I dumped the planks in the room where I'd left everything yesterday.

I wanted to go straight back, but then I thought a couple of minutes wouldn't make much difference and I needed a short breather. It was not worth forgetting for a single minute that haste might cost you your life in this world of zombies. And I was not planning on dying. For the entirety of my previous life I had not lived but merely existed, while here I was just flourishing. This world seemed specially created for me, and I did not have to be a gray misery, but could be whoever I wanted, thanks to my achievements.

I filled the kettle and sat down in the kitchen. On the table was an aromatic and still-warm baked pudding, which helped me understand that things were looking up.

I had lots of boxes and caskets, so I could try my luck and open a couple.

A red trinket casket produced a regular sword, which was garbage as far as I was concerned, but I didn't get upset, and proceeded to open another few. Thus, I became the proud owner of two more swords, one long pike, and two maces. It appeared that randomness was not for me.

It would be more profitable to sell the trinket caskets. It would be good to land some cards, of course, but simple weapons would suffice.

Time was running out fast, so I needed to visit the trading platform now.

During the next seven minutes, while the kettle was coming to the boil, I looked at hundreds of items and tried to figure out how much they were worth.

Then I got up and made a cup of tea, blew on it to cool it down, and dived headfirst back into trading.

CHAPTER 15

THERE WAS SO MUCH of so many useful things that I couldn't believe my eyes, but I still couldn't figure out what was absolutely necessary and what would be gratuitous expenditure. By which I mean, nonessential outlay of boxes and trinket caskets.

The question is, will a feisty arrow go right through a shield? Perhaps they just have harder heads than basic arrows?

And the potion of metamorphosis? What would it metamorphose me into? A bloodthirsty vampire or a dumb monster? Or perhaps a fluffy bunny? In which case I was toast. I wondered if I might find a potion that would cure me of my phobia of human love. No, too good to be true. My biggest phobia, my weakness, seriously stressful and capable of sending me into a tailspin, was heightened personal attention and uncomfortable questions. How complicated everything was.

First, I put up for sale everything I didn't need, accompanied by a note reading, "Will buy any archery equipment." You never knew, I might get lucky and land something truly vital.

I was immediately inundated with offers, and some real corkers there were too. For example, "Will exchange curved sword for gray box or potion-of-nausea card." *Why are you offering me that when I've clearly stated what I'm looking for?*

After the twentieth rejected offer, I at last understood what their game was. They were bunging me all manner of garbage with incomprehensible names, in the hope I would think the items had something to do with archery.

As a result, I had to give a curved sword away in return for ten red boxes. I did not see a better offer there, and the sword was of no use to me whatsoever, less so because it had no level. On the other hand, the boxes could be exchanged for five or ten arrow cards, which they soon were. You could never have too many arrows.

After a short pause for thought and a weigh-up of the pros and cons, I began to buy up all the arrows I could, the most basic ones. I had two coins and could look back at the trading platform later, and with a decent stock of arrows I could gain more levels and rewards several times faster.

Someone was selling a crystal-tipped-arrow card for three food boxes, so I completed the exchange without the thinking, and in doing so, gained something I needed at a bargain price.

Then, in return for some "**Reinforced leather vambraces, level 2**," I gave away ten red boxes. Never before had I held in my hands an item higher than level 1 — largely, I thought, because they weren't exactly common — yet here was a pair of level 2s. I took them just in case I should find myself too close to a zombie with no way out, and I'd be able to put them on my arms and let the bastards chew away at them.

I checked the marketplace for dark pears but, to my chagrin, found nothing. I was already daydreaming about becoming a nocturnal cat.

Of the rarer things I saw, I took three cards for new kinds of arrow: serrated, 15 pcs; explosive, 12 pcs; and most interesting, holy arrows for protection against the undead, 5 pcs.

They would not go amiss. In fact nothing archery-related would go amiss, but my resources were not unlimited. I had seventy food boxes and ten red boxes left, but there was much more I wanted. I exchanged all the red boxes for arrows. I would need a plentiful supply; I could feel it in my water.

After another ten minutes scrolling through the trading platform, I snapped and spent the remaining boxes on basic arrows. I didn't bother to count them, but there were over five thousand, a laughable number when you considered how many zombies were roaming the city streets.

It did cross my mind to buy various potions, enticed by names such as "potion of strength," but after giving it a certain amount of thought, I decided to level up by myself and wait for strength to appear naturally, along with everything else. Yesterday in the shower, I'd noticed positive changes to my body. And no, I hadn't grown a tail, or chubby hamster cheeks. The changes were in the relief of my body. I had never done anything apart from archery before. Well, maybe a bit of calisthenics at home on occasion, but now I looked pretty trim.

The only disappointing thing was other survivors' offers. They wanted me to trade my stuff for either chickenfeed, or crap that was worth chickenfeed, while I was counting on exchanging it for something useful.

So screw them, I was better off doing another store run. I unloaded all my superfluous weapons into a storage closet. I'd never used them and they took up a fair amount of space in my inventory.

The closet was a cubic meter in volume, and had a lockable, strong door. I figured it had been the generals' valuables safe. Were it not for the lock, I would never have risked leaving all my bladed weapons in it. And not out of fear they might be stolen, but more out of fear that the curious Liza might crawl in there to play and end up getting injured. Back when we were kids attending weapons-oriented clubs, we had one fundamental rule drilled into us: any weapon should be kept in a safe place. It was a rule you did not play fast and loose with.

I recalled an incident when an experienced archer disregarded the rule and ended up having a crossbow bolt extracted from his leg. His young son had found the "toy," somehow managed to load it, and shot his father, in play, when the latter walked into the room.

On the landing of the second floor, I bumped into an old acquaintance hurrying somewhere.

"Varg, hi, how are you?" he said, smiling and reaching out for an embrace.

Damn, it seemed his attitude to me was becoming less and less formal with each passing day, as though I were his brother, or godfather to his child.

"Shatun, you're strangling me, let me go," I said hoarsely. It worked. He let me go.

"Hehehe. I wouldn't strangle you, but you'd do well to avoid a hug from brother Clubfoot, otherwise he might."

He appeared to be joking, but for some reason I believed him.

"I was doing superbly until I bumped into you. I'm off on a jaunt, and a shopping trip while I'm at it," I said, seeing no need to hide my plans from him.

"I wanted to thank you personally for the ammunition you left us. It came in very handy yesterday." He was truly grateful. After all, if it hadn't been for my help, who knew how many people would have died yesterday?

"It's a shame I wasn't around yesterday, I could have increased my inventory." I had already thought about this and truly regretted it, for an inventory was a lifeline, as were trophies.

"Stay and live with us then, and next time you won't miss out on such an opportunity," he suggested.

I thought for a moment. "Do you think they'll be back?"

"I'm sure of it," he replied in earnest, and from his face I could see how worried he was.

"I'll think about it, but right now I have to go," I said, trying to bring the conversation to a close.

"Good luck," Shatun said as I turned to leave.

That was the kind of news I liked. By killing their enemies, I would become stronger everyday due to gifts from the system. And at the same time I would earn some authority with the people living here, which would also be an advantage in the future.

I went out via my now habitual balcony route, not forgetting to lock the door behind me. This time I decided to try jumping down. It was risky and silly, of course, but I had to test out what I was capable of.

To my surprise, I didn't even notice my landing, as though I'd jumped from the first floor as opposed to the second.

Now I knew I could land like a paratrooper and remain intact.

I headed off back to the hardware store. The journey was practically the same as before, except for a chomping sound coming from a dark side street. Naturally I was curious and went to see what was occurring.

Fuck. Such was my reaction when I saw what

was making the noise. In the city center, in a side street between rows of houses, a massive canine thing was chowing down on a zombie. Its snout was abnormally long and covered in foul slime. With each bite, its maw opened enormously wide, like a snake's, and it shoveled the food inside, where hundreds of crooked and razor-sharp teeth finely ground whatever fell between them, including bones and clothing.

Sidling very quietly, trying not to breathe, I left that dreadful side street, hoping the beast would not notice me. I didn't even want to shoot at it, for if I missed, or it dodged the bullet, I was a goner. I wouldn't get far running from such a monstrosity. What if it had armor or some other surprise up its sleeve? Nah, something like that needed taking down from above, and from the safety of a fortified building. Able to sneak safely away from the cute little doggy, I now tried to put some distance between us.

Unpleasant news greeted me in the store as well. Yesterday I had broken only the bottom part of the window in order to crawl inside, but now it was completely gone, and a hulk would be able to climb through the hole. The shop looked like a bomb site and had clearly been visited by marauders. Shelving was overturned, and some of the items I'd made a note of yesterday were gone. Fuck, and the store detective was smelling none too sweet.

I would now need to hurry before the store was looted completely. I started scooping all the larger items into my inventory: sheets of metal, planks, sections of iron fencing, and rebars, which would all come in handy for constructing barricades. When my inventory was full, I found some rubble sacks and filled them with smaller bits and bobs. I needed a load of screws and nuts and bolts, and I filled one sack to overflowing with them. Then I threw it over my shoulder. It was a bit prickly, but tolerably so, and the weight I practically didn't feel, which meant I could manage another one. I filled another sack with a variety of tools. Then another, then another, then another.

When I looked at the six bursting sacks, I figured I might have gone overboard. Shoot, surely I hadn't gotten so greedy I'd decided to take half the store home?

I was never going to take all this on my shoulders, but it was a shame to leave it; I didn't want to have sorted it all for the sake of others. The sacks were loaded with lots of useful gear: pliers, hammers, saws, and electric tools, along with a dozen items the names of which I didn't know.

I wandered around the store, pondering how to get everything back to the dorm in one go. I even had the idea to take a car, but immediately rejected it as being too noisy. But then I saw a handcart and had a lightbulb moment. It was heavy, meant especially for carrying weighty loads.

I loaded the cart to the max, then I found some machine oil and lubricated the wheels so they wouldn't squeak.

Then I trundled everything back to the dormitory. The route was already familiar, there were next to no zombies, and if they did suddenly cross my path, they would present no problem. I knew I could make one other person next to me invisible, or a small item, and I did so for the handcart, which was fantastic, because I could imagine people's reaction when they saw a heavily laden self-propelling cart.

The journey home took twice as long, because I was forever having to skirt around zombie corpses and piles of trash. Chaos reigned.

Another problem cropped up by the dorm: it was impossible to approach with the cart.

I had to run up to the apartment, unload everything from my inventory, run back down to the cart, fill my inventory from it, and run up to the apartment again.

On the last trip something unpleasant happened as I was climbing over onto the balcony. The windowsill I was holding onto suddenly came loose. It would be a joke to be beaten by a simple windowsill.

The main entrance needed clearing of zombies, because at this rate I was definitely going to do myself some damage by climbing up onto the balcony every time.

At a rough guess, there were no less than a thousand down there, surrounding the building on all sides like sharks circling for a feed.

Since I'd decided to stay here to live, it was worth helping the soldiers with materials to build decent barricades through which they could easily fight the zombies.

Perhaps it was worth them digging a moat?

Wait, what? Since when did I decide to live here? I wanted to vet these people first.

Dang, I really had decided to stay, although I was damned if I could remember making the decision. I felt incessant discomfort in the company of people, so why on earth...? The interesting thing was that I reacted differently to different people. Some incensed me so much I wanted to quit their company immediately, while others were sometimes even interesting to be with. You could probably call it egoism. Polina fed me wonderfully, and I could communicate with her almost calmly, while Combat provided important information and fulfilled all my conditions.

My mind worked so strangely on occasion that I didn't understand it myself. Never mind, I would cross bridges when I came to them. In the meantime, I took out my telephone.

"Combat?" After a couple of rings, my call was answered, and I wanted to be sure I wasn't mistaken.

"That's me. Glad to hear you, Varg. Has something happened? Do you need help?" The man sounded alarmed. I was not the sort to call for a chat.

"Well, yes, I do need help. I don't know how best to describe it," I said, faltering. Out of nerves, I wanted to destroy all the zombies. I was sure I could hear them laughing right now.

"Tell it like it is, and I'll understand and certainly try to help," Combat replied in a friendly manner. He'd had to work with all sorts of people during his long military service, and he'd learned to find different approaches to different types.

"Well, I need the address of an art-supplies store, and one that sells ladies clothes." My embarrassment made me want the ground to swallow me up.

"I see. I honestly don't know, but I'll ask my fighters and send you a message." I was prepared to swear he was smiling as he spoke.

"It's not what you think, Combat. And don't tell anybody, consider it our secret." If the dorm occupants found out, they would ridicule me and I'd feel terribly embarrassed. I seemed to have goofed up.

"Relax, I understand. You've been taken in hand," he said, no longer concealing his glee. "I can assure you I won't tell a soul."

"What hand? Hey, what are you talking about?" But all I could hear were the beeps at the other end of the line.

The conversation with Combat only served to confuse me further. What had he meant by "taken in hand"?

I was strong and independent. Who could possibly take me in hand? Even this dorm... Nothing was keeping me here, I could take off at any moment and cope perfectly well by myself. The only thing I liked about this place was Polina's delicious cooking. And of course I did not relish the thought of running around in dirty clothes all the time. It was a shame I could only wash clothes with the aid of a washing machine.

Or maybe he was joking and this was army humor? Yes, that was probably it. I hoped.

While I was waiting for Combat's message, I decided to shoot some zombies to settle my nerves.

By the time I'd killed about thirty and collected the rewards, Combat still hadn't written. Not wanting to waste time, I took the handcart and headed back to the hardware store.

Back in the store, an interesting idea occurred to me when I saw a bunch of bricks in the stockroom. Why did I want to cover the windows with metal sheeting when I could block them up with bricks?

Definitely a great idea, but how would I get them back to the dorm? Each window would require at least thirty bricks, and they weighed approximately three kilograms a piece, which meant one trip per window. However, if I could find a bigger cart and load it to the maximum, three trips should suffice.

Pondering the situation, I couldn't decide whether it was worth the time. It would doubtless be a sound investment in my future, and if Polina was killed by a spirited zombie, who would prepare my meals? And if anything should happen to Liza, Polina would start grieving and stop cooking such tasty grub. Everything came down to food. As well as my safekeeping in sleep. I had twice already lost convenient accommodation and all my possessions, and that was enough. I wasn't going to let it happen again.

Facilitating the girls' security was absolutely the best way forward. But when had I managed to fall in love with Polina's cooking? It was probably a hangover from childhood trauma. My grandmother and I had always had very little money, and what we ate was meager and not tasty. That said, if you go hungry for three days at a time, then any food, even the simplest, is delicious.

But Polina's cooking was unparalleled, her meatballs deserving of special note, as well as her borsch with sour cream and whole chunks of meat floating in it, not to mention her baked pudding.

I could not cook like that by any stretch of the imagination. I simply didn't know how, and I was dead lazy to boot.

So lost was I in thought that I didn't even notice how quickly I found a large handcart. All problems were of woman born, as they said, and here was I, contemplating all sorts of nonsense and at the same time becoming depersonalized.

The good thing was that I could apparently keep abreast of my situation on autopilot. Inside the store there was a single roving zombie, which I pacified instantly with my spear.

I began shunting bricks into my inventory, and the final result came to: cart 100 - inventory 30. When I tried to budge it, the cart moved, but the wheels produced a loud and unpleasant squeak. I oiled them again. The squeak was gone, but the cart was still heavy and slow.

No message had arrived from Combat. I hoped he hadn't gone to find Polina to ask where to find those shops, otherwise my situation would be doubly awkward. I did not like asking anyone for anything. I didn't know why, but it made me feel very out of sorts.

It was better to be a maverick, a lone wolf, trusting only myself and dealing with everything by myself. The only pity was that survival was always a problem for a lone wolf. Sooner or later, they were always suffocated by the crowd.

I pushed the cart and tried to remember where I might find the store I needed. There were lots of clothes stores, and I'd even spotted a couple on these trips, but how was I to know what was trendy and what wasn't? What if I brought home something she didn't like and which didn't suit her.

Perhaps I should have brought Liza with me? Or is that a bad idea? Yes, definitely a bad idea; Polina would castrate me. Although I could say I was going to help her level up. As a mother, Polina must be interested in her child's future. What nonsense is this?

I thought I heard laughter from a passing zombie. I turned towards it. It didn't appear to be laughing.

Is it me, or did it just turn its head aside to pretend it was ignoring me?

"Are you joking with me?" I asked, approaching the creature to a distance of a few meters.

"Aarrghh."

I didn't know how I understood, but from the zombie's eyes, I saw it was poking fun at me. I took its head off with a swift spear swipe.

That's better. Otherwise, any old zombie might start poking fun at me. Pfft.

As I walked, I realized my head was slowly beginning to leak, and it was all down to two chicks. Or rather it was down to one chick, and one little girl whose ability to screw with my head was no worse than any grown-up's. Then again, perhaps it was useful for my head. Grandma used to say it wasn't worth retiring totally inside my beloved shell, or else one day I might lose my humanity.

When I made it back to the dorm and unloaded, Combat's message arrived at last, telling me the addresses of the stores I was looking for.

The first, an art shop, was on May Street, which was close, a twenty-minute walk.

I sent a return message of thanks and set off in search of the store. May Street had once been quite busy with people; now it was busy with hundreds of roving zombies. One of the first buildings I came to was inhabited by people. Hmm, they even had food and weapons. Life was evidently not bad.

Then my eyes lighted on a truck overturned onto its side.

"Excellent, just what I need!" I said, delighted by what I saw.

I approached the truck and clambered up onto the roof of the cab. Now I had the zombies in the palm of my hand. I produced my bow and got busy with my favorite pastime. First, I took out the zombies nearest to me. When they were all dead, I deactivated invisibility and started on the ones now coming for me. The zombies here were regulars, no jumpers or archers, which provided a perfect opportunity to earn myself some easy rewards.

Unfortunately, all good things come to an end all too soon, and I quickly ran out of zombies. I climbed down and gathered my trophies, mainly gray boxes this time, and put them straight into my inventory.

The shop was a brick building, no less than two hundred years old, its walls decorated with stucco. The door was locked and it would be a shame to break it down, for it looked the same age as the building itself and might be considered of architectural value. I had no choice, however, as I urgently needed... *That's a point, what exactly do I need?* My knowledge of artists was negligible. Never mind, I would figure it out once I got inside. I shoved my dagger into the gap between the door and the wall, as a lever, and threw all my weight against it. Unable to cope with that level of brute force, the door opened with a creaking sound. It was certainly going to require some restoration now, since a huge chunk of old wood fell out of it. But what was I thinking? What restoration, in this apocalypse, when the only thing on people's minds was how to survive?

Never mind, screw it. I needed to quickly find artists' materials to curry favor with Polina.

Once inside, the first thing that caught my eye was the counter behind which the storekeeper used to sit. The walls were hung with pictures accompanied by price tags. *Maybe I should take her some pictures? No, that would probably make me an idiot in her eyes. Although, I already am an idiot, breaking into an art shop during a zombie Apocalypse.*

After scouring the store for five minutes, I found just what I'd been looking for, in a separate section for blank canvases, paints, and brushes. There was also a selection of sketchbooks, pencil sets, and easels.

I took thirty canvases of varying sizes, all in wooden frames, and five easels. Now for paints. I raked together at least ten kilograms, not reading too much into their names. If Polina could draw, she would soon figure out what was what. Then I swiped all the pencils and sketchbooks.

After practically cleaning out the young artists' department, I still had twenty kilograms' worth of free space in my inventory, so I threw in those pictures which looked the best to me. They happened to be the most expensive ones. If Polina didn't like them, they could always be given to somebody else.

Upon leaving the store, I realized what a birdbrain I was, to put it mildly. I had filled up the entire inventory and not left any space for clothes.

What was I to do now?

Shoot, it would soon be getting dark, and I still had to do one more brick run to the hardware store. On the other hand, if I didn't find any clothes now, it might not be worth going home. The expression "a zombie hath no fury like a woman scorned" was oft quoted with good reason. Or was I making that up? Anyway, it didn't matter.

I had to establish supremely trusting relations with Polina. I needed at least one reliable person in the dorm who would be squarely on my side, and so far she suited me down to the ground.

That meant I had to get home as fast as possible, in order to hide the pictures and everything else before going out again in search of the clothes store.

Art dogs.

Chapter 16

AS I'VE SAID BEFORE, chicks are an evil, but a necessary evil. I had never before had to spend hours on end in conversation with a girl. On occasion I'd tried to get to know the girls from the archery club, but relations usually came to an end all too soon. Who wants anything to do with a weird shy guy, who on a date might suddenly jump up at any moment and just run off? But everything was different now, and I didn't seem quite so strange in this new insane world.

I only got around to dealing with the presents late into the evening, when I eventually found the clothes store and packed everything into my inventory. There wasn't enough space for everything I wanted to take, so I was forced to put the remainder in two rubble sacks and haul them home on my shoulders.

There was still nobody at home, so I threw

everything into the supply closet and headed back to the hardware store for bricks, cement, and buckets of sand.

Frankly, it had been an exhausting day. Running about the town was more draining than killing zombies, and selecting clothes could only be exclusively with the system test.

Returning home again, I quickly laid out all the gifts on the sofa in the living room and went to take a shower. What with Polina not having been home all day, I figured I'd have to fend for myself as far as food was concerned, but no, dinner awaited me on the table along with a note. How convenient! Nobody at home, yet there was food on the table and all the creature comforts in a clean and tidy apartment. I was warming to this life more and more. I'd always dreamed of having a housekeeper, like in the old movies, only the money had never been there.

As the night drew on, I became mildly concerned about the girls' absence, but when I searched the building, I discovered them up on the fourth floor. Polina and a few of the other ladies were having a chat and a laugh over tea, while the children amused themselves in play.

The girls returned home just before ten, bringing a piece of cake to go with my tea. Way to go! They'd even found time to bake a cake while visiting friends for a cup of tea. We sat at the table for five minutes, then they left, no doubt to sleep, which suited me just fine. I remained sitting there, drinking my tea, eating my cake, and planning my future. Life was changing, and I was drawing ever closer to my goals.

All that was required now for total happiness was victory in one more test.

Polina suddenly crept up behind me.

"Thank you," sounded in my ear, then I felt her lips on my cheek.

The fork fell from my hand and my head buzzed. When I snapped out of my shock, she scampered off, wishing me *bon appetit* as she left.

For me it was unusual behavior, but I have to admit it provoked no negative emotions, if anything just bewilderment.

"Well done!" Liza ran into the kitchen, gave me the thumbs up, and run back to Polina.

And for the umpteenth time I was convinced communication with zombies was easier and more understandable.

Had my gift really been so pleasing to her?

Finishing my tea, I decided to wash the dishes after myself.

"Leave it, I'll clear everything away. You have a rest, you've done so much today," said Polina, appearing alongside me again.

What is she talking about? What have I done?

Deciding instantly to find out what I'd done today, I turned sharply around and found myself face-to-face with Polina. Blushing, I span quickly back around and took two steps away from her. Distance was our everything.

A smile played on her face.

"Surely killing a couple of hundred zombies

must mean something to you?" she hinted. "The whole dorm is humming with tales of your heroic feats and how you helped everyone."

"It's all baloney," I said. The smooth-talking redhead was making me blush beet-red once more. "There was nothing to it," I said, waving away the adoration.

"Uh-huh, nothing," she said, staring at me with an unceasing beam. "My girlfriends have been driving me mad today with their questions about you."

Not good. I totally did not want to be popular. I did not like this at all. Just one hint of stardom was enough to give me the willies, and I was in a real state I by now.

"Polina, I brought a load of different building materials," I said, nodding towards the room where they lay. "I'm going to run and find Combat and ask him to designate some people to board up the windows. Can you keep an eye on the process tomorrow?"

"Haha, so that's the way it is." The girl laughed sonorously and took a step towards me, looking me right in the eye. "You don't just kill zombies, you can lug bricks around as well. I would never have thought you were so domesticated."

"I wouldn't have said you were an artist," I retorted.

"You doubted me?" Her eyes flashed cunning and danger.

"Possibly." I returned her smile. "I didn't see

any pictures or drawings in your last apartment."

Calmly, she replied, "You didn't see any because there were none. Half a year ago I was forced to sell everything. I didn't have any money for Liza's daycare, so I had to make some sacrifices."

"Sorry, I didn't know, I didn't mean to offend you." My mind did not work well in conversation with people and often got me into unpleasant situations. My phobia was my biggest weakness.

"Are you capable of offending? You look very kind." Her mood was somehow playful today, and that did not bode well.

"How should I know? Sometimes I don't know what I'm capable of," I replied indifferently. "As you've noted, I'm very strange."

"Right now the whole world is quite strange, don't you find?" she said. I didn't know how to answer, and she didn't need an answer. "Anyway, run along and find Combat, since that's what you were going to do. It'll soon be bedtime."

I did not need telling twice. I was only too glad to bring this meaningless conversation to a close.

"Try not to be late to bed, please. Liza's afraid of sleeping without you in the room now. She says she's not scared when you're close by."

Well, shoot. I was almost out of the kitchen, just by the door.

"You've just given away your child's secret," I said, turning the screws on her conscience.

"That child gave away my interests, so there's nothing to worry about." She waved it away and set to washing the dishes.

Life with a chick was oh so difficult, but her cooking was something else.

There was no one else in Combat's room, and we sat there for about an hour, during which time we solved all my problems. He was glad to learn he'd been able to help me, and he thanked me for my assistance in destroying the zombies. There were still plenty out there, mind, but nobody was banking on me offing them all in one day, and the fighters had spent at least three hours helping me with that job.

He promised to send some people tomorrow to brick up the windows, and I promised he could have whatever materials and tools were left over when that work was done. Win-win. I'd been planning to give him everything anyway, since the current state of the building's defenses left much to be desired. And it was stupid to lose people when they should have been slaving away at jobs too dull and unstimulating for me.

He also shared the news that he was trying to conduct negotiations with the band that had recently been attacking them. By all accounts they were total psychos, a mob of ex-cons who had discovered a bunch of opportunities in this new unstable world. They had no problem killing, but as for work, they were certainly not up for that. They'd proposed that the soldiers give them thirty chicks, and five guys who could handle a sledgehammer.

Of course Combat told them to go to hell, but

now everyone in the dorm was worried about repeat attacks. The bastards claimed to have a ton of weapons and ammunition, no doubt the result of trading in them.

According to information gleaned, their band consisted exclusively of men and they had a problem with women.

But the most shocking thing he saved for last.

"That's not all, Varg," he said, before falling silent and fingering the cup of tea on his desk.

"I'm all ears."

"They also want us to give them some of the children." This was a curveball. "Those bastards know nothing of honor and morals. My informers tell me their favorite pastime of late is seeking out survivors and killing them to level up, as well as pressganging anyone who takes their fancy. That's the men. What they do with the women you can imagine for yourself."

My hands involuntarily clenched into fists, and the word "KILL" sounded in my head. I had no problem killing people like that by the dozen.

"How are you for equipment?" The time for joking was over.

"Better now, thanks to your assistance, but we're seriously low on bullets."

"Take these, then," I said, handing him seven of my red boxes. "Also, let me know as soon you hear the band is on the way here. I'll make them regret their decision to attack you."

Life in the dormitory was beginning to look up. Enemies were appearing, and killing them would allow me to expand my inventory.

Combat thought a moment and shook his head.

"They've got firearms and you've only got a bow. It's too dangerous." He seemed to be concerned about me. "Don't take this the wrong way, but you're the only one who can destroy zombies with relative ease. If something happens to you, it's our loss."

"I'm not going to die, you can trust me on that, Combat. I have killed people before, and not just the once."

"Have you thought about what will happen to Polina and Liza if something happens to you?" He unexpectedly took a different tack.

"What could possibly happen? They've got an apartment, and enough food for a few weeks," I said. I couldn't see the problem.

"What a fool you are, Varg." Combat smiled. "I sometimes think you feel more at home among zombies than among people."

How right he was. "You're right there."

"My advice to you, from someone who has lived through and seen much more than you, is this: don't spurn good people; they help people like me and you to remain people."

His words set me to thinking.

"People like you and me?" I asked. What was he talking about?

"That's right, we are alike," he said with a weary smile. "Life for us is easier on the frontline than in a relaxed domestic atmosphere. At least you know where the enemy is."

"Wise words."

I exited Combat's office in a ponderous mood. There was a certain sensible logic to his words.

I got home as the girls were getting ready for bed, and Liza was sincerely delighted I would be spending the night at home.

After wishing them a good night, I closed my eyes and tried to sleep. Sleep, however, evaded me, old Combat's words whirling around my head.

I tossed and turned for two hours, until Polina was awoken by the squeak of my bed.

"Is everything okay?" she asked. "Why aren't you sleeping?"

"I can't get to sleep. I'm thinking," I replied quietly, trying not to make a sound.

"Who are you thinking about?"

I replied only after a pause. "About life."

"You'd better get some sleep. We don't know what tomorrow will bring, and you need your strength." Polina was concerned about me; I'd taken so much on myself, and I was strange enough as it was. I did not understand many things and my reaction to people was unrivaled. Yet she was immensely grateful for everything I'd done for her and her daughter.

*   *   *

Today Polina stayed with her girlfriends until nearly midnight, the result of her conversations with me. Everyone was interested to know everything about me, amazed how I'd managed to get hold of so much food and feed them so easily. They oohed and aahed to hear that boxes of food meant nothing to me, and at a difficult time for everybody, when others were starving. This morning she'd risked asking me for some food for a girlfriend with two children, and I hadn't refused.

She had even been a fraction concerned that she'd overstepped the mark, but I merely waved it away as though such trifles didn't bother me. By contrast, when she or Liza approached me with their jabbering, I would immediately flush red and become fidgety, my restless eyes creating the impression I was seeking an opportunity to make myself scarce.

On the rare occasion she was able to observe me, Polina could never understand what I was thinking about. I was an enigmatic and weak-looking guy, so where did these fearful stories come from, the stories told by everyone who came anywhere near me?

Rumors were already doing the rounds about the test I was said to have completed, and this morning practically the entire dormitory had gathered at those windows not yet boarded up, to watch me masterfully take out zombies with my arrows.

She hadn't been entirely truthful today when she told me about Liza. She herself was calmed by my sleeping presence in the same room. It seemed there was no enemy in existence capable of frightening me, and I could solve very quickly any problem that arose.

When the zombies had attacked them in the previous flat, I had saved them, before providing them new accommodation and food. As I was leaving the following day, I'd said I wouldn't be back for a few days, and it had saddened her that she might never see me again. But when I returned the same day, it had delighted her. When the bandits had attacked, my absence worried yet at the same time it consoled her, since I would not be able to charge into the fray and be killed.

I'd upset her yesterday by, according to hearsay, putting the screws on Combat in my search for addresses. Combat was respected by all, and feared by many who knew what he was capable of. Yet here was Varg posing absurd questions to him and seeing no problem in that. Combat's attitude to me was also unusual, and he did everything I asked, hoping to retain a valuable fighter. And I'd combed half the city in search of gifts for her, and she liked that very much. Despite my not understanding what I was doing, she was most appreciative of the gesture.

Polina's thoughts were rent asunder by a thunderous explosion which made the whole building shudder.

"Attack," Polina realized with horror.

Igor leaped groggily from his bed. No, it was Varg who jumped up, ready to do battle and kill.

"Mommy, I'm scared," Liza cried, rudely awakened by the explosion.

"I'm here, everything's going to be okay,

darling," replied Polina, stroking her daughter's head fitfully and wondering what was actually going on.

Was this the end?

* * *

I was just beginning to drift off when the deafening explosion tore me from the darkness, and judging by the cries and the shuddering of the dormitory building, we were under attack from a tank.

The first explosion was followed closely by a second, and I frantically pulled on my armor.

Liza was crying and Polina placating her, but at least they weren't hurt.

"Bastards. I'm off. You wait here, I'll be back soon. Just as soon as I can get this shitty armor on."

"Let me give you a hand," said Polina, skipping over to me in just a nightie.

I froze at the sight, and very soon she had done everything herself, even pulling the straps tight.

"Thank you." I nodded and attempted to tear my eyes away from her breasts, which were clearly visible through the thin material, for it was not polite to stare at a girl in that way.

Okay, it's time to kick those bastards' butts. I headed quickly out of the apartment, but Polina ran after me and grabbed me by the arm.

"Be careful. Please."

My heart clenched. She was frightened, tears

in her eyes, and I was overcome with a bitching hatred towards the aggressors.

"I'll be back soon," I said with a sharp nod.

I ran out onto the fifth-floor landing and into a crowd of people. Everyone was already awake, the women huddling together, panicked, and the men running downstairs, their faces serious.

Since the attackers were obviously coming from downstairs, I followed the men. By the sounds of gunshot, I had a rough idea of where the fight was. The ground floor was all chaos and zombie growlings. My eyes sought familiar faces, and found only the sentries. After an instant's contemplation, I grabbed a uniformed man running past, in order to get up to speed on the situation.

"Hey, fighter, what's happened?" I had to outshout the crowd.

Initially he tried to free his arm, but on failing in this, he looked up to curse me. When our eyes met, he recognized me.

"It's not looking good, Varg. A rocket-propelled grenade just hit the first floor." The report was delivered in haste. "There's an enormous hole in the wall down there, and zombies are flooding in from the street. I must report to the management urgently."

"You better run then," I said, before shouting after him, "tell Combat to get barricades built on the second floor, and I'll try to hold them off."

The fighters threw themselves at the zombies with whatever weapons they could find, but they were outnumbered. One guy fired three rounds from a pistol, and three zombies collapsed to the blood-spattered floor, but new ones quickly arrived to take their places. They were the fighter's last rounds and he beat a hasty retreat. Well yes, they weren't exactly snowed under with weapons. Or protection.

I looked along the length of the corridor to see that the wall by the main entrance no longer existed, replaced by a massive hole through which zombies were pouring. *Fuck, another one of those shots and the building might collapse.*

I drew my bow and began to shoot on the hoof as quickly as I could.

"Over here, Varg! He'll help us. We need guys with shields," shouted someone in the crowd when they saw me.

Another male voice added, "We need to buy some time, even at the cost of our lives. Our wives and children are up there; we can't let the monsters through."

I fired nonstop, killing zombie after zombie, yet their numbers were not decreasing. I decided to use an explosive arrow.

"Everyone take cover! This is going to be big," I warned the fighters. I gave them a few seconds to heed my advice, then I let the arrow fly.

The arrow flew a good fifteen meters before exploding, but it was close enough for us to feel the shock wave.

"Varg, you'll blow us all to high hell," shouted the frightened men.

Fuck. I already realized I'd done something dumb. I should have tried one out somewhere else first. But kudos to the system, a fire did not break out, although the now singed zombies' stink was even worse. Clearly not the right arrows for zombies, the stench not worth the little damage caused, and people now found themselves having to hold the line while wrinkling their noses at the smell. It was clearly no way to go, so I switched back to basic arrows. There was the option of blocking up the new entranceway with bodies, which would make the building easier to defend, but I would have to kill three hundred zombies first.

"Fuck, my shield broke!"

I looked in the direction of the exclamation and saw the speaker holding just the straps.

Things looked seriously bad.

Soldiers ran up, fired off their weapons, and immediately retreated. I moved with them, shooting over and over, and then suddenly I had nowhere to retreat to. Behind me was another wing of the building, which contained no stairways, and if we continued on that course, we'd be trapped.

The guys were doing okay, though, and trying to hold the zombies at bay. They had come to fight with whatever weapons they could find, some wielding chairs and stools instead of shields, while others slayed zombies with swords and spears.

"Varg, there you are. You need to retreat. We're going to set up barricades on the second floor and hold the fort from there." It was Fedya who had found me, out of breath. He had evidently seen action already, for his face, hands, and uniform were covered in blood.

"Fedya, you do understand not all the fighters are going to get out alive? As soon as we retreat, the zombies are going to chase us upstairs."

"I know that, and Combat knows it too." His eyes reflected all the pain of the decision taken. "They understand there's no other way out."

How maddening is all this? Simply infuriating. I knew it would be nothing but trouble with soldiers. I was on the verge of telling him what I thought, but then I had an interesting thought. *What would be happening now if I wasn't here today? I've killed no fewer than a hundred zombies, and yet they're still arriving in droves. Without me, these beasties would have been on the upper floors and killing everyone ages ago. And my plans would have gone up in smoke, and that's no good. I've done loads here already, so I'm not going to admit defeat.*

"Fedya, order everyone to retreat, and I'll try to buy you some time. Don't worry about me." I was acting the total idiot, I knew that full well, but I had no choice.

The man stared at me displeased before looking at his comrades. I was nobody to him, while they were his battle buddies. I had no one, no nearest nor dearest, while they had families waiting for them.

"Combat would tear my head off for you," he said with a heavy sigh. "But thanks for your gallantry. If you survive, I'll owe you a huge field," Fedya said, extending me his hand to be shaken, and giving me a tight embrace into the bargain. *FFS.*

"Listen up, fighters. On the count of three, drop everything and quick march up to the second floor," he shouted at the top of his voice.

"But what about...?" The fighters began to object.

"That's a fucking order!" Fedya shrieked in a frenzy.

Now that is a commanding voice, I thought.

The troops did not stampede like a herd of rams, but retreated in an organized fashion, discipline coursing through their military veins.

They quickly rounded the corner, and soon all that could be heard was the stamping of boots on the staircase.

Meanwhile, I remained face to face with a hundred hungry mouths and pairs of eyes, my heart beating so loudly I could feel it knocking in my head, and my adrenaline level off the charts. It was these moments that made life worthwhile, for it was in battle that you were tempered and became stronger. If you didn't die, that is.

And I did not want to die, for I had only just begun to live life.

CHAPTER 17

I HAD TO LURE THE ZOMBIES away quick smart, before they began to wonder where all the people had disappeared to and turned back to look for them. This entailed retreating into a corridor which appeared to be a dead-end. The zombies gladdened me by obediently chasing me en masse, having sensed fresh meat in close proximity.

Arrow after arrow flew from nigh point-blank range — there were ten yards between us — and the zombies may have been shuffling slowly, but there were an awful lot of them. No matter how many I took down, they kept gaining on me, if only by half a step at a time, and they would very soon have me pinned in the blind alley.

Gunshot sounded in the distance, the soldiers popping off zombies from the roof. Of course this eased my task somewhat, ever so slightly reducing the flow. No more than that, mind. And I was made to dwell bitterly on boxes I could not reach, although that was trivial. Right now the main thing was to fell as many zombies as possible.

The further I enticed them, the more dangerous for me, but it was such a rush to feel the adrenaline bubbling in my blood, and my nerves were stretched as taut as my bowstring. It was at moments like this I understood that survival for a single person was impossible in this world without the help of others. Zombies mutated too fast, as though controlled by a system whose aim was not to let people drop their guard in their battle for survival.

Completely out of the blue, one of the zombies turned out to be a jumper and caught up with me in one massive leap. I had no time to react, and all I could do was dodge it by taking a step back, but it was too late. The razor-sharp claws scraped across my chest, leaving scratches in my armor and sending me flying. Falling backwards, I smacked my head against the concrete wall. However, as the system had promised, I was now much stronger, and so I did not lose consciousness, only orientation. I was also in fucking pain, but there was no time for self-pity. The jumper was smart, and when it saw I was still alive, it jumped at me again. But this time it was pinned like a butterfly on my spear, which I had opportunely taken from my inventory. How's that for confidence in my strength?

I threw it to the side and finished it off with a

bow shot.

Damn, there wasn't even time to replace the spear. Every second counted and the distance between me and the zombies was shortening.

I very much hoped the soldiers had managed to prepare themselves by now, for I was tuckered out and my head hurt since the scuffle with the jumper. Never mind, I would tease the zombies some more and then make my escape.

On a subconscious level, I had come to consider this place my home, and I was trying to defend it. I could still remember my previous home and the things it had been a shame to leave there, but not to worry, I would find and wreak my revenge on those who had ousted me from that department. It was only a matter of time.

The thoughts in my head did not hinder me shooting zombies on autopilot, but the situation did not change. *How many beasts are there? I must think of something urgently, before I get eaten. But what? Perhaps I should make a run for it?*

Okay, I'll risk it.

I took out a disposable-crossbow card, loaded with a cold-explosion bolt, and activated it. In my hand appeared a heavy, medium-sized crossbow, carved from mahogany and loaded with a bolt that would spread an icy cold all around. After a second's thought, I shot at the zombie in the middle and jumped back as far as I could, just in case. Good job too! The wave of cold nearly reached me, but I managed to evade it by squeezing into a narrow nook in the wall. The zombies were not so lucky. The explosion adopted a cone shape and froze everything in its path to a distance of three meters. The first row were definitely goners, instantly recast as stalagmitic icicles, while those further back were merely frozen to the floor but still showing signs of life, and therefore required shooting sharpish. Jumping up onto a ledge, I had a clear view of all my targets and quickly shot all the frozen zombies within range. The wall of ice gifted us all ten very necessary minutes.

The piles of dead zombies continued to grow. Suddenly a pike whizzed by, missing me, thank fuck, and I immediately put an arrow in the bastard who'd launched it. Walking along the ledge, I looked down on the crowd in search of zombies with surprises. I hoped these monsters would not be joined by a hulk or one of those sweet little doggies. I did not want to rumble with any of them right now. After killing yet another zombie, I was rewarded with a long-awaited message of joy.

You have gained level 7.

Your body has become stronger. Your stamina is increased as a result of a number of bodily improvements.

Leveling up is all very well, but I've still got to survive today.

No matter how fast I was, I was also tired and therefore beginning to fire wide of my targets. Were that to continue, I would very soon be eaten. I had to take urgent measures, and I decided to flee. I'd given people enough time to prepare for repelling boarders, and there was no way I could keep fending off zombies until morning. Yes, I had taken the next level and was feeling very pleased with myself as I tried out my new-found strength against a whole horde of zombies, but I was still very weak and urgently needed to think about how to become stronger yet.

I had recently become too caught up in the arrangement of accommodation and lifestyle, totally forgetting that this world did not pardon weakness. Only absolute strength would help me achieve more.

In my retreat, I inched my way into the depths of the corridor, seeking out a convenient door or window to break through. If the worst came to the worst, there was another grenade, but I had other plans for it. Fortune eventually smiled on me and I found a window which seemed not reliably boarded-up. I was forced to cease fire while I jumped up onto the windowsill. The sheet of plywood came away easily, and beneath it was a thin piece of iron bolted to the window frame. This would obviously require a good few kicks, and as I watched it dent but not fly out of the window, I got a bad feeling. The remaining living zombies were almost upon me, and I would need to hurry before they sank their talons into my feet. However, everything had its durability margin and iron was no exception. Another couple of heavy kicks, and the metal sheet flew out, providing me a view of the half-empty yard outside. Zombies wandered about below the windows, and jumping down into their midst was not the best idea. Activating invisibility,

I walked quickly along the window ledge, before jumping down to the ground and disappearing around the corner. At last I could catch my breath and relax. I walked a short distance from the dormitory building and dialled Combat's number.

"Varg, are you alright?" asked the man straight off the bat.

"Uh-huh, everything's fine, I'm just tired and a bit mauled."

"Are you injured? We've all been worried about you? Polina and her daughter are here with me, freaked out with concern," Combat said.

"Everything's fine. Tell them not to worry, I'm okay. More importantly, did you make it?" This was the most important question for me right now, for if not, then all my efforts had been in vain.

"Your help was invaluable today. You bought us enough time to construct barricades on the second floor," said Combat.

"Good, I'm glad." There was no time for a long chat, so the conversation needed a drawing to a close.

"I'll be back towards morning, so hang on in there, don't go dying on me. And another thing, Combat, keep an eye on my girls, okay? I trust nothing will happen to them in my absence."

Combat knew who I was talking about, despite my struggling to squeeze the words out.

"Don't you worry, I'll do everything I can. You look after yourself as well."

On that, the conversation ended. I still had business to attend to in town.

When Combat had told me about the gang who'd launched the RPG at the dormitory, I immediately wanted to drop in to see him, but hadn't had time. Now I didn't want to put off my little payback mission until later. They had seriously gotten my dander up.

It was not difficult to locate their position, a simple-looking and ugly building with not all of its windows boarded-up and many of them with lights on, which meant they were not afraid of anyone, to be demonstrating the fact so hubristically.

There wasn't much to be seen from a distance, and it was dark, although I did now have night vision. Two sentries on the roof, armed with machine guns, sweeping the locality with spotlights and wearing webbing packed with spare magazines. No shortage of ammo, then.

They were way better prepared than the soldiers in my dormitory. They had found a tractor somewhere, and were using it to build a perimeter wall out of abandoned cars. The wall was not big, just three or four vehicles in height, but it was enough to keep out the zombies, preventing them coming too close and making them easier to pick off.

I was over the wall in no time, such things being no obstacle to me now, but I had no idea how to get inside the building unnoticed. These bastards had attacked my new home, and I'd gotten myself so worked up I could not let them go unpunished. They had to pay.

I wasn't about to kill them all. I couldn't in

fact, what with being so exhausted. But give them a thorough thrashing? Oh, I was definitely up for that.

I walked around the perimeter and found an easy way in. Beginning from the second floor, an old rusty fire escape led upwards. The first floor had no apartments, and the windows were boarded-up and sand-bagged. Unhurriedly and noiselessly, I climbed up to the roof, where I saw the bored sentries whispering quietly to each other as they observed something down at ground level. I calmly produced two arrows and sank one of them into each of the enemy heads.

You have killed a survivor.

The capacity of your inventory is increased by 3kg.

You have killed a survivor.

The capacity of your inventory is increased by 2kg.

Patting down the bodies, I found a key to the main entrance, and needless to say I relieved them of their machine guns, grenades, and ammunition, loading everything into my inventory. The only thing I didn't take was an unfinished bottle of vodka which lay nearby.

Before entering the building, I scanned it thoroughly to find the safest route.

I entered to sounds of merriment: laughter, voices, and the tinkle of glasses coming from rickety doors throughout the whole building, in celebration of today's successful sortie. What surprised me was the absence of female voices, which suggested nastiness was afoot. Either they killed their women, or this building was not their main headquarters, but more like a warehouse.

The first loser to exit a room and head for the bathroom got unlucky. I stabbed my dagger into his heart and, gagging him with my hand, dragged him back into his room. The dorm was completely different to ours, with two communal bathrooms and everything absolutely filthy. Also, it was difficult to walk stealthily because the floor squeaked and seemed it might give way at any moment.

You have killed a survivor.

The capacity of your inventory is increased by 8kg.

I took this guy's weapons too, and also discovered at least a hundred rounds. If the one single bed was anything to go by, he probably lived alone. I wanted to leave the gang a gift in the form of a grenade-loaded trip wire, but unfortunately I didn't know how to set one up, and I didn't especially want to learn. Why would I, when I had half a dorm's worth of specialists trained in precisely such operations?

I found the armory on the second floor, housed in a separate enormous apartment, which was fantastic. On the way to it, I killed another two drunk fuckers who had come out of their apartment for a smoke. This resulted in new notifications.

You have killed a survivor.

The capacity of your inventory is

increased by 5kg.

You have killed a survivor.

The capacity of your inventory is increased by 1kg.

I wasted more time when another two idiots decided to have a scrap in the corridor. I was forced to wait until they'd punched each other's faces, shaken hands and embraced, and returned to their debauchery.

As I closed the armory door behind me, I could not believe how easy it had been to find it. They didn't even lock the door with a key or post guards by the door. I understood the need to be able to hand out weapons as quickly as possible in the case of a zombie attack, but even so. If one of these idiots felt the urge, in a drunken stupor, to wipe out all his dorm-mates, getting his hands on whatever took his fancy would be a cinch.

The first things into my inventory were a crate of hand grenades and another of rocket-propelled ones. I could not have them being launched at people. Following these went two dozen pistols and ten Kalashnikov assault rifles, and the remaining spare space I filled up with as many bullets as would squeeze in. I had thought to put a serious dent in their reserves, but this was not even a half, which was a great shame.

There was obviously the option of blowing up the building, but that also involved the chance of blowing myself up along with it. Had Fedya been there, he would have mined the whole building by himself, whereas all I could do was kill people individually. I mean, of course I could try to kill them all myself, but in a narrow corridor a bow would certainly lose out to a machine gun. Or at least it would so far.

While I was contemplating how to proceed, I glanced through the other rooms. On the second floor was a communal kitchen where they cooked their food. It contained three stoves, and a table at which currently sat five men playing cards, two of them chefs, judging by their dirty aprons. I decided to try taking them quietly one by one, and so I selected the best-hidden corner of the corridor and hunkered down there, waiting quietly for them to finish their game and for one of them to need to visit the bathroom.

Meanwhile, I overheard snippets of their conversation.

"The next watch'll be along soon, then we can chill. Jack! I win!" shouted one of the men before doing a jig of joy.

"Fuck," swore his opponent. "Wait here, I'm gonna take a piss, then I'm gonna even the score. Don't touch anything while I'm gone."

And so appeared my client. He stepped out into the corridor, cursing, and plodded off towards the bathroom. A colorful character, arms heavily tattooed, he wore old sweatpants, and a bulletproof vest on his otherwise naked torso. He died cock in hand, and fell face first into the toilet.

You have killed a survivor.

The capacity of your inventory is increased by 4 kg.

There was no point in hiding the body, for he had smeared the wall with his blood, and even without the corpse, any fool would realize someone had been killed. Still, not to worry, I was monitoring the entrance and would have the next candidate in my sights.

The next candidate did not keep me waiting long. After ten minutes, the senior men sent a scout to check where their comrade had gotten to. The kid looked about eighteen, and was lean and bald and missing two front teeth. He looked like a rat. He did not immediately carry out his orders, but first ran to the food store and snaffled several tins of food and a whole baloney, shoving them into his inventory. He tried not to make any noise as he worked, and when he left, he looked shiftily up and down the corridor. He would not, however, escape his destiny. I shot him just a meter from the first guy, as soon he'd opened the door and seen the corpse.

You have killed a survivor.

The capacity of your inventory is increased by 3kg.

The system gave me three kilograms for him, which meant he had previously killed people. I dragged his body into the cubicle where the other one lay, closed the door, and returned to my position.

The rest of the guys in the kitchen were now cussing to high hell. Two players were missing, without whom they could not begin a new game, or so their shouts had me think. This continued for twenty minutes as we all waited for one of them to get bored enough to go in search of the lost men. Then destiny shined on me.

One of the men expounded a theory: "Lads, d'you think that bitch went to the storeroom to fill his face? He's been gone too long. He didn't bother looking for Borislav, I tell you, he's eating."

"Why don't you go take a look?" one of the other two suggested to the theorist.

"Yeah, sure. If I catch him red-handed, I'll throw the motherfucker to the zombies, I swear," he said with a scowl.

This time I dragged the corpse to the food store, which was of course a risk and would have to be done quickly.

You have killed a survivor.

The capacity of your inventory is increased by 6kg.

A whole six kilograms. Wow, not half bad. At this rate I'd soon be able to load up my inventory even more. I even entertained the thought of sprinting to the armory to gather more ammunition, but then reconsidered. Too little time.

I went back to the kitchen to keep an eye on the remaining two men as they drank beer and chatted in expectation of their comrades' return. I noted it was the two chefs who had stayed in the kitchen, and behind them, on a rolling boil in large pans, was a brew for the inhabitants of the building.

I got bored of waiting for them to leave. They

might become really suspicious and raise the alarm by walkie-talkie, and then I'd be compelled to leap into action. Edging the door open with a foot, I put an arrow in each of them, the first finding its intended target, but the second going marginally astray and entering the second chef's neck. He grabbed at his neck and his mouth gaped in shock, but he couldn't cry out, too loud the bubbling of blood and bloody foam. Yet the man would not die and he reached for a gun lying on the table. I could not allow that, so I finished him off.

You have killed a survivor.

The capacity of your inventory is increased by 3kg.

You have killed a survivor.

The capacity of your inventory is increased by 5kg.

Dropping by to visit had been an excellent notion.

CHAPTER 18

AFTER KILLING THE LAST of the kitchen dwellers, I quietly closed the door so that nobody would interrupt me. There was no point scouring the entire kitchen, for I had already picked out the things I needed. While waiting in ambush, I had hatched a plan to take revenge on these creeps for their attack. They had no right to encroach on my territory, and they needed punishing for it.

Just in case, I quickly examined the whole building again and found nothing suspicious. From the top shelf of a cupboard I took a pile of tea towels and tablecloths. I threw them into the sink, soaked them, and wrung them until they were lightly damp. Then I removed everything from the stovetop and switched on the gas rings, before carefully laying the damp cloths on top in such a way as not to extinguish the flames.

It was no doubt a bizarre way to exact

revenge, but it was all I could do. Had Fedya been there, he would have mined the whole building a second time. The flames still burned, which was good, and the material began to smolder. I had five minutes, no more, since the building was wooden and very old, and I was hoping that when the towels caught fire, the house would burst into flames like a match being struck. I figured no fire-fighting zombies would come running in response to the alarm call. For greater effect, I placed several boxes of bullets on top of the wet rags, which would hinder the timely quenching of the fire by exploding and making people scared to approach.

Done with my business in the kitchen, I could now leave. A stink of burning rags was rising, accompanied by smoke, and I did not want to be in the building when the bullets exploded. I exited by the main entrance, which was guarded by two men. Only they weren't guarding it, but snoring loudly, so I approached at a relaxed pace and shot them at point-blank range, not remotely concerned about nappers being shot. They had only themselves to blame. The door was locked with a massive dead bolt that had clearly been applied after the beginning of the apocalypse. I raised it, opened the door wide, and emerged onto the street. Then I climbed up onto the defensive wall constructed of cars, settled myself comfortably on the roof of a blue sedan, and feasted my eyes on the fussings of the people in the building.

Shouting orders, their leader was among the

first to run to the kitchen, where he immediately wanted to put out the fire, but just then the bullets began to explode one after another and fly off in all directions. Frightened people ran from the kitchen; my plan had worked. The situation quieted down and the explosions ceased, but the kitchen was engulfed in greedy flames. Everything had gone to plan. Wicked.

You have killed a survivor.

The capacity of your inventory is increased by 4kg.

You have killed a survivor.

The capacity of your inventory is increased by 6kg.

This time the system reacted slightly tardily to tell me about my trophies for the killing of the two guardsmen. I wondered for a moment whether they hadn't died slowly, but no, there was no way they could have survived without a super skill, and the system must have decided not to interrupt me while I was busy. It had happened before that the system did not reward me immediately.

The dead sentries were eventually discovered and it now occurred to people that they'd been visited by an interloper, and the wide-open door was a sure sign I had escaped through it. The leader was shouting and gesticulating towards the door. Excellent, the fish had taken the bait, and all I had to do was wait for them to chase after me.

Ten people exited the building and began combing the territory in search of me, figuring I couldn't have gone far since there were crowds of zombies on the other side of the barricades. Five arrows, five men down, inventory up by 17 kg. The remaining five made themselves easy targets in the dark by splitting up to look for me separately.

I could not hang around any longer, however, because they soon found the bodies of their comrades outside and began firing willy-nilly. They might easily have popped a cap in me. In one enormous leap I flew over the flocking zombies, before somersaulting along the ground and rising to my feet.

I had today taken revenge on the gang and reaped a pretty good harvest, expanding my inventory in the process. Staying to live with the soldiers was probably not such a bad idea after all. Thanks to them, I would have no problem finding adversaries, and by leveling up I would become stronger and stronger with every day. And, which was most important, my conscience was absolutely clear. Those bastards attacked us first and all I did was retaliate. The only downer was not having killed all of them. But who was to say I would be leaving them in peace now?

I didn't want to rush anything today, for I was still not exactly a standard fighter. I could not openly go up against a crowd, and these people weren't so stupid as to impassively allow themselves to be shot. Which was to say nothing of the survivors' skills that might be capable of producing unpleasant surprises.

Taking one last look back at the smoking building, I lobbed two grenades at the barricade to clear a path for the zombies. It was lucky that pulling the pins did not take too much brainwork, and after the two powerful explosions, I took to my heels. The explosions stirred the zombies, many more now joining them from neighboring streets, and they rushed through the new opening towards the building.

Those fuckers were in for a rough time. It was far from certain they would be able to save their dwelling as it was, and now they had zombies to cope with. The ones that had made it into the building would need clearing out, and that would be no walk in the park.

It was dusk when I got back to the dorm, and my phone displaying so many missed calls and messages was not a welcome sight. Out on maneuvers, I'd put it in my inventory so it wouldn't disturb me, and no sooner had I retrieved it than messages began to ping up thick and fast. Unsurprisingly, there was no coverage inside an inventory.

"I don't want to reply now while there's still one more matter to attend to," I said to myself as I put the phone in my pocket. The throng of zombies around the door had thinned somewhat, but not totally. I desperately wanted to sleep, but first I needed to wash off the sweat, dirt, and dried strangers' blood I was caked in. I took out my bow, activated invisibility, and cleared the vicinity of the remaining zombies.

Once or twice I pulled back the bowstring so hard that the arrow pierced two bodies, but this was the only thing of interest in an otherwise monotonous and robotic bout of arrow flinging. At the same time, however, I did get my second wind from the joy that archery afforded me. I killed, I gathered trophies; I killed, I gathered trophies; and so on until I was nearly out of arrows. I only stopped firing when I came across a yellow trinket casket. *I wonder what surprise awaits me this time?* Not wanting to delay the moment for a single second, I instantly gave the mental order for it to open.

You receive: a skill book: blink, level 2.

At first I was disappointed. What the hell was blink? And how could it possibly help? I'd never even heard of it before, so how could I know what it might be?

Evaluation.

Skill: blink, level 2.

This skill allows teleportation to a distance of 15 meters. You can only teleport upon visual contact, i.e. if you cannot directly see your potential destination, you cannot teleport there. Blink does not work through walls.

Important note: blink uses its bearer's internal energy and will not work when that energy is depleted. The higher the skill level, the less energy it uses.

Important note: learn to sense your internal energy and spend it wisely.

Important note: the volume of your internal energy cannot be increased at this

level of evolution. Until level 30, your energy reserves grow only when you level up.

Attention: for these three hints, the system confiscates three blue trinket boxes.

Forgive me, dear system, for doubting you. And forgive me also, respected skill, for disrespecting you. And while I'm at it, forgive me, my dear precious, for dropping you, in my shock. This last appeal was to my bow, which had fallen from my hands when I was reading a system notification.

I studied blink there and then and felt my knees trembling with worry. This is probably how girls feel when they're about to be proposed to, although it's probably sacrilegious to draw a comparison between two such different things. My blink was a hundredfold better than any, even royal, offer of marriage. Never mind being asked for my hand; I wouldn't balk at giving away a heart for a skill like that. Although not my heart, obviously. Someone else's. Those were ten a penny.

The system may have relieved me of fact boxes in exchange for full disclosure concerning the skill, but I still had two facts in reserve, which I would definitely use, although later, and at home. That said, I did not understand fully the thing with internal energy, and I would gladly have traded another box for more detail.

I raised my head to the sky.

"System, how about a swap? I give you another trinket box, you tell me about energy.

What do you say?" I asked, putting out a feeler.

As expected, nothing happened. Never mind, it wasn't the end of the world, for now I had blink, and the instructions for it were elementary. I activated it and was instantly teleported to a second-floor balcony. I wasn't even sure how to describe what happened: a momentary teleportation or a tear in space. *I was just there, and now I'm here, yet I feel nothing out of the ordinary, but for a light fatigue. If that is energy, and fatigue is a consequence of it, then no worries, I'm all for it.* According to how I felt, I figured I could easily blink another ten times. The main thing was not to zone out at the most inopportune moment.

Standing on the balcony, I started on the zombies I hadn't been able to shoot from below. In the front few rows I saw some dangerous-looking beasties: jumpers and shooters, very nasty adversaries which had to die first.

The balcony afforded me an excellent view of the whole yard, and I noted that the quantity of zombie corpses had grown significantly since yesterday. At long last the soldiers had decided to fight back. Good lads. About time too!

I began jumping from balcony to balcony using blink, my reduction of the zombie headcount more productive now as I continued to shoot the deadmen from ever newer positions. And how convenient the gathering of trophies now was! After laying waste to a couple of dozen zombies, I would jump down using blink, collect my prizes in one fell swoop, and jump back up. Prior to this, the difficulty had been the zombies padding around by the trophies while I was on the ground, but now I could kill them first, before collecting my rewards.

* * *

The clock said 10 AM and I stank like a mofo. I'd run out of arrows a couple of hours ago and been compelled to take up my sword. Unable, unwilling even, to leave them down there, I descended to the yard, which was now sparsely populated with zombies, although fresh faces were likely to show themselves while I was gathering my arrows.

With the aid of blink, it took me approximately an hour to finish them all off, and now, hopefully, there remained only the ones inside. Leaning back against the wall, I looked wearily down to see mountains of corpses lying everywhere, clusters of flies circling above them. The stench from the decaying bodies was rank, and something had to be done otherwise there would soon be no fresh air to breathe in the dormitory. If they weren't removed in the near future, an epidemic would break out, and that was the last thing we needed, what with all our other woes. I realized that with increased level came improved immunity. But not everyone was at my level.

After a brief rest on the balcony, I blinked down and entered the dorm. It took me another hour to clear the remaining zombies, which I did using old arrows plucked from the corpses littering the place. As a bonus, I was lucky enough to collect a bunch of boxes and caskets that had dropped during the night. It was odd nobody else had claimed them. They weren't afraid to touch my goodies, were they? Perhaps they just hadn't gotten this far?

As I approached the stairs leading up to the second floor, I saw they were blocked with piles of dead bodies. The soldiers had not sat idle in my absence. One corpse had a sharpened stool leg protruding from its eye. I stood there blankly for five minutes until I realized what I wanted to do. Fatigue and sleep deprivation really did have a terrible effect on the mind, and I just zonked out, like a zombie, and stared into space.

Upon deactivating invisibility, so as not to scare people, I was spotted immediately. Faces told me I'd done the wrong thing, looking at me with fear in their eyes. The women stepped hastily away, while the men reached for their weapons. They didn't know whether I was human or zombie, but they did not hurry to attack, and I had to thank them for that. I do not like such focused attention on me, and this was way too much. Hesitant to attack, they eyed me as I walked past, but just as I got to the bottom of the stairs, Shatun shouted out to me.

"Bro!" said the man in delight as he looked me in the eye. "I was sure, I knew you'd do it." It seemed he intended to embrace me, but then he wrinkled his nose and sprang back. "Sorry, let's not hug, you don't smell too good, you'd better go take a shower. And a visit to the doctor wouldn't harm you, you look like shit."

"I've got to see Combat first," I managed to squeeze out through my exhaustion. Despite his good mood, Shatun also looked pretty wretched.

"Let's walk, it's on my way."

Folks continued to stare at me, and I wanted to use blink to make myself scarce. There was a meeting underway in Combat's office, attendees including Clubfoot, Quartermaster, and Fedya.

"Fedya, we have to urgently close up the hole in the wall. Those beasts might attack again, we can't even get out of the building, and we..."

Combat didn't finish. His words became stuck in his throat as his gaze landed on me entering the room. The claw marks on my armor, in fact my whole appearance, told everyone I had given my all last night.

"Varg," said Combat, shocked.

"In the flesh," I replied, before plunking myself down on an empty chair without waiting for an invitation. "Can I have some tea? Plenty of sugar."

"Fedya." This one word from Combat was enough to make Fedya leap to it without even arguing.

"Varg, are you okay, are you wounded?"

I didn't immediately catch what he said. My consciousness kept trying to switch off, and only by employing incredible willpower was I able to maintain a grip on myself.

"I can't be sure, but I don't think I'm

wounded. I spent too much strength. It was a very difficult night." Everyone saw my struggle to squeeze the words out, but one look at me couldn't fail to have made it clear I'd been in the wars.

"Yes, we had a rough night as well. My guys haven't had a wink of sleep, and we're still expecting a repeat attack," said Combat. We managed to give them a few rounds each, but we've got nothing left. We got lucky and picked up a couple of red boxes of bullets by the stairs."

"They won't attack for a while yet," I said, to appease them, so they wouldn't panic for no reason. "Go down and clear all those corpses away instead. And patch the up hole while you're at it," I said with a yawn.

"How do you know they won't attack?" Quartermaster asked, beating Combat to it with the question on everyone's lips. "And about the hole in the wall, we'd be only too pleased to fix it, but the zombies won't leave us alone."

I liked Quartermaster. As a person. He spoke infrequently, but when he did it was to the point. He was also fanatically dedicated to his duties, spending all his time in the storeroom dealing with our reserves.

My eyes were becoming heavier and heavier with sleep, yet sleep was not on the cards just yet.

I stood up and approached Quartermaster.

"Tell me, do you believe in miracles?" I asked, leaning on a table with my hands and looking him straight in the eye.

He frowned. What was this nonsense I was

talking? Never mind, just play by the rules.

"If miracles can help us get out of this shitty situation, I'm prepared to put my faith in a can of stewed meat," he snickered.

"Well in that case..." I said, emptying my inventory of all the munitions I'd stolen.

A grenade accidentally slipped from the table, and two people dived to catch it at once.

"Oops, sorry, I'm so beat," I said, making my excuses after spotting what had almost happened.

"Where did you get all that from?" Combat couldn't believe his eyes, and Quartermaster could only stare wide-eyed at the mountain of weaponry.

"Last night I paid a visit to those bastards who attacked us, and put a small dent in their numbers," I said, not wanting to conceal the truth. "And we need to decide quickly what to do with the rest of it. They've got a whole warehouse full of goodies like this."

A deathly silence hung in the office, so I figured I'd drop another surprise.

"I committed arson there as well. Then I threw two grenades and created an entranceway for the zombies to access the building, so it's all shit and giggles there right now. Plus I cleared almost all the zombies from outside the dorm, and the few that are left will be no sweat for you to deal with."

Quartermaster hiccupped.

Combat rubbed his tired eyes. I couldn't do that, for fear of rubbing today's dirt into them.

Combat stood up and held out a hand to me.

"Varg, I don't even know what to say. You

saved us all today. This morning you bought us time to erect the barricades, and now, thanks to all this ammo, the snipers on the roof will not miss any attempted incursions," he said, sincere gratitude in his voice. "If you need help with anything at all, just say the word and we'll do what we can."

It was precisely the reply I would have expected from the man. He had accepted me, giving me to understand that he acknowledged my right to independence.

I took his hand. I liked this strong-willed fellow, who had taken such a crippling burden on his shoulders at this difficult time. I would not have been able to take command in the way he had, sending people on tasks in the knowledge that their death would be on my hands. I may have been indifferent to people's fates, but killing them indiscriminately was something I could not and would not do. It was probably all down to grandma. She had raised me alone and taught me much. Were it not for her, I would have become a real monster, and I now realized the energy it had cost her to instill me with just a drop of humanity and a minimum level of morality for life in society.

"Good," I said with a reserved nod, giving him to understand I'd heard him. "Now, if we're done with business, I'm off to get some sleep." With enormous difficulty I rose from my seat. It was going to be a struggle to get to my apartment without falling over on the way.

"Thanks again for all you've done. And there's

one more thing" — Combat smiled and paused — "Polina is waiting for you." I didn't have time to ask what he was talking about before he spoke again. "Fedya, take our hero home. He's so tired I'm afraid he might collapse in the corridor."

In one gulp I drank the tea Fedya had brought, paying no heed to how hot it was.

We walked in silence until people started goggling at me too openly and whispering to each other, at which point Fedya barked at them and they hastily made themselves scarce. He had a certain reputation, I noted.

"Here we are," he said as we reached the door of my apartment.

I made to enter, but he stopped me.

"Varg, I just wanted to thank you personally. What you did today as we retreated was very important. I apologize for my behavior in the first days of our acquaintance. I'm not used to trusting civilians. Ten years' service in hotspots, you understand."

"Forget about it, everything's fine." In my current state I would have forgiven a zombie.

"Take care then," he said, waving a parting hand.

The door was closed but not locked, and I entered without knocking. Polina was sitting at the table chatting with her girlfriends.

"Igo-o-or," she shouted, making my ears pop. "You're alive!"

The next instant, she came at me like a whirlwind and threw herself upon me. I was lost and didn't know what to do while she trembled and sniffled and sobbed and buried her face in my shoulder.

Apart from returning her embrace with one arm, I could not think of anything else to do.

"Everything's okay now," I said, giving the girl's back an awkward stroke. "Erm, I'm really dirty."

"That doesn't matter," she snuffled. "At least you're alive." Polina was not about to let me go.

We stood like that for half a minute before I was able to free myself from her clutches.

"Oh, you must be starving, look how pale you are," she lamented, wiping her tears to the smiles of the other ladies. "You run along and take a shower while I heat some food up."

My reaction to her was somehow different now, better than before. I was probably becoming used to her. Perhaps she really could help me get rid of my complexes? I must admit I was very glad of my decision to stay and live with her and her daughter. On top of which, today's gift from the system, in the form of the **blink** skill, had already made up for much. Perhaps this was karma recompensing for services rendered?

"Well, don't just stand there," said Polina, interrupting my philosophical musings. "Get in the shower, then come to the table."

"Yes, ma'am," I replied, raising a sluggish hand to my head in a military salute, before about turning and marching towards the bathroom.

Titters of amusement burst out behind me.

There you go, they're laughing at me again. Never mind, I won't say anything, I'm not the only one who had a difficult night.

"You're supposed to salute with your right hand," said the petite 38D brunette with a smile. Now I realized what had brought the smile to her face.

"What's the difference?" I could not see the difference.

"One fu—"

"Katya!" Polina snapped. "Stop messing with his head." Then she turned back to me and said, "Go already. Pay no attention, it's just silly army humor."

It may have been unusual, but it was also nice to have your own place to live and people waiting there for you.

CHAPTER 19

WHAT A PLEASURE IT WAS TO BE in the shower after a whole day running around. I spent nearly an hour luxuriating in jets of hot water. The dried blood did not wash off easily, and the dreadful smell only disappeared after my third soaping.

After eventually managing to make myself look half presentable, I remembered my armor, and although it was torn in places, I put it in the bath and covered it with water to soak. The sponge and loofah I had washed with were put in my inventory, with a view to throwing them away later since they were irreparably mangled.

Nothing had changed during my absence from the living room. I never understood, and I never will, how women contrive to prepare so much food in such a short time. It would take me about an hour to boil pasta, and if I was in the mood to make a salad, the whole meal would take about an hour and a half.

"Sit down and stop looking at us like that," said the brunette whom Polina had called Katya.

"Uh-huh," I muttered, and with a dumb nod approached the table.

The hot soup with its big chunks of meat smelled so flavorsome I could not help myself reaching for it with my fatigue-trembling hands.

"Let us help you." Polina obligingly offered her assistance.

"Thanks," I mumbled, mildly embarrassed. "My hands don't seem to be working."

"That's hardly surprising. The whole dorm's buzzing with tales of your heroic feats. We're soon going to have crowds of people at the door wanting to catch a glimpse of the hero," Katya sniggled.

"Yeah? Well, let them. Just so long as they don't give me any hassle. If they want to give or tell me anything, then it's via Polina." I did not want to speak to anyone.

Katya and Polina exchanged glances, then both stared at me with a strange expression on their faces. A look of gratitude? Or not? I couldn't tell.

I felt uncomfortable. I'd done nothing heroic, so what was all the thanks for? I lived here as well, so all I was doing was protecting my... my...? Wait, why was I thinking that? I was merely protecting my home, but I'd found it to be quite a lucrative business in terms of enhancing the capacity of my inventory. And I'd rounded up a week's worth of rewards, including three hundred white boxes. I was generally pretty pleased with everything.

Actually, that's a point, how much have I enhanced the capacity of my inventory by?

Status.

Name: Varg.

Level: 7.

Skills: invisibility, level 10; regeneration, level 2; evaluation, level 1; blink, level 2.

Inventory: 181 kg.

Now then, not bad at all!

At this rate I would soon be able to carry half a ton's worth in my inventory.

"How's the soup? Good?" Polina asked. "Eat up, don't be shy."

"I'm not shy. Why would I be shy?" I retorted, fixing my eyes on the bowl once again.

"Uh-huh, he's not shy," said Katya with a smile.

"That's enough, leave him alone, or I'll send you home," said Polina, looking sternly at her friend.

"You crosspatch," said Katya, taking umbrage. "But she's right, you eat up. Polly's cooking is simply divine, and she's wonderful too," she continued, turning to me.

Shoot, chicks, huh? Why were they so difficult?

"What are you doing here? Aren't there things to be getting on with after an attack like that?" I asked.

"Polina invited me round. It's dangerous downstairs and she said I could wait out the attack," Katya replied. "I mean, if you're not against the idea? It is your flat."

"Don't you worry about it. I really don't mind," I said, to appease her. "Polina's the boss around here, and she can invite round anybody she likes."

"Aren't you worried we might eat you out of house and home?" Katya asked.

Her question stumped me. I sat for a minute, blinking and not knowing how best to answer it. Then I succumbed and burst out laughing.

"Do you seriously think... hehe... I'm interested in food?" I had not laughed so genuinely in ages. "I killed a thousand zombies today. I don't care in the slightest about food."

"Pfft," exclaimed Katya and Polina in chorus. "And here was us thinking you'd gone mad after all that nastiness," Polina said with a chuckle.

After that, everything was pretty relaxed and informal. The girls chatted about various things, discussing news mixed in with gossip, and I listened, glad not to be dragged into their empty conversation.

Katya bemoaned the fact that she and her daughter had been kicked out of their apartment and moved into some utility closet. It was a familiar story, and I recalled Polina being evicted.

She hadn't kicked up a fuss, but their new residence was cold and damp and she was concerned her daughter shouldn't get sick. They didn't so much as glance at me as they were chatting, which suited me just fine.

"Level her up, then she won't get sick," I said,

before wondering why I'd interrupted their conversation with something so asinine.

"She's seven years old. Do you think she's capable of killing a zombie?" said Katya, her eyes displaying a mixture of irony and mild reproach. "Perhaps you know how a child might be able to kill a zombie safely?"

I'd bungled yet again, blurting without thinking. Why was I so smart and astute in the privacy of my own mind, but so dumb and blundering with other people? Anyway, it was too late now and I would have to think of something.

"I could give her a crossbow," I said with a shrug, as if to show I saw no problem in that. "I could find her some grenades too. They're dead easy, just pull the pin and throw." I said, messing with Katya now.

She set to thinking.

For fuck's sake, what are you thinking about, woman? It was just a stupid joke!

"Okay, I'll think about it," she said.

Our conversation was interrupted by a knock at the door.

Knock, knock, knock.

At the door stood a man.

"Come in," I said.

"Varg, our boys have just earned a bunch of trinket caskets with arrows, and Quartermaster sent me to give them to you," the man said, showing me the cards in his hand.

He did not enter the room. Perhaps he was afraid, or perhaps he clocked me staring at his dirty boots. Whatever the case, I approached him myself and took the cards. Then I returned to my seat at the table and continued to listen to the ladies' conversation.

Their chatter even allowed me to forget my fatigue. Though I didn't forget to continue stuffing my stomach with Polina's tasty treats. I had already realized food helped me regain lost strength. Perhaps it was a side effect of **regeneration**? And now **blink** on top of that!

I tuned back into the girls' conversation. Or the ladies' conversation? I didn't know what to call them. What if I offended them each time? It was definitely a problem of mine. Even thinking about it confused me. I had never known, and I still didn't know, how to address whom, and I consequently found myself in sticky situations.

"Katya, I'll give you some pasta and meat to take home for you and Anya," said Polina, snapping me out of my meditations.

"I'd be very grateful," Katya replied, blushing. "We haven't had a proper meal in two days. If it wasn't for you, I don't know what we'd have done. We're still waiting for provisions from the management."

For some reason they were both looking at me now, as though I would start shouting not to give anything to anybody. I had already told them I didn't care, and that food was merely a consumable. If cooking was how Polina earned a reputation in this community, then so be it. She was now in my team and also had to develop herself.

"Varg," said Katya, turning to me. "Are you sure that's not a problem? I don't want Polly to get into trouble on my account. You don't be shy, tell me what's what and I'll understand. Such times we live in. Nobody's even loaned me bread in the past two days. Everybody has a family to feed, everybody's afraid of instability, and nobody knows how long this siege of our walls is going to go on."

Jeez, how much more of this?

"Polina, does your friend think I'm going to hang myself over a crust of bread or something?" I took the direct approach. "Why is she looking at me so weirdly, when all we're talking about is food?"

"Igor," she began softly, "you just don't understand. People are starving and there's a catastrophic shortage of food, so everyone's trying to economize. She's concerned you might think she only dropped by because of food. Katya's not like that. We've been friends for ages."

Hmm, like that, is it?

"This is for you, Katya," I said, throwing ten boxes of food down on the table. "And don't look so plaintively at me."

It meant absolutely nothing to me, absolutely nothing to worry about.

"By the way, Polina, what's our food situation like? Do we have much left?"

Polina lowered her gaze to the floor and was clearly in no hurry to answer my question.

"Pol?"

"Sorry, there's almost nothing left," she replied guiltily. "It's the children. I shared some food with them a couple of times."

It seemed she was about to burst into tears, and I felt even worse now. It wasn't much fun to see her in that state, especially over something so trivial.

Remembering my childhood, when we lived and fed ourselves on grandma's pension alone, I understood very well that children should not go hungry.

"Calm down, I told you I don't mind. Take this," I said, pulling thirty boxes from my inventory and putting them on the table. "If you want to feed the kids, go ahead, it's no problem."

I approached her slowly, lifted her chin up, and looked into her eyes, saying, "Just don't forget people are base and ungrateful creatures. Today you give them a crust of bread, tomorrow they rock up demanding to be fed. And know this: if anything should happen and anyone does us any harm, I'll kill them all without a twinge of conscience, so before you go helping people, have a good think about who they are and what problems might arise as a consequence."

I knew what I was talking about. I'd been different before, but then I realized humankind was no peak of evolution, more like a parasite, able to adapt and live at the expense of others while destroying all the goodness it comes into contact with.

"Excuse me, but not all people are like that." The comment was spoken softly and from behind my back.

I knew not everybody was like that, for I did occasionally come across the odd normal person, but they were few and far between.

In my mind the words conjured a scene from long ago, when grandma was still alive. One day I'd announced to her that when I grew up I would take revenge on all bad people. How I remember her kind eyes, which just then reflected sadness as she said to me, "How will you be any different to them, then, little Igor?"

"Perhaps not all, but I have come across, and continue to do so, my fair share," I said with a shrug, rising and heading for the bedroom. "I want to say one more thing. Everyone who's tried to harm me in this new world, most of them have been dead."

"How big is your inventory then?" asked Katya, changing the subject. They had all heard about how to increase your inventory, and the girls were very curious.

"Are you sure you want to know?" If I told them that, they might think a murderer and psychopath was living among them.

"More than twenty?" was Katya's guess.

I thought for a second before replying, "more than a hundred." Then I disappeared into the bedroom, leaving them to digest the information. It wasn't exactly classified information, but they needed to understand who they were dealing with.

Climbing into bed, I listened to their reaction, interested in whether they would stay and talk about me or leave and talk about me. It would certainly not be nice if Polina did that, but if she was going to, now was better than later.

They surprised me.

"You've got yourself a keeper there," came Katya's rhapsodic voice.

What are they talking about?

I didn't hear any more. I fell asleep. Before my head hit the pillow.

"Hi, how are you? Everything okay? You're awake, yes? Are you rested? Am I disturbing you?" Upon opening my eyes, I saw a cute and curious face looking down on me.

"Liza, leave him alone, he's asleep." Polina intervened on my behalf.

"He's not asleep," replied the girl quickly, "his eyes are open and he's looking at me."

"Aaagh, can I go on a raid again today?" I groaned in desperation. "Zombies aren't this tortuous."

"You see, mom, he's not asleep, and that means I'm not disturbing him. Are you going to play with me? Draw with me? Can you read me a story? Can we go for a walk?" Her questions were relentless.

"Can I have some poison?"

"Nope, then I'll get bored. Yesterday you asked me to wake you up. You said you had a lot of important things to do," Liza said, reminding me I had plans.

I had slept, apparently, until midday, so Liza had decided it was high time to wake me up.

Such an awakening did not exactly help to get me out of bed on the right side, which I announced to everyone present in the form of a variety of cuss words uttered beneath my breath. Although in truth what upset me most was that I'd slept for so long.

The situation changed dramatically, however, just as soon I clapped eyes on the spread on the living-room table. I got the sneaking suspicion Polina was planning to properly fatten me up. The table creaked beneath the weight of the food, which would easily have gone around five people, yet there were just the three of us. And Liza was a child and probably didn't eat much.

"Fried fish?" I asked, unable to believe my eyes. "I haven't eaten fish in so long I never thought I would again."

There was no fresh fish to be found in the shops, and I certainly wasn't going to go fishing in the river.

"Uh-huh," said Polina, beaming at my astonishment. "Two of the boxes you gave me yesterday had live fish in them."

"Cool," I said, not standing on ceremony but immediately forking two pieces onto my plate along with some fragrant herby rice.

There was only one word for her cooking: heavenly.

Whenever I thought, *what am I doing here?* or *it's time to do a runner*, I would try some of her cooking and immediately understand I did not want to leave.

"How did you sleep? Do you feel better?" Polina inquired after my health at the table.

"Much better, thank you." I wasn't used to others caring about me. "I was just really exhausted yesterday after running to and fro all day. I'm going out again today to give those fuckers a hard time."

Her expression turned to alarm. "Maybe you shouldn't go anywhere today? You looked really bad yesterday, like a revenant. You should rest today and build your strength up."

You see, I wasn't the sort to take orders. Yet in a way she was right. I had nigh checked out yesterday; too much going on. Added to which, I had no armor anymore, and I was almost out of arrows. *Perhaps it's worth using another trading coin to buy the necessary consumables? Come to think of it, that armor saved my life yesterday. The system promised my body would become stronger, but there was no guarantee beastie's claws wouldn't have gotten through to my skin.*

"I'll think about it," I replied, and continued chowing down.

After breakfast I needed another rest. I had overeaten, and yesterday was probably still catching up on me.

As I lay on the sofa in the living room, I noticed something interesting. Within the space of an hour, Polina walked past me in two different outfits.

I wondered if she was doing it for me or she just liked to dress beautifully, unlike me, without my own clothes, only the hand-me-downs she'd given me. It was time to revitalize my meager wardrobe. The zombie blood would never wash out, it would leave stains.

I don't remember falling asleep again, but I did hear a loud knock at the door through the haze of my slumber.

When I awoke I looked straight at the apartment door, where a small girl was crying and hammering furiously on the door with her skinny hands.

My heart jumped. Had they broken through? Somebody died? What could possibly have happened that they'd sent a child to fetch me?

"What happened?" I asked of the girl on opening the door.

"Anya, what happened? Has something happened to your mom?" Polina repeated my questions, having recognized the child as Katya's daughter.

"There's a man hurting mommy," the girl said through her tears.

I felt ill at ease. Basically it wasn't my problem, and she was a child so she may have misunderstood the situation. That said, if the dorm had developed a louse, it required punishing. I didn't want to intrude upon others' business, but the matter was decided by Polina's beseeching look and the pistol she was now holding. I wondered how far she would go now she had a weapon in her hands.

While she was getting ready, I decided I would go check and what was actually happening.

"Are you coming?" I ask Polina. She nodded in reply.

Polina took the child in her arms, and we ran. Was it me on level 7 or Polina? How the hell could she run as fast as me? She kept up with me right from the very start.

We ran down to the third floor, where at the end of the corridor were a couple of utility closets.

"I said you're gonna be mine whether you like it or not. I don't care, get it?" These were the first words I heard, and they were enough for the speaker to have signed himself a death warrant. I hated people like that.

"Go home to your wife, you jerkoff, and stop saying that," Katya shouted at the man.

"You bitch, you made your own choice, now strip, and quick."

Slap. Just as we were approaching the wide-open door and could see what was happening inside, we heard the sound of a face being slapped.

A bald man of about forty, with a large round belly, held the girl's arm with one hand while slapping her again with the other.

Frankly, it was a shocking picture. Even more so for my seeing something I shouldn't have been seeing, which was Katya's beautiful figure dressed only in a transparent nightie.

WTF? How had someone like this been able to worm his way in among the soldiers? Perhaps the system had had this effect on him? After all, it had changed me. Not that much, mind.

"Dmitri, have you totally lost it?" screeched Polina in her shock.

"Ah, you're here as well. Come on in, I promise you won't regret it," said the man as he looked at my Polina with a repulsive leer.

At that moment, I didn't notice myself thinking of her as mine. I was trying to keep my cool so as not to go mental and kill him in front of the child.

Just then Katya's daughter wriggled out of Polina's arms and ran to the man.

"Don't touch my mommy," she cried, trying to unclench the hand he was gripping her with.

"Get lost, squirt! Don't worry, I'm gonna be your new Papa and I'll teach you some manners," he said, waving away the annoying little girl so hard that she smashed into the wall and crashed to the floor. "I'll teach you to interrupt, you piece of trash."

That was the last straw.

A wave of anger washed over me, yet with it came a surprising calm. I slowly approached the man.

"Any last words, Dmitri?" I asked in with a smile.

"Who the fuck are you?" he asked, now having the grace to turn his attentions on me.

"Varg."

"Varg. The name rings a bell. Ah, that's it, you're Polina's fella," he speculated with a smile.

"Now, Varg, feel free to fuck off, get it?" And he burst into a fit of cocky laughter.

"As you wish." I shrugged my shoulders, used blink to come right up close to him, and sliced off the hand with which he'd struck the child.

"Huh?" he managed, looking in bafflement at his new stump.

"F..." I teased. "You're fucked, my friend."

Level 3. Well I never, loverboy. For five minutes I tenderized him like a steak, paying no heed to the gathering crowd. I did not put too much into the strikes, however, not wanting to kill him too early. I pummeled him to unconsciousness, deriving a colossal amount of enjoyment from the process.

The throng of people in the corridor grew and grew, but I was not about to explain anything to anyone, nor justify my actions. Polina did that, and in the event that somebody might not be satisfied, I could not have cared less.

With one hand I grabbed the man by the scruff of the neck and dragged him along the corridor towards the stairs.

On the way down I bumped into Combat, who was catching his breath after a quick sprint upstairs. Our eyes met, he looked at my prisoner, said nothing, and let me past.

The whole dormitory would probably be scared of me after this, but I didn't care. He'd done something he shouldn't have, and such people were fair game to me.

"Open," I said calmly to the two sentries

318

posted by the main entrance.

The soldiers exchanged glances, unsure of what to do, but did not reach for their weapons. Instead they obeyed and opened the door.

I dragged the man out towards the zombies. Bumping down the steps brought him to his senses, and he now tried feverishly to break away. When they saw us, the zombies standing fifty yards from the dorm ambled limpingly over to us.

"No. N-o-o-o!" the man shouted. Before being eaten alive.

There was no way he was getting out of it. I waited until there was nearly nothing left of him, and only then did I shoot the zombies.

Reentering the vestibule of the dormitory, I was met by a whole delegation.

"You know why, yes?" I asked Combat, who was waiting for me by the door.

"I do." He nodded, his angry hands clenched into fists.

"Any questions?"

"No. He was a scumbag. It won't happen again. Anyone does anything like that again, I'll shoot them myself. If it weren't for you, I'd have killed him."

"So that means I deprived you of that particular pleasure," I said with a weak smile. "I hope after today everyone understands what will happen to anyone who thinks they're higher than others and have pretensions towards what is mine. And another thing, I hate rapists. Tell that to all your people. If anyone tries to repeat what he did, I'll repeat what I did. Although next time I might think of a more sophisticated means of doing it."

Combat thought.

"I assure you nothing like that will happen again," he said. I wanted to believe him. "How are you, anyway? Don't want to kill anyone else?" It was hard to say whether it was a genuine question or a joke, but the people standing around tensed a tad.

"Don't you worry, I'm not a psycho, I just don't like rapists," I said, attempting an embarrassed smile, which came out as a scowl. "And another thing, don't hold your weapons so tightly, fighters. If I wanted to kill you, you'd already be dead."

"You think so?" a young show-off buffoon said with a chuckle.

He didn't have time to close his mouth before I was behind his back and holding an arrow shaft to his carotid artery. I figured this was better than a knife, otherwise those present would get even more worked up. I didn't want to start killing them when I was just beginning to get used to them and their home.

The spectacle made Combat break out in a coughing fit. "What was that? A new skill?" he asked.

"Uh-huh. Kill more zombies and you too will know this ability," I replied.

I returned to the apartment to see the rescued Katya sitting with the children. Polina was feeding her hot tea to calm her down, and the children were feasting on candies.

"Igor." Seeing me in the doorway, Polina threw her arms around my neck again, just like yesterday. "Thank you," she whispered into my ear, before returning to her friend.

"Thank you," Katya said awkwardly.

"Uh-huh, thank you," her daughter said, tearing herself away from her candy.

"And thank you from me also," Liza said, running up and embracing me.

So much attention. Once again I froze, but this time it was nice.

"It would appear we've broken him," Katya said, breaking out in a smile.

"It happens." Polina looked at me and also smiled, foxlike.

CHAPTER 20

FOR THE SAKE OF DECENCY, and tea and biscuits, I was compelled to join them at the table and pretend to be interested. It was indeed boring to listen to their chat to begin with, but then everything changed.

As it transpired, at the last meeting, Combat had introduced an emergency harem regime. There were plenty of women and children in the dorm, but very few men. So, they had concocted a situation whereby a man could take a second wife if he so desired, along with her children of course, if she had any. The only rule was that it had to be by mutual consent, no coercion.

In his joy at the situation, one man had lost the plot, deciding he was an Arab sheik and figuring he would live life in the dormitory as he pleased. How mistaken he'd been. He got very unlucky.

"It's a good job you killed him. He was a real asshole," said Katya, bloodthirstily but nonetheless cringing at the unpleasant recollection. "He was always following me, suggesting I become his lover. And all he ever did was drink, exchanging food boxes for vodka. His wife and son went hungry, and they were always covered in bruises after his beatings. The other men explained to him several times that it was no way to behave, but he didn't give a monkey's. Mind you, this was the first time he crossed the line. He seemed a regular guy before all this madness began, but then it was like he'd been swapped out. He started bemoaning the futility of our resistance all the time and claiming that taking care of civilians was a pointless waste of resources."

"How did Combat not notice it?" I wondered.

"He wasn't one of us. He used to live not far away, but when everything kicked off, he came running here with his family. He was immediately sent out on a zombie clearance with the other men, and evidently his sense of his own importance went to his head."

"I'm very grateful for your help." Katya said sincerely.

"Any time. If anything happens, I'm here to help," I replied.

"Like right now?" she asked, narrowing her eyes.

"Try me," I said with a shrug.

"Better let me try," Polina interrupted.

Something about the way they looked put me

on my guard. What were they plotting? Shoot, I had to get out of there. But how? The window? Boarded up. The door? Too long. Ah, man, how could I possibly leave a place where I was so well fed?

"Well? What are you planning?" I said, sighing a heavy sigh of resignation.

"Igor, can Katya and Anya live with us?" Polina asked to my surprise. "You saw the conditions they have to live in. There's no heating there and Anya's already coughing. And all sorts of weirdos keep showing up, thinking that since she lives alone, she either has to beg for food or spread her legs." These last words she whispered because of the children in the room.

Frankly, she'd surprised me again.

"If you let them live with us, I'll be able to play with my friend every day and I won't bug you so much," Liza added with a smile.

A fairly weighty argument. And two pairs of hands were better than one.

"Fine, I'm not against the idea. I'd even go so far as to say I don't care. I told you ages ago to do what you want," I said with another sigh, of relief this time.

I thought it was going to be worse for my psyche, but it turned out to be no big deal at all.

"Thank you," they all said in unison.

"Don't think I'm a sponger," Katya jabbered, cheering up in a wink. "If there are problems with food, we can go hungry, and I'll help Polly with the housework. You can't even imagine how much work Polina does by herself."

I could very well imagine it, actually. Previously, I'd had to do my own housework, and I didn't like it.

It sounded logical, for I had seen Polina elbow-deep in housework many times. She was forever cleaning the flat, washing something, cooking, or tending to her child, who also demanded her care.

"I can spare food, so eat as much as you can. Just don't go pop," I quipped.

For some strange reason, goosebumps were running up and down my back. There seemed to be no danger in the vicinity, except the four pairs of eyes looking at me in adoration.

I hoped I wouldn't regret my decision.

It was decided that Katya and Anya would be given the second bedroom, currently empty.

Thinking about my new roommate, it occurred to me that everything had happened somehow too quickly. I had actually been planning to hire a couple of girls to do the housework, but not just yet.

When I tired of sitting with them, I went for a stroll around the dorm, thinking I might pop in for a chat with Combat. The only person I found was Shatun. He clapped me on the shoulder and congratulated me, saying he would have done the same in that situation. He also inquired whether I wasn't being tortured by my conscience, before letting on that he'd also been forced to kill fairly frequently, so if I ever needed a heart to heart, he was always ready to listen and dispense sound advice.

Ah, if only he knew just how many I've killed. And without the slightest regret. When it comes to douchebags like that, my conscience is spotlessly clear.

While I was thinking what to do now, I received a message from Combat asking me to drop by his office when I had a moment. So that's exactly what I did. He was sitting alone in his office, pouring over some papers. After a short nod, he cut to the chase and asked me to escort a group of soldiers to the hardware store in the city. There were practically no zombies left anywhere near the dorm, which provided the opportunity to go and appropriate the building materials everyone needed. It was not a demand, merely a friendly request he knew I would not refuse.

I agreed without hesitation. I was still too weak to go on a solo raid today, but to take a stroll in company was doable. And should anything happen, I'd be able to disappear at any moment. Although it remained to be seen whether I would leave them by themselves. It would have to be an extreme circumstance, but I would consider it. I was so used to the turmoil of the past few days that I couldn't sit around kicking my heels now if each new dead zombie brought me closer to the next level.

* * *

"So what do I have to do?" I asked of the squad leader, my friend Shatun. Combat had known who to send.

"Damned if I know," he said, scratching his head. "Combat said you were independent. It's probably better if you go twenty yards ahead in invisible mode and eliminate any danger. And if you can give us advanced warning, we'll be able to avoid it."

"Maybe it would be simpler for me to just kill them all myself?" I asked. I saw no problem with that.

"Most of them, but not all. Our soldiers need to gain experience, and leveling up is good motivation. And if we manage to pick up a few boxes and trinket caskets on the way, then so much the better."

"I see."

"Oh, by the way, I forgot. Take these, I was asked to give them to you," Shatun said, taking four cards from his inventory and handing them to me. "That's everything we managed to claim this morning."

They were basic-arrow cards; two hundred arrows.

Very timely I must say, since I hadn't gotten around to visiting the trading platform.

I took the cards and activated them immediately, before preparing to leave, along with the other fighters. There were just twelve of us, all young guys, but they looked nothing like career military personnel, a bit ragtag, if I was honest. All their armor was different, the makeshift stuff as well as the system stuff, and one guy wore bright red boots and chain mail over his camouflage gear. Still, as I knew from first-hand experience, any armor might save your life in a sticky spot. As I sat smoking, I saw Shatun signal the beginning of the operation, as they were calling it, although for me it was just a stroll in the fresh air.

We progressed very slowly, the group constantly stopping and waiting for my reconnaissance reports. On the way to the store, the guys killed various lone zombies and small groups, taking delight in the boxes dropped, while I wiped out those groups that numbered more than ten.

As I walked, I observed the soldiers. Give them my level and skills, and I wasn't sure how easy it would be for me to deal with a squad like that. They had discipline and military experience, and they were quickly learning how to kill zombies with swords and spears.

"Halt!" I commanded, deactivating invisibility and stopping the squad. "We'll have to make a detour here."

Up ahead I saw an ambush waiting, five armed men sitting in the building opposite the shop and keeping watch over the entrance. On the doorstep of the shop, a dead man lay face up. I had a clear view of the enormous hole in his head, and the fresh blood hadn't yet had time to dry, meaning the wound was recent. Zombies were shuffling towards him from all directions.

I relayed a detailed description of the situation to the soldiers, and they discussed the matter.

"We must stop those bastards, they're killing simple folk," said one of the soldiers.

"We have a task which must be carried out," said Shatun in disagreement.

"It would be inhumane to just walk on by."

"Right now we have to think about our home and families. Our priority is to patch up the hole in the dorm wall."

They argued for two minutes without coming to a concrete agreement.

"Perhaps I should just kill them all, huh?" I interrupted, taking the decision on myself. Those people were my bonuses, and walking on by and leaving them alone was just plain silly.

The collective focus was now on me.

"Could you?" asked someone.

"Of course I could," I said with a confident nod.

"It's risky. What if something goes wrong?" Shatun was concerned for me. Or maybe for himself.

"Okay, wait here, I'll be quick. If anything goes down, write me a message and I'll be back in a flash."

"To save us?" a guy asked with a snarky grin.

"Uh-huh," I replied, returning his smile. "Or

to bury you. But first I'll cut all your heads off so you don't go wandering the streets like zombies."

That was decided then.

I reached the building quickly, but there I came across an obstacle. The main entrance was closed, and I worried that opening it would produce noise and attract attention. The apartment I needed was on the second floor. I had big children back there unsupervised, so there was no time for thinking and I had to act quickly. I produced from my inventory an empty glass jar and threw it in the direction of the shop, making a noise that would instantly attract the attention of people and zombies. One observer was joined by another two, and they each took up their position by the window. Although truth be known, it was a window in name only, no glass, only curtains.

I selected the first guy, the unluckiest one, and in my opinion the most dangerous-looking, and put an arrow right in his eye. He didn't have time to squeal, slumping instantly to the floor.

You have killed a survivor.

The capacity of your inventory is increased by 3.5kg.

Momentarily a second arrow was drawn back along with the bowstring and let fly at the next victim. This time I misfired. The arrow went through his cheek and entered his brain, and in his dying breath his finger reflexively pulled the trigger of his weapon and a shot rang out.

You have killed a survivor.

The capacity of your inventory is

increased by 2.5kg.

Damn, not good.

The third man who dared to peek out the window was smarter and took cover, while his remaining comrades, having witnessed the deaths of the first two, did not approach, instead vacating the apartment in double quick time. Cowards.

I did not want to chase them; fighting indoors was not my cup of tea and I had to get back to my squad.

"Here I am," I announced, exiting invisibility and frightening the men, cataleptic in their stress.

"Fuck! Don't scare us like that!" someone hissed. "Are you injured?"

"Everything's fine. One of them just managed to pull his trigger before he died."

"You raised a proper ruckus," Shatun said, displeased. "Now we'll have to change our route."

"Let's just go another way, it's no problem," I said. I saw no reason for them to be so concerned. "I'll go on ahead, shooting zombies, and you pick off the stragglers. Then back at home you can tell everyone about your heroic deeds. It's the lucky ones who get to bring home spoils, like real cavemen."

"Don't mock us, lead us. It sucks around here as it is. We're not accustomed to fighting monsters like this. It's much easier killing people."

The next alley was very narrow, yet managed to fit quite a lot of zombies. You could tell it was rarely used and hadn't been cleared, and maybe some fresh ones had joined the crush.

There had been good hunting to be found on the main street and I'd reaped a good harvest.

See a zombie, shoot it; see a zombie, run it through with my spear, which coincidentally had been found and returned to me, after a thorough wash.

We were nearly at the end of the alley when I had to halt the squad again.

"Shatun, we've got problems," I announced with a frown. "I don't know what's going on, but I can see somebody at the windows of those two buildings facing each other over there. I think they're archers."

"What? Are you sure you're not mistaken?" he asked in surprise, looking at the neighboring houses but seeing nothing suspicious.

"I get the feeling the zombies have set up a people ambush, and I've never heard of that before. If I'm right, those beasts are very accurate, and their spikes are all covered in a disgusting sticky slime. I reckon any wound will immediately become infected."

"Should we go round?" he asked, after a short pause for thought.

"No," I said with a negative shake of the head, "we'll lose valuable time. I'll go ahead and kill them, you stay here for a couple of minutes."

"That might be dangerous."

"No more dangerous than anything else in today's world." I waved him away and strode forward.

Choosing a convenient spot, I looked around

to check no zombies could see me. The place seriously spooked me, but I couldn't quite put my finger on why. All around was quiet. The only problem was that these zombies did not give the impression of being dumb idiots. They appeared to have set up an ambush, although they hadn't exactly selected the best place for it. Finding a good position to fire with my bow, I got busy. It was important to find a point at which two zombie positions would shoot at once.

My first arrow found the first zombie no problem, entering its head with a crunch and settling there. Then I noticed something odd. The second zombie could not see this, but it did twitch its head to the side as though it had sensed it, and now stared at the spot, shouting hysterically. *Shoot, were they friends or something? Or twins?* I couldn't even ask it now, because my second arrow had already found its mouth and killed it on the spot. Returning hastily to Shatun, I thought about what I'd seen. If zombies were beginning to think, then that was really bad. Shit even.

The soldiers had developed problems in my absence. I didn't know how, but they'd been attacked by a gaggle of deadmen. Seeing them in the midst of a zombie battle, I did not hesitate to activate blink to get back to them quickly and join in the game, popping off infecteds.

There were at least three zombies to every squad member, and little by little the fighters retreated, not doing so well in the fight. Out of the corner of my eye, I observed one of them chopping at a zombie. *What's the point of chopping off its arm?* He may have been aiming higher and just missed, but it was always best to go straight for the head.

And here came more zombies from the other end. Excellent, I would continue to reap my harvest. After my twentieth arrow, the system decided to cheer me up.

You have gained level 8.

Your body has become stronger and your brain more productive.

Now that was interesting. Did that mean I'd become smarter? Perhaps my reactions would be faster? And my memory better?

"System, will that help me stop being afraid of people and falling into a stupor in their company? Oh, please say yes, I beseech you." As always, my question remained unanswered, and all I could do was sigh a groaning sigh.

Distracted by the system's gift, I came close to overlooking Shatun. He was trying to fend off five beasties at once, and when he took a step back, he tripped over a child's bicycle lying on the ground and fell onto his back. Another two seconds, and he would have been eaten alive. I took four shots, killing four of the zombies and leaving the last one to Shatun, so he could prove he was worthy of leading a squad alone, not just with my assistance.

Of course that was easy for me to say, considering my range of skills, but each man works with the tools in his toolbox, as they say. I had never studied properly, but invisibility had helped me superbly in the beginning.

Having wiped out the zombies, the soldiers began to regain their wits, breaking out in smiles of satisfaction.

"What would you do without me, soldiers? You nearly got eaten by a small group of zombies." I understood the situation, of course, but they needed a bit of ridiculing, otherwise they would relax totally.

"That's easy for you to say. Although actually, you did pretty well to make the sides even," said one of the guys, wiping the sweat from his brow.

They had not done too badly, even doing some quality zombie crushing and earning a few rewards.

"So what's the difference between you and me?" I was interested to hear his opinion.

"With your skills, any of us would become a killing machine." He was not about to give in.

"I'll let you in on a little secret, soldier." I felt like bragging. "To begin with I only had one skill; now I've got five. I got them not by sitting around, but by constantly killing zombies to earn new skills and levels. Get killing, and everything will come to you. But you won't get far by looking at others and envying them."

The fighter was evidently very tired and did not want to get mad at or argue with me.

"Forget it, Varg, that's not what I meant," he said dismissively. "But you're right about one thing, we do need to kill more beasties. I don't think they were this nimble before."

"Shatun, how are you? Need to change your pants?" I said, switching to a new target.

"Screw you, Varg." He did not share my mirth.

He gave his fighters a five-minute breather to check their ammo, which was running very low, and then ordered them to move out again. I may not have been their commander, but guide could also be seen as a job. We reached the store without incident, except for one of the soldiers managing to get level 2 on the way and Shatun leveling up to level 4.

"Take everything you need from the store, and I'll keep watch. But you keep one eye on the door as well," I said, activating invisibility and blinking up onto the roof.

The roof was flat and therefore easy to move around to keep watch over the surrounding area. From up there I shot zombies attracted by the noise, some of which I made myself by occasionally throwing things down onto the road. I did not want to kick my heels, so I shot zombies and kept the soldiers on their toes at the same time. I liked having my little jokes with them, because sometimes they were too serious. *It would be fantastic to earn myself a skill today.* What I was missing was a skill that would generate arrows and have them appear right in my hand.

Ha, dream on.

That was clearly not going to happen, since the only things that dropped were gray and brown boxes. The brown ones I did not like at all and gave them to Polina, who in turn gave them to Quartermaster. They were worth very little on the trading platform and therefore of no use to me, more fuss than they were worth. I had not forgotten the business with the tent.

That was just me moaning to myself out of boredom. And what wasn't to moan about with so few zombies left? I suppose I could have spent the whole night reducing the monster headcount. That was worth thinking about, although Polina was right when she said I was still weak after yesterday. My first experience of blink had had a powerful effect on my body, and I still needed time to adapt.

The soldiers had not limited themselves to their inventories, as I thought they might, so I was honestly astounded when I saw what they were doing. Perhaps I'd missed something and Quartermaster had shown his face? They'd built a veritable train out of shopping carts, each man binding three carts together with wire and loading them right up to the top. Now I knew why they needed me. They would now be slower that the slowest zombie, a notion I found amusing.

They had piled in everything they could find. I swear to the system, one the soldier had a whole cart full of cable ties. Was he going to handcuff the zombies? A second had for some reason filled his with screwdrivers. I became concerned to be sharing living space with these people; they were quite evidently out to lunch. The only normal one was Shatun, who was taking nothing, merely giving orders.

"And don't forget to take all those screws over there in the corner," came his commanding voice.

Oops, my bad, he was actually overseeing all this insanity.

Anyway, the system would be their judge. Let them take everything they wanted, especially if it might make them go out zombie killing more often instead of lounging around in the dorm.

They'd taken pretty much all the remaining bricks as well. Which reminded me, I would have to remind Combat of the debt. I had loaned them my bricks, and now they would have to return them and brick up the windows in my apartment. At home I was always on the alert, forever peeking out of the window and sometimes convinced a beastie was about to come flying in.

I was glad the fighters had adapted quickly and were improving all the time in their zombie killing, acquiring a taste for the system's gifts. I also had to keep active and level up. I could not cohabit with folks who were stronger than me in everything. That said, I could of course leave them anytime, but that would be to deny myself the occasional chat with somebody, to boast of my successes.

I viewed everything through a prism of practicality, and that was probably not right. After all, these were by and large common folk in need of help. It was another matter that I was not about to befriend every single one of them.

CHAPTER 21

THE SOLDIERS HAD EVENTUALLY FINISHED loading up their carts and were now scouring the area in search of me. No one thought of looking up at the roof.

"Are you done?" I asked, creeping up soundlessly on Shatun from behind.

I immediately had to duck an attempted sweeping strike.

"Jesus, bro, don't do that!" he said,

"Okay, I won't," I replied.

The journey home was uneventful, except for a tiny bit of shooting. There were moments when the heavily laden wagon train couldn't squeeze through a space, and the road would need clearing of corpses and garbage. The carts were very noisy, their clangs and squeaks audible along the whole street.

We were spotted, or heard, to be more precise,

as we approached the dorm, and a group came out to meet us, Combat himself at the head. In turn, I spotted the snipers who had taken up positions on the roof. Most importantly, there were now fewer corpses in the yard.

It was definitely good that they'd begun to clean up the area around the dormitory. It was now neat and tidy; much better. Groups of three people were patrolling, not only inside the building, but also out on the street. They were killing stray zombies that dared come too close, and earning themselves experience and boxes.

"It's good you managed to do everything and stay alive," said Combat, greeting us cheerily.

"I promised I'd bring them back safely," I said with a smile.

I hadn't actually promised anything of the sort, but that wasn't important.

Combat and his people understood the joke and smiled, while the soldiers behind me bored into my back with heavy, angry looks.

I even heard someone behind me mutter, "showoff."

"Thanks for your help," Combat said, extending me a hand and firmly shaking mine. "You brought loads of stuff we need. That's good news. Unfortunately, I have no good news to share."

I understood from his face that something unpleasant had happened.

"Should I be worried?" I asked coldly, staring into his eyes.

He understood me.

"No, they're all okay, don't worry about them," he said. My sharp change of mood had unnerved him, and he hurried to reassure me. "The problem is a blackout throughout the whole city, and it's not going to be possible to restore the electricity supply."

"What happened?" Shatun asked, stepping to the front.

"We were told there was a large explosion at the power plant," said Combat. The news shocked everyone present. He continued, "I don't know the details, but it's very bad. It's back to the Stone Age for us."

"Fuck," I said, unable to contain myself. "That's a catastrophe," I said, pulling a face and trying to figure out how I might be affected.

The obvious thing was the fridge, and the electrical appliances Polina used for cooking. After that came the two little ones, who were always busy with the games console and therefore did not particularly hound me anymore.

"How is everyone?"

"Everyone's in shock. Some were even in hysterics and needed some serious calming down." Combat attempted a smile but it came out unconvincing. "All our phones will soon be out of juice and we won't be able to exchange information with other survivors."

"What about generators?" Shatun asked. He did not want to let it lie.

"They consume too much fuel, and they're

very noisy. Although they might be enough for charging phones," Combat said, looking back at me. "Okay, let's not stand around out here. Let's go back inside. The snipers are doing well to keep them at bay, but the fliers are out again tonight." He beckoned us to follow him.

So there I was, back in that fucking place again. How else could I think of Combat's office, where all people ever did was argue about things they couldn't change? Listening to that was seriously boring. That said, there were things that demanded my personal input.

The meeting lasted about forty minutes, during which time I managed to scoop out some interesting information about the world around us and the gangs populating it. For future reference, I made a mental note of places that would need checking out later. At the end, I did not leave with everyone else, but gestured to Combat that I wished to speak alone with him.

We didn't speak for long, about ten minutes, but he willingly shared the information I required. The meeting itself had only superficially covered some obvious potential threats from outside. Everyone else knew what they were from their daily meetings, but I needed clarification. I did not want to bump into a group of people with such skills as the ability to paralyze me with a stare, or poison me with a light breeze wafted in my direction. There might well be even worse, for I didn't yet know all the surprises the system had in store.

Combat didn't know much about the gangs, but what he did know he told me, which was mainly basic stuff like approximate numbers, places of residence, and approximate arms volumes. It was enough for me to build a bigger picture. Clearly there were already strong communities in the city, which it was too early to go sticking my nose in, but there were also smaller groups that could easily be eliminated.

"Thanks for the information," I said, rising from the table.

"Wait a minute." He stopped me. "Am I to understand you're going out for a walk now? Can you look for a few things I need in town?"

He produced a notebook from his desk drawer and held it out to me.

I ran a quick eye over the list and chuckled, not knowing what half the items were.

"Sorry, I'm not interested. If I accidentally see something, I'll put it in my inventory, but I don't see the point of specially running round the whole city in search of all this. And anyway, you can leave the dorm safely yourselves now."

"I see," he said, before continuing, "I didn't mean go looking specially, but just if you happen to see anything."

"Fine. See you," I said, waving from the door.

"Be careful. If you get into trouble, call, while you still can," Combat called after me.

Darkness was still three hours away, just enough for a walk.

I had killed very few zombies today, so why

not put that right? I would not stray far from home, and I had a rough idea of the danger zones inhabited by hostiles, so nothing to worry about.

I walked along a familiar road, killing oncoming zombies. When I tired of this, I began sticking them with my spear. My arrows were not limitless, so it was worth using them sparingly.

I meandered and meandered, and before long, surprise surprise, I came across something interesting.

My attention was drawn to a clothes store set back from the main drag. Through the smashed window I saw lots of clothes. I myself had no decent attire to speak of, and I'd long been wearing hand-me-downs. I entered the store, and in the men's department selected a pile of random stuff in the hope that Polina and Katya would help me figure it all out at home. My taste was, frankly, not up to par. The apocalypse was all well and good, but I did not want to walk around looking like a chump. I was Level 8, after all. *Replacing my old sweatpants wouldn't hurt.*

Running a hand over a superb-looking jacket, I looked at the price label. I had never earned that much in a month, but now I could just take it, I didn't want it. Pity I didn't need one. But then I thought for a moment and took it anyway. You never knew. Done shopping, I headed out the door.

As I stepped onto the street, a couple of zombies appeared, so I skipped effortlessly over to them and removed their heads. Then I saw another, standing by a drugstore. It wasn't stirring, but it was staring fixedly at the wall, zoned out.

Oh yeah, that's a point, drugstore. There had been no medicines on Combat's list, but they would always come in handy. I spent five minutes inside, taking everything that came into my field of view. I knew precious little about medicine, except for ascorbic acid and antiseptic. I hoped someone in the dorm would be more knowledgeable.

Right, now I could go home. Except that I would make a little detour and approach from the other side, for reconnaissance purposes, and also to shoot some more zombies.

As I walked I examined the houses, and I noticed quite a lot of survivors. They were evidently joining together into groups. I was very surprised by a nippy lad of about fifteen who killed three zombies as I watched. An interesting skill: in his hand was a small laser pointer, with which he decapitated the zombies.

It occurred to me he might be very useful to us, but not this time; it was too early for us to be looking for new people. I had to strengthen up significantly first, so that no one would so much as think about looking at me awry.

Then I helped some people who were in a spot of bother. Ten survivors were trying to protect their house from zombies clinging to it on all sides and trying to bust through the boarded-up windows. *So that's what life on the first floor is all about.* And whoever had parked their car beneath the windows had done the inhabitants an enormous "favor." It was possible they might have coped with the beasties, were it not for the zombie archers that were here in numbers. It felt slightly odd to see so many of them in one place.

The people were throwing various objects through the holes in the boarded windows, receiving sharp spikes in return. Victory would not be on the side of the humans in this particular battle; the zombies were winning. I drew my bow and began selectively popping off zombie archers and jumpers, and as the number of dead jumpers grew, so things became easier for the humans. They were so busy fighting fiercely back that they didn't notice my intervention.

I approached unhindered and collected my trophies while the battle with the beasties raged, then I left. I was not going to help them right through to victory, but I had given them the chance to deal with the zombies by themselves. And I would not have lifted a finger if they'd been just men. I had decided to help when I saw the women and children.

From here my return to the dormitory was uneventful, even disappointingly so. The most routine and laid-back of days.

I did not visit Combat, for fear he might drag me into a meeting. I could pop by any time to discuss things with him *tête-à-tête*.

Instead, I went to see Quartermaster. He was an upstanding man, and he didn't ask too many questions.

"Ah, Varg, greetings. Do you have something

to make an old man happy?" he asked with a smile.

"Uh-huh, I've got you some medicine," I said, emptying everything onto his table without going into too much detail.

He immediately began covetously inspecting it all.

"Not a bad catch, a lot of stuff we need," he said, clacking his tongue approvingly and smiling. "Do you require anything in return?"

"Me?" I said, thinking what I might possibly need. "Well, if Polina comes and asks you for anything, you could let her jump to the front of the queue."

"Agreed, no problem," he said without arguing. "You provide me with more than anyone else, and you don't ask for anything in return, unlike the others. Those layabouts come here with two or three things, and demand the Earth in return. They get squat, no handouts."

"Okay, take care, I'm off," I said, waving him good by as I left.

My apartment greeted me with an odd silence. Everyone was sitting in the candlelit living room, doing their own thing. The children were playing, while the girls were looking through the clothes I'd brought earlier and discussing them in hushed tones. But the second I walked in, all eyes were on me, making me feel very awkward.

"Uncle Varg's back," Liza said, flying to me and hugging me tightly. "Come and play with us, we're bored."

"Liza, Uncle Varg's busy," Polina said, coming to my rescue.

"Uh-huh, busy. I'm very busy," I said, with a quick nod of my head.

"Doing what?" asked Liza, narrowing her eyes in suspicion.

"Um..." It took a few moments to think of something. "I brought you a sack of clothes, and now your mom and Katya are going to help me sort through them."

She continued to stare at me for a while longer, as though she didn't believe me, before saying, "Okay, fine," grabbing her friend by the hand, and running to the other room.

She was, no doubt, offended, but I was able to breathe a sigh of relief and return to the ladies.

Jeez, I did not know why their cunning, satisfied looks frightened me so.

"Everything okay?" I asked with a smile, testing the water.

"Come in, come in, don't just stand there by the door," said Polina, also smiling.

For the entirety of the next hour, I paid for my mistake. Each item of clothing I'd brought was thoroughly inspected and discussed, much of it criticized and rejected. Mind you, there was no way I could have foreseen it, and eventually they were done and I could breathe another sigh of relief. Although as it turned out, all too soon.

"Igor, what do you think about our clothes? We've spent all day choosing outfits."

This cannot be. Surely they can't be doing this

to me. They can't, can they? Ah, they can.

For the next two hours I looked, or more correctly, given the poor lighting, *tried* to look, pretending I was interested. I was eventually rescued by the children, who came running and dragged me away to play with them.

"Liza and Anya, why don't I find and bring you everything you want, and you can play by yourselves," I suggested just as soon as we'd decamped to the room which served as the playroom.

Buying off the children was the best tactic.

I always reacted well to the children, despite having no idea what to actually do with them. I found an easy way out by telling them stories from my life, and they tried to listen, but my life was so dull that I soon lost them.

Then we were called to dinner, which I was unspeakably glad of. The potential for dish variety was seriously low with no electricity, but they had managed to heat something up in a pan over a fuel tablet. I did not like the situation at all. The question needed addressing urgently and a solution finding.

"Slim pickings," was my verdict as I inspected the spread. "That bad, huh?"

"Sorry." For some reason Polina felt guilty. "We'll think of a way to cook. If the worst comes to the worst, I'll ask them to build a Russian stove."

There was no point blaming her; it wasn't her fault.

"Tomorrow I'll go and see Quartermaster and

ask him to think of something," said Katya. "And I won't leave until he does."

The girls looked dejected and didn't look at me while we ate. They seemed very worried.

"Don't worry, it's not your fault," I told them, putting another spoonful of cold ragout in my mouth.

The worst thing was that the gas had disappeared along with the electricity. At this rate, we would very soon be back in the Stone Age and cooking on campfires.

Beep

Hmm, apparently I wasn't going to be allowed to eat in peace. A message from Combat: *We've got company.*

"Ladies, I have to leave you, something urgent has come up," I said, becoming suddenly serious and heading for the door. "While I'm gone, don't go anywhere near the windows. And keep together."

Four heads nodded in unison. I ran quickly to Combat's office, to find out what was going on. The snipers had spotted a group of armed people near our sanctuary and raised the alarm.

"Varg, are you sure you want to go alone? There's a group ready to go out on a sortie." Combat did not approve of my idea.

"Definitely. I'll be quick, you won't even notice I'm gone," I said, seeing no reason for me not to go alone.

"Fine, but it's just reconnaissance, as we originally planned, and the takedown team will do everything else, okay?" he said, trying one last time to change my mind.

"Let's do it like this," I said, thinking of a way out. "I'll check out the situation, and I'll deal with it myself if I can, but if I can't, I'll come back to you."

He gave me a hard stare for several seconds before waving a hand.

"The group moves out directly after you," Combat said, having the last word. "And don't take any stupid risks."

A state of affairs that suited me just fine.

I went down to the second floor, before blinking down to the ground from the already familiar balcony there.

I did not want a repeat of recent events, and I did not believe that people were just milling around down there, but the thought that a shell might land in my apartment made my blood boil.

I found the spies quite quickly, in the building opposite, in an apartment with a superb view of our dormitory. The first thing that caught my eye was the enormous amount of weapons they had. And then there was the grenade launcher lying in the corner. There were seven people in the apartment, two observing the dorm from cover, two tinkering with weapons, and the remainder lying on the floor and chatting among themselves.

I blinked over to the open window and listened in on the conversation there.

"They definitely didn't see us, Quiet?" said one man.

"Definitely, I tell you, everything's fine. Our

guy says things couldn't be worse for the fighters right now, and they have problems with weapons," replied another.

"But they've got loads of babes," said another wistfully.

"So we wait here until nighttime and then we leap into action," said yet another, appearing to be the leader.

"I can't wait to annihilate those soldiers. It's just a shame the zombies will get the chicks instead of us." Regret sounded in the voice of the speaker. "Maybe we shouldn't be so rough with them, Fedot, huh? We'd be better off just kidnapping the chicks. We've got a whole prison full of hungry men who are going to start pouncing on each other soon."

"You know they killed our people and set fire to the warehouse," said someone, giving me to understand where they'd come from. "They're relatively weak at the moment, but they might become a powerful force in the near future, so it's better to do away with them straightaway. We'll find chicks elsewhere. There are thousands of people in the city."

"By the way, I heard from Company there's someone over there with abilities, apparently quite a high level. Won't he get in our way?" He was speaking about me. And it was damn nice to be spoken about in such terms.

"No, he won't. We're going at night. I'm hoping he'll be asleep and will only be woken by the explosion," said the leader with a sneer. "With any luck it'll squish him."

Then I saw a new skill.

"Rom, all clear? Sniffed anything out?" the leader asked one of the observers by the window. "We're seriously relying on your skill right now."

"All clear. Only the smell of decay," the man said, wrinkling his nose after another deep nasal inhalation. "But you know I can only sniff out a person at fifty meters."

"Keep it up. Something's giving me the willies."

"Is your skill out of whack again? Your animal instinct?" asked the sniffer with a smile.

"Yeah, it apparently only works when it wants to, the bitch," the leader cursed.

By now I was bored of listening, and I figured I'd heard the interesting stuff. The bastards had come to kill us, and most importantly, kill me. I could not let them get away with it.

I didn't care that there were seven of them and only one of me. Nor did I care what levels they might be. They would die today. Although no, not all of them. I would leave one as an appetizer and take it to the soldiers as a gift they could disembowel to retrieve any vital information. They would appreciate a goodwill gesture like that. Besides which, I would also receive information I needed.

I blinked my way back out onto the street and went around to the left side of the building. I now had a clear shot at the two watchers in the window. They weren't looking down, but at my dorm through binoculars.

The first arrow struck the sniffer's neck. The fucker couldn't even sniff it out, useless filth that he was, with his useless skill. Without wasting time, I pulled my bowstring back until the bow creaked, before putting a crystal arrow in the head of the second man. He didn't die immediately and he tried to shout out, but it was too late. His brain was already pierced and he could not afford such luxuries as a voice, even or a life.

You have killed a survivor.

The capacity of your inventory is increased by 6kg.

You have killed a survivor.

The capacity of your inventory is increased by 11kg.

The reaction of the rest of the group was instant. I was even surprised to see a grenade thrown from the window. I was very lucky (praise be to the system!) to have blink. By the time the grenade exploded, I was already introducing my dagger to the neck of a third man, then sticking a fourth with my spear.

You have killed a survivor.

The capacity of your inventory is increased by 6kg.

You have killed a survivor.

The capacity of your inventory is increased by 2kg.

"That's another two down. Where is that animal?" roared the commander in his impotence. I was killing his people with ease, yet he couldn't even see me.

I blinked back outside when an aimless random shootout began inside, between three previously self-confident people who now found themselves victims trying to figure out what was killing them off. Standing on the neighboring balcony, I spotted one more, who held his machine gun tight while looking nervously all around. My arrow got him right in the eye.

You have killed a survivor.

The capacity of your inventory is increased by 15kg.

What a fruitful kill! How many people must he have killed, to have such a levelled-up inventory? A pleased smile appeared on my face, for my level would now be upped significantly.

"We gotta get out of here," came the whisper of one of the men, addressed to his boss. "We fucked up big time here. We gotta... khhaheee..." He took a crystal arrow to the throat and collapsed to the floor.

You have killed a survivor.

The capacity of your inventory is increased by 6kg.

How lovely, system. Maybe screw the gift for the soldiers and I'll kill this bastard myself and take home just his head?

Wait a minute. From my position on the balcony, I saw a squad from the dormitory moving in my direction. They were running towards the shots. Damn, if he looked out of the window, the leader could fell half the squad with his machine gun. I had to act quickly.

"Scared?" I asked him tauntingly as I blinked onto another balcony to dodge the bullets.

While he was looking at the balcony I'd just vacated, I crept up on him from behind.

All I had to do, according to what I'd seen in the movies, was strike his head with the blunt edge of my dagger, and he would be out cold. I crept slowly closer to my enemy, but then was very surprised when he turned around sharply in my direction. Using blink, I was on him with a strike that made his body crash into the wall, but on autopilot the son of a bitch managed to pull his trigger and shoot me.

Fuck, he got me. In the leg. Ah, it hurts.

He lost consciousness from impact with the wall, and his head was bleeding, but I knew he was still alive, since the system had not given me a bonus. Holy shit, my adrenaline levels were dropping and the pain was rolling in with doubled intensity.

Damn, I never thought it would be this painful. I took a T-shirt from my inventory, tore strips from it, and wound them around the wound to stem the flow of blood. The shot had come from practically point-blank range, so the bullet should have exited, but no, it had remained in my leg, which hurt hellishly when I took even the shortest step. And I could not sit around, for this was no holiday camp, but rather the end of the fucking world, and life meant movement.

Wincing from the pain, I hobbled over to the

motherfucker and bound his hands with some cable ties I'd taken from the hardware store just in case. Then I quickly gathered up all the weapons; they would come in handy for our troops. All the while, I felt worse and worse as the bullet made its presence known with each step I took, and the blood was now seeping through the makeshift bandage.

Damn, I feel really bad. Regeneration. It would be a disaster if the wound healed with the bullet still inside. My body's damned strength had prevented the bullet coming out the other side of my leg, a huge disadvantage of this skill.

On the plus side, the capacity of my inventory had grown, which without doubt made the trip worthwhile. If only it weren't for the unpleasant surprises.

As I looked around, I realized I was trapped, for there were already zombies beneath the window. I wondered where they'd been hiding to get here so quickly. I could not use blink with my prisoner, and I would not be able to get away from here in invisibility mode. Added to which, the blood would attract the zombies, if it hadn't already. While trying to imagine how best to deal with the situation, I saw the soldiers and realized it wasn't quite so bad as it seemed.

My dormmates were already here and rushing to my aid, although there were only two dozen of them against a hundred zombies. If I could put in just a little effort, they ought to be able to cope. However, there was another question: might they not kill me because I was injured? They didn't know about my blink skill, which allowed me to vanish from a dangerous situation. Was it worth the risk to my life? On the other hand, it was an excellent opportunity to test these people.

I took out my bow and limped over to the window to help them, since they couldn't quite reach me yet.

As I killed my twentieth zombie, I realized I should be pleased to have been shot in the leg rather than the arm. With my arms intact, I still had full combat effectiveness, despite the intensifying pain in my leg.

CHAPTER 22

FINALE

SHAME. THAT'S WHAT I FELT when the soldiers picked me up and hauled me back to the dormitory. My strength had not deserted me, and I would have made it by myself, but Shatun and Clubfoot wouldn't hear of it, saying right off the bat that such a leg injury must not be stressed, in order to avoid further damage.

I'd landed myself in trouble. A hero... Fuck. So much swagger, only to get shot so stupidly. All I can say in my defense is that the prisoner was no simpleton and was inevitably well-informed. He was taken straight down to the basement for questioning.

"Don't worry. Fedya and Combat can make anybody talk," Shatun said, allaying my fears.

"Can I sit in Combat's office while I wait for the results?" I asked Shatun hopefully, leaning on his shoulder as we set off.

"Nah," he said, smiling, "you need to get to a medic to get that bullet out."

I sighed joyful relief at the news. A medic, excellent, that meant not home to Polina, into whose eyes I did not want to look right now. I had promised her to rest for a day, but then I'd broken my word.

"Shatun, are you sure this is the way to the sick bay?" I asked, suspicious of something amiss, and looking for somewhere to hide.

"Of course not, I'm taking you home," he said with a smile. "We don't have a sick bay yet. But we do have a doctor." His words were like an alarm bell in my head, auguring my doom.

"I'm dead," I said, dropping my head fatefully.

"Did you screw up?"

"Uh-huh. I promised not to go looking for trouble today," I said. There was no point hiding the truth from him. After all, you could say he'd saved me.

All the way home I was expecting a stab in the back. To my shame, I did not trust these people fully yet, and it would have been easier to do me in now, while I was wounded, than if I was fighting fit. But they turned out to be better people that I thought.

"My sympathies. Polina will definitely go mental at first, but she's a smart lady, she'll understand," said Shatun, clapping an enormous hand on my shoulder. "Although I would advise you to make reparations. A man must not break his word."

"How?"

"How should I know? Think for yourself," said Shatun, shrugging in surprise.

Entering the apartment was like going to my execution. A whole delegation awaited me, Polina at its head.

I never thought the looks they fixed me with could be so heavy. Liza's expression was exactly like her mother's. Only Anya, Katya's daughter, seemed to pity me. The silence did not last long. They soon recovered their voices and began fussing around me.

"So this is you taking a day off, is it?" Polina asked.

"It just happened," I said, lowering my eyes.

Then Katya confronted me with the fact that it would be her removing the bullet from my leg, and warned me it would be very painful. News I did not care much for.

"Katya used to work in a hospital and she has experience of wounds like that," added Polina.

The ladies wanted to drag me up onto the table, but I was categorically against it and somehow crawled up onto it under my own steam.

"Don't be shy, brother, cry out all you like," was Shatun's advice. "I've had four bullets removed without anesthetic, so I know all too well how pleasant it's going to be for you."

Cheers for that, I feel really calm now. I will not be reduced to tears and shouts. I'm not that kind of per... arghhhh.

Bastards! Without warning, Katya had begun digging around in the wound, and not with a scalpel, it seemed, but with a red-hot nail. Where had she found an instrument like that? Surely she didn't carry it around in her inventory?

"You have very tough skin," she said, surprised and pushing harder.

Despite the infernal pain, I can honestly say nobody saw me cry. They just listened to my snarlings and hissings. Katya found and removed the bullet, before stitching up the wound very quickly, shooting her up at least a hundred points in my estimation. The thought of her digging around in my thigh for five hours was a fearful prospect.

"Now you lie up for two weeks and you'll be as good as new," she said, stroking my cheek and making me squirm from her touch.

I could not agree with her. And when Shatun said goodbye and left, I told the girls so.

"One day, maximum two, and I'll be good to go. My regeneration will deal quickly with the wound."

"And then you're going to go out solo again and beat up all your enemies?" Polina asked, her brow puckered. "I can see I'll need to have a word with Combat."

"Naturally," I said, sighing heavily. "What else is a sociopath supposed to do in a community of humans?"

"Stop being so stupid, maybe?" Polina asked, one eyebrow raised questioningly. "You nearly got killed today, and you don't even want to rest and restore your strength."

I had no words to respond with.

I was saved by Liza, who said she wanted to sleep. Then Katya remembered it was also Anya's bedtime.

No matter how much I wanted to sleep, lethe did not come. All I could do was ruminate about the day and how reckless I'd been. Evidently I was too accustomed to relying on my invisibility.

I recalled the hundreds of bizarre objects on the trading platform which I had not considered for fear of buying a dud. And now I figured that if, for instance, someone else bought a kinetic artifact or a paralyzer there, then death might catch up with me.

The schism between me and the people around me had narrowed significantly. It had become easier for me to communicate with the soldiers, and a mutual trust had developed. Despite their munitions problems, their military experience was colossal, which could not have been said of mine. I really had been a fool to go out alone. Hero, my ass! Various thoughts crept into my head to the accompaniment of the increasingly heavy rain and thunder outside. It was the first storm, indeed the first rain, since the start of the apocalypse. I wondered how the zombies would behave in the rain, and in my curiosity I took a peek out of the window. Approximately a dozen fliers were circling the building but so far not attempting to break into it.

My observation of the beasties was interrupted by a loud female shriek inside the apartment. I rushed to Katya and Anya's room to look for signs of danger, but saw only a trembling mother holding tight her weeping daughter. Katya was dressed in a thin nighty, and oh, her breasts! My ears burned red at the sight, and I hastened to turn away. It was not polite to ogle.

"She had a bad dream, it's only to be expected," said Polina, who had also not been sleeping.

I could understand them. They were regular folks, weak, and they didn't know what awaited them in the near future. Were I in their shoes, I would also be afraid. I was sure of my strengths, and my sleep was sound, whereas the ladies were having a hard time of it, and that was to say nothing of the children.

* * *

"Are you sure nothing hurts? Maybe I can get you something?" I was hearing these questions for the hundredth time today.

Katya and Polina had been fussing around me all morning, trying to do whatever they could to help. They did not yet understand what regeneration was or how it worked, and so they were worried about me.

All attention had been on me since first thing in the morning. They changed the bandage on my leg and then brought me food in bed. Regeneration ate up a lot of calories, and my appetite was bestial.

The slightest squeak of my bed, and one of them would come running into the room with an offer of assistance.

And my attitude towards them began to change for the better. It was a pleasant change to be cared for and mothered, as opposed to attemptedly killed off.

While I had some free time, I decided to do the things I'd been putting off until later.

I activated the trading platform and began rooting painstakingly through it. I needed armor, arrows, and if possible, one or two things that would supercharge me.

Luckily I had amassed a fair number of boxes and caskets that could be used for trading purposes.

I didn't yet know what to do with the red trinket caskets. They might contain useful weapons. Or they might just as easily contain unvarnished trash, and if it wasn't in the form of a card, then I wouldn't even be able to sell it. Yet red trinket boxes were highly valued on the market.

The first thing I did was buy fifteen basic-arrow cards. Interestingly, one trader was selling them for forty-three gray boxes. He was probably in the habit of killing zombies by the shedload and could simply sell them on.

Next, my attention was grabbed by a **level-1 invisibility potion**, priced at a hundred gray boxes. Evidently, invisibility was highly valued among the people. Or maybe it was a get-rich-quick scheme. Of course I didn't buy it. Though had it been on sale for ten boxes, I might have, purely out of interest. I did, however, by a dark pear for ten red boxes. Night vision was quite something, and I considered myself lucky to have noticed it in good time.

The trading platform was so massive you were spoiled for choice, although in truth there was an awful lot of junk for sale as well, like a sink card, a fur-carpet card, and a bearskin. This garbage dropped from brown boxes, of which I had nearly a hundred, but I wasn't planning to open them, what with the tent saga fresh in my mind. Of course I could give them to Quartermaster, who could use them to get supplies for people, but it was too early for gifts like that.

It was strange that I still hadn't come across a single brown trinket casket. There were also things being traded for green caskets, something else I'd never seen with my own eyes. I thought I was destroying zombies by the bucket load, yet thus far my loot had been very repetitive.

I entered the word *electricity* in the search bar, thinking I might get lucky and solve the problem. Electricity potion, electric snare, electrodynamic motor, and dozens of other items I had no clue about.

I bought some electricity potion for five gray boxes and was immediately disappointed.

Evaluation:

Card: Quality Electricity Potion.

Your resistance to electricity is increased for three hours.

If we were going to war against Zeus, the potion would be just the job, but right now it was worthless.

After this particular purchasing fail, I began to select items more carefully. Now I pondered whether to buy an Electricity-Production Artifact or an Electricity Distributor.

If the name was anything to go by, it might come in handy, but on the other hand it might well be more trash. I bought an Electricity Distributor card.

Evaluation:

Electricity distributor.

A craft item.

More of the same. Three red boxes spent on nothing.

Fortune smiled on me at last with my final purchase, which was good, because I'd already given up on finding anything of any value.

Evaluation:

Card: Small Electricity-Production Artifact.

Provides electricity inside a building. Not for outdoor use; only for indoor use.

Important note: to activate, install on any wall.

In anticipation of once again having hot water in the shower and normal food, as well as the children being occupied with their gaming console for days on end, I forgot about the pain in my leg and limped about in search of a wall to hang the artifact on.

I chose the bedroom, away from prying eyes. I opened the card, and in my hands lay a small crystal approximately the size of my palm. It was simple to operate, and all I had to do was approach the wall and it immediately attached itself very firmly. It even seemed it would be impossible to move it to another room. Not everything went according to plan, however, and no light appeared in the bedroom. Was the damned thing defunct? Perhaps I'd missed something?

Hmm. I pondered the situation for five minutes before plumping for a new evaluation.

Evaluation:

Activated small electricity-production artifact. To initiate activity, charge with experience.

Important note: to initiate the activity of the artifact, within twenty-four hours you must gain experience equivalent to killing ten zombies. The transfer of experience to the artifact is activated by speaking the word "Charge."

So that's it, I thought, scratching my head. *That's why the system so obstinately refuses to divulge people's experience levels or how much we gain for zombie kills.* The system complicated many simple things. Why not just say I needed twenty experience points and would get five for each zombie?

Anyway, screw it. The main thing was there was light in my apartment again.

When I thought about it, something like that would be a luxury for some. Not everyone could kill ten zombies for the sake of electricity, and it struck me these figures were not accurate. A hulk or a zombie dog could provide more experience than a regular zombie.

Uh-oh, here comes trouble. I hobbled quickly back to bed, lest I got chewed out for taking this important stroll.

"Igor, you did that." Polina was not asking, but more like confirming.

"Uh-huh."

"How?"

"I got an interesting reward," I lied.

I did not want to tell them about the trading platform. That would be tantamount to signing myself into slavery, and they would start using me all the time as a vending machine on legs.

She noticed the crystal and beamed a smile.

"Oh, that changes everything. Life will be much easier now. I'm only concerned the other residents will be envious." Smiling joyfully, she skipped over to me and kissed me on the cheek. "Thank you so much for the light. I was racking my brains thinking how to organize our daily life without electricity."

Again I crashed. She had kissed me again. *Damn, at this rate I might get used to it. If only I could react normally and not like an idiot.*

* * *

We sat having a relaxed cup of tea, when suddenly Shatun burst into the apartment without knocking, breathing noisily after his sprint up the stairs.

"Varg, something urgent's come up. Combat needs to see you." Evidently something had happened.

"Hey, he's wounded," said Polina, looking wrathfully at Shatun with her hands on her hips. "Surely you can cope without Igor?"

"Igor?" He was hearing my name for the first time. "Never mind, it's not important now. We've got an emergency situation. Combat ordered me to bring Varg, even if it means having to carry him. It's very important."

It was as though they knew I'd drunk the **healing potion** I'd bought for fifteen gray boxes. My leg was already practically healed and didn't hurt anymore.

"Shatun, you do realize I'm not obligated to come running at your behest?" I asked, for confirmation.

"Varg, believe me, it's a very strange situation. And it has directly to do with..." He fell silent, looking first at Polina and then at me. "It has to do with you."

Now this was interesting.

"Okay, let's go then, since it's so important." I had no clue what was going on and could only hope they weren't all going to attack me together.

As we moved quickly down to Combat's office, Shatun kept looking strangely at my injured leg.

"Thanks for coming so quickly, Varg," Combat began. "Sorry for dragging you away so suddenly. An unpleasant situation as developed."

"I'm all ears." Despite my relaxed appearance, I was tense inside.

"Your prisoner cracked and told us a bunch of interesting stuff. We're dealing with a gang of already two hundred mugs under the leadership of one Fedot Spikey. They call themselves the Spikes."

"Am I supposed to know him?" I raised an inquisitive eyebrow and took a seat at the desk.

"Not you, but Polina should know him," Combat said. I felt so uncomfortable I wanted to kill someone.

"Before, when life was peaceful, he was the director of the city prison. Now he heads up a gang of survivors, half of whom were banged up in his prison. There was a time when he tried to get close to Polina, but he got knocked back. He's an acerbic and unforgiving character."

"Where is he?" I asked coldly. Then I realized one silly question was not enough, so I asked another. "What's the likelihood his attempts to blitz the dorm are because of Polina?"

"Actually fairly minimal. We don't think he's quite that stupid, although it could be a contributing factor to his aggression," Combat said to appease me.

"Now he's got lots of people under him, and according to information we've received, he's zealously kidnapping and killing people in order to level up. In addition, they're much stronger than us now. He's got lots of weapons, and whole barracks full of thugs who used to do shady deals in town, so they've got lots of hidey-holes throughout the city."

He was going to die no matter what. The property owner in me was foaming at the mouth. Polina may not have been property, but in some sense I already considered her my own.

"Does Polina know?"

"No, we wanted to tell you first and let you decide how to take it from there."

"Thank you," I said with a nod of gratitude. "What's that burning smell?" I realized something was stopping me thinking.

"We've been lighting a fire in a bucket to make tea," Fedya said with a grimace.

Shatun didn't mention the electricity in my apartment. Had he been in such a rush he hadn't noticed? It was possible he'd decided not to interfere in our affairs.

"But that's not all," continued Combat.

There were ten people sitting in the office, all roughly the same age as Combat, and all preferring not to get involved in our conversation. Had he forbidden them to speak? So they didn't insult me or say too much? Commendable; I was pleased.

Everyone looked attentively and somehow

nervously at me, as though their futures depended on me.

"So, the prisoner tells us Fedot has organized his own group," said Combat, before going quiet in expectation of my reaction.

"I get that. You already said he has a large group," I replied, confused as to why he was repeating himself.

On hearing my reply, he nodded to himself before saying, "That means you don't know the main thing."

My curiosity was piqued. What was it I didn't know?

"We also didn't understand at first what the prisoner was talking about. Turns out he created a group via the system, and now they're a one-of-a-kind clan, or tribe. Call them what you like, it doesn't alter the fact, or the danger they pose."

Interesting. So you can officially create a clan via the system. Perfectly logical, I suppose.

"Did you find out how he did it?" I asked, twigging at last what he was driving at.

"That's the thing." From his inventory, Combat produced a round stone and put it on the table in front of me.

Evaluation:

Stone of group creation.

It is easier for survivors to survive if they unite together in a group. Group members are offered more tests than loners.

Important note: In time, the status of a group may be raised to clan.

Interesting.

"We've already created a group, and called it 'Honor.' And I would like to invite you to join it."

What a military-sounding name! "Why would I want to do that? What responsibilities would I have? Would I be able to leave the group at any time without hassle?" I asked the questions most important for me personally.

Combat's mind was eased by my questions. Judging by his expression, he had been expecting an immediate categorical refusal. And since I was not actively against the idea, he would try to talk me round.

"Basically, we'll always be able to track your position. And if you get killed, we'll find out the name of whoever did it. It is also possible to send messages to other members of the group directly, just like the system does. There are lots of factors, but one thing I can say is that it's already proven very advantageous for us. So far, our group has only gained level 3, but all new recruits get plus ten kilograms to their inventory."

"So the more people, the higher the group's level?"

"We reckon it depends on people's skills rather than numbers exclusively," said Combat. "And regarding whether anything will change for you in the group, I can assure you everything will be just as it is now. You can do whatever you like, and you won't have to report to anyone. The main thing is that you don't go nuts. But I understand you're a regular guy, despite words like 'subordination' and 'discipline' being unfamiliar to you."

His words made me smile. It was a serious proposition, and I reached for a cigarette.

"I don't see the advantage to you," I said honestly. "Why do you need an uncontrollable guy who can't even be called on to work? What use will I be to you?"

Combat laughed. "Did you hear that? He's asking what use he'll be. After everything he's already done."

Combat's battle buddies smiled as he continued, "Varg, just do what you always do, and that will be enough for us. And as for what use we'll be to you, you understand it's not every day you stumble across a reliable rearguard. And besides, we've got lots of enemies. Although by all appearances, you like killing them, right?"

It was a dangerous person who was able to read me so easily, so it was good we were on the same wavelength. The main thing was that he should never consider me a threat, for if he did, I didn't know how much blood it might cost him.

It was all madly interesting. I understood the system did not do anything for the sheer hell of it. And since it had given people the opportunity to join together, there must be some reason for it. And now I was going to follow the system's path and would be bound to use its gifts.

"Fine, I accept your invitation. But on one condition. You stay out of my business, and I don't have to answer to you." I had taken ten minutes out to mull over the proposal, and it had been a fast ten minutes. "My chief aim is a comfortable life and, naturally, leveling up. So if you understand and accept that, then we can work together. I don't mind how I level up, whether it be running around the city by myself or covering your fighters on a task."

"It's agreed then. That's pretty much what I was expecting." Combat did not conceal his delight, just like the other men in the office. "Here's your invitation."

The survivor Combat invites you to join the Honor group.

I had considered everything carefully and it was the correct decision.

I accepted the invitation mentally, and received another notification.

Congratulations! You have joined the Honor group of survivors.

"Welcome to the group, Varg," said Combat, rising from his seat at the table and extending me a hand, which I shook.

This should be very interesting. I'm one of them now. Where will this road lead me?

END OF BOOK ONE

Want to be the first to know about our latest LitRPG, sci fi and fantasy titles from your favorite authors?

Subscribe to our **New Releases** newsletter:
http://eepurl.com/b7niIL

Thank you for reading *An Ideal World for a Sociopath!*

If you like what you've read, check out other sci-fi, fantasy and LitRPG novels published by Magic Dome Books:

Reality Benders
a LitRPG series by Michael Atamanov

The Dark Herbalist
a LitRPG series by Michael Atamanov

Perimeter Defense
a LitRPG series by Michael Atamanov

League of Losers
a LitRPG series by Michael Atamanov

Chaos' Game
a LitRPG series by Alexey Svadkovsky

War Eternal
a LitRPG series by Yuri Vinokuroff

The Hunter's Code
a LitRPG series by Yuri Vinokuroff & Oleg Sapphire

An Ideal World for a Sociopath
a LitRPG series by Oleg Sapphire

The Healer's Way
a LitRPG Series by Oleg Sapphire & Alexey Kovtunov

A Shelter in Spacetime
a LitRPG series by Dmitry Dornichev

Kill or Die
a LitRPG series by Alex Toxic

The Way of the Shaman
a LitRPG series by Vasily Mahanenko

The Alchemist
a LitRPG series by Vasily Mahanenko

Dark Paladin
a LitRPG series by Vasily Mahanenko

Galactogon
a LitRPG series by Vasily Mahanenko

Invasion
a LitRPG series by Vasily Mahanenko

World of the Changed
a LitRPG series by Vasily Mahanenko

The Bear Clan
a LitRPG series by Vasily Mahanenko

Starting Point
a LitRPG series by Vasily Mahanenko

The Bard from Barliona
a LitRPG series
by Eugenia Dmitrieva and Vasily Mahanenko

Condemned
(Lord Valevsky: Last of The Line)
a Progression Fantasy series
by Vasily Mahanenko

Loner
a LitRPG series by Alex Kosh

A Buccaneer's Due
a LitRPG series by Igor Knox

A Student Wants to Live
a LitRPG series by Boris Romanovsky

In order to have new books of the series translated faster, we need your help and support! Please consider leaving a review or spread the word by recommending *An Ideal World for a Sociopath* to your friends and posting the link on social media. The more people buy the book, the sooner we'll be able to make new translations available.

Thank you!

Till next time!

Made in the USA
Las Vegas, NV
03 August 2024

93331302R00216